MAKING
A
MOVIE!

MAKING

A

MOVIE!

Or How to Stop Worrying

About the Budget and Save Your Ass

A NOVEL BY

STEVE NICOLAIDES

MILL CITY PRESS

Mill City Press, Inc.
2301 Lucien Way #415
Maitland, FL 32751
407.339.4217
www.millcitypress.net

Paperback ISBN-13: 978-1-66285-753-9
Ebook ISBN-13: 978-1-66285-754-6

DEDICATIONS

TO CAROLINE, there at the beginning, there at the end, and every moment in between. From my heart.

AND to my Yodas, Dick Rosenbloom, Bill Finnegan, and Dick Briggs, who taught me production is war, and to win with meticulous attention to detail, kindness, hard work, and laughter.

SPECIAL THANKS to Elisabeth Seldes Annacone, Robert Eversz, and Scott Campbell for their continuing support through the many months of this endeavor.

BIG THANKS to Mitch Marcus, Toni Devereaux, Allen Koss, JB White, Tim Cummings, Dean Drabin, Bruce Cannon, Eric Klosterman, and Larry Nimmer for their early and enthusiastic support of this effort.

> "Friendship is the hardest thing in the world to explain. It's not something you learn in school. But if you haven't learned the meaning of friendship, you really haven't learned anything."

> —**Muhammad Ali**

PART ONE – EARLY PREP

RICH – LOCATION MANAGER

Okay, I admit it. My panties are in a righteous twist right now. This guy I worked with a couple of years ago as a second AD on a big feature is now running his own production company, and yesterday he called and begged me to head out to the Owens Valley on a picture he just secured financing for. A modest indie that has to be finished in nine months, prep-shoot-post, so the sprint is <u>ON</u>, and he needs me to start looking for locations ASAP times fifty.

My slacks won't be back from the cleaners 'til tomorrow, and I'm very particular about the crease in the legs and this place does it perfectly, and I've got to pack for six months, from spring until fall in the mountains. And there's the mess with my camera charger, and this woman named Lois who I really like but she's been married before to a guy in the movie business and wants nothing more to do with that shit.

I'm not a hurry-up guy, never was. Slowest eater in my family, in school I liked to sit in the back (rule number one—don't raise your hand) and never dated a cheerleader, never even thought about it to be honest. That race was way too fast for me. I've worked in the film industry for the past twenty-five years. By trade I'm a location manager.

I get hired, they give me a script, and pretty much right away the question is, 'Where are we shooting this?' If there's a director or a production designer, I immediately get with them, try to get a feeling for what they want, what they see. These days, I'm often the first one hired.

This I like, feeling like a Cavalry scout going into Indian country, the first man on the moon, whatever. No one sitting on my shoulder asking when this and that is going to happen. When I'm alone, I'm on my time. I'm the first to feel the excitement of the hunt, the danger of the expedition. What is the world we're trying to find, or piece together? In a creative void, that's a scary question. The script says, 'Ext. Neighborhood Street'. What pops in your mind? That's where it starts.

The movie YOU see is what you start looking for. Can't help it, human nature. But you're alone, scarfing a burrito in your car while you wonder if you should knock on the front door of that house. The street is perfect to you. The house is perfect too, half-way down the block, beautiful exterior architecture, old, tall trees. Where every American would want to live.

You knock on a door as a location manager, you never know who or what will answer. Sick older people with wheelchairs and smells and endless health problems. Young families with wild kids who scream all day while their parents hit each other and down a twelve pack before lunch. Movie stories may be about these people, but you don't want to film in their homes.

Like I said, a producer I know called me. He's bankrolled by money from Russia. In this case, no director or anyone else is on board, but he does have a tight script. And he must spend twenty million dollars before year's end. That's nine months from now.

The script is called WOMEN IN WHITE. It's about a rural town in the eastern Sierra Nevada desert of California, tumbleweeds and pickup trucks, snowy mountains to the west, endless dirt roads to the east. A dried-up town with one woman's clinic, no hospital, and two schools: first through seventh, eighth through see-you-later.

Pregnant teenager goes to said clinic and vanishes. She's found wandering on the back roads nine months later with no memory of where she's been. Turns out she's not the only one. A troubling pattern exists in the town. An investigation is organized, once again. The last two went nowhere.

Three pages in we meet the angry female sheriff who leads the team, tired of the men who run the town and never even tickle the problem. Now things have changed. The sheriff has a teenage daughter herself, and she's not about to let this go quietly. The script leads to a compound in the wilderness where 'women in white' birth the girls' children and raise them as anti-abortion fighters.

The locations seem clear: small rural town, the women's center, local police station, character homes where the girls live, and the great vast nowhere to search for the crazy ones who do crazy things. And finally, the brutal, bloody attack on the compound.

At first, I think it's not a difficult assignment. But then I remember: every movie is a difficult assignment.

It's given we're in a small town. Where to house the cast and crew? Are there sixty hotel rooms available for three months during tourist season? Where do the director and the stars stay? Are there restaurants open for dinner every night? How many? When do they close? Where does the caterer set up shop at day's end to prepare for tomorrow's on set meals? Where is the warehouse for the set builders, set dressers, wardrobe storage, and all the equipment that comes with night filming? It's a tent show with lots of needs.

The search for places to shoot is left to me. The list of locations rarely gets smaller in prep. I need a scout immediately. Someone with a car and a camera and a good eye for locations. As usual, I'm told there's no money to bring someone I know and trust from Los Angeles. Union wage, hotel and per diem...same old, same old.

On Thursday morning I'm ready to roll, my large suitcase, my espresso machine, my computer, cameras, all the chargers neatly packed in the back of my Subaru. If you're going to nowhereville and forget your chargers, you're fucked. Happened once, never again.

By mid-morning I'm past Lancaster and on my way north into the mountains. After an hour of driving through the bleak part of western Mojave, I hook up with the I-395, one of the most beautiful highways in America, running along the forgotten part of California through the Mojave Desert and into a long stretch that nestles to the west under the backside of the Sierra Nevadas.

The 395 eventually cruises into the Owens Valley, in spring awash in small lakes, gentle streams, and eventually the small but strong Owens River. It's the landscape that was raped and pillaged to create suburban Los Angeles. Chinatown, Jake.

I was born in the seventies. I missed all the great Western movies in theaters except *DANCES WITH WOLVES*. But my dad didn't. He loved them. When VCR took over the world, we rented every one of those great ones, made popcorn over the stove, and enjoyed the best days of my life. My Dad was my best friend. Our friendship kept him alive for a long time.

Even on a modest color TV, I felt in my bones the wonder of a great location. It puts you right there. I still don't understand abstract art, but for me, a little boy with his Pop watching TV, the majestic vistas and hidden rocky dangers in these westerns.... man, that was art.

As the light in the stunningly clear blue sky turns soft, I pull into Lone Pine. There's a movie museum on my left. I know the town thinks it's legendary for the early cowboy and gangster movies. The Alabama Hills and all that. But shit, it's tiny.

Getting a hotel room now becomes a worry. In length the town is maybe five active blocks, two traffic lights on 395, with five motels. Each has a lighted "Vacancy" sign so I'm fine. But immediately I think, what happens when the circus comes to town?

I pull into the Dow Villa. The 1950's neon-sign has not yet come on. A few cars and trucks parked in the lot. Good, maybe it'll be a quiet night. Of course, a huge F-350 takes up two spaces by the office door. A location manager by nature should be a Buddhist. You can't let the eccentricities of most human beings get under your skin. The pilot light for my "incorrect rage" clicks on when I see this fat fucking truck hogging the front door.

When you're on the road for work you always must choose between plastic and cash. Like in the Westerns, cash feels like the long rifle you carry in your saddlebag, insurance against the worst. You want to save the cash for emergencies.

The cash comes from the company. If you're putting hotels and meals and gas on plastic, it's your money. You'll have to get reimbursed. And you can go to your grave waiting. Companies want answers yesterday, but it takes them five weeks to get you a reimbursement check.

I park and head into the office. A six-foot-three guy in shorts and flip-flops wearing a No Doubt t-shirt is having trouble with his credit card. A tall young man from India is behind the desk, rolling his eyes. The No Doubt guy finally gets his card to work. I step up to the counter.

"I'm a location manager from LA, and I need a room for probably two weeks, maybe a lot longer. Can you help me?"

The young Indian man is handsome, dark-skinned, and gives me a barely disguised smirk as he drops his head to the keypad. "Do you have a reservation?" he asks.

"Unfortunately, no. Didn't think it was necessary."

"Fishing season is about to start."

But he continues to work the keyboard, and then smiles and looks at me. "I've got two rooms available for that stretch of time. Shall I block the second one too?" Obviously, he's been around film teams. He knows the needs get bigger, not smaller.

This is when I feel like the scout ahead of the Cavalry. They're making decisions and I'm rarely a part of that. If I put money down on the bet they are coming, they won't. If I hedge my bet, they'll be here two days early.

"Book mine for three weeks, the second one for two weeks starting next Monday."

"Excellent. And how will you be paying, sir?"

I realize I haven't even asked the rate. "What's the rate? And for this many room nights, what's the discount?"

"Normally $149 per night, tax included. For this many room nights, $134."

"That's the best you can do?"

He looks up at me.

"I may be bringing a big movie to this town. Let's start off on the right foot, huh? What's your name?"

"Dev, sir. My name is Dev. My family owns the hotel. I too certainly hope we can start off on the right foot, but it's $134. That's 10% off, sir."

THE GLOVE – LINE PRODUCER

I'm at Hugo Boss in Beverly Center when I get the text, trying on t-shirts, waiting to see if the Showtime pilot I produced in Wyoming is going to series. Not really worrying about another job, wondering how a fifty-year-old man can ask a twenty-five-year-old Persian salesgirl out to dinner tonight. She's slim, smoky-dark eyes, gorgeous. Then another text sings out and I fish the phone from my front pocket.

It's my agent, Peter. 911 text. This is a good sign. I buy three shirts. Hugo Boss is the best. While I'm paying, two more texts come in. Urgent. At the food court, I call him. "What's up?"

"There's a twenty-million-dollar movie fully funded, and they need a sharp line-producer. It's busy, my A-listers are jammed. Can you take a meeting?"

Peter tries to be funny. But he's an agent. Fatally serious and humane, not especially funny. I gather the facts. Euro-funded indie company, abortion story about them that fight and them that don't, couple of movie stars, small town location. Ten weeks prep, eight weeks shoot, four weeks wrap. Two-hundred and twenty-five grand. Feels like a nice bridge before the series.

"Okay. Who and when do I meet?"

"3:30 today at Paramount. I'll text you the details."

"But I haven't read it. Can we do this tomorrow?"

"No."

At Paramount, the pass allowing me to park on the lot isn't at the gate. I pull over and wait. Three minutes later a young Asian woman in her security uniform strolls out of the kiosk and comes to my BMW. She smiles and tells me to come ahead. I park in a big empty lot.

It's always weird going to a job interview. I persuade myself I'm totally confident, because I know the people I'm coming to meet are looking for any crack in the mirror. I'm the guy responsible for the money.

Beyond the old buildings from the thirties and forties are a row of newer, modern structures, glass and steel. This is where I'm going. A young woman sits at the reception desk. I ask for Matthew Kaufman. She picks up her phone, punches some numbers. A small, handsome man around forty hurries out of a large conference door and smiles.

"Hey, I'm Matthew. Do they really call you the Glove?"

I like him right away. "My last name is Glovetick. Hungarian. The family fled the Soviets in the Fifties."

"Show biz," he laughs. "Great to meet you. I've heard nothing but wonderful things."

"It's a town full of liars. You know that, right?" I laugh.

He smiles and ushers me into the conference room. A man and a woman stare up at me from their chairs, almost smiling. The dance begins. First, everyone expresses enthusiasm over the project. It's current, meaningful, a great adventure, a real thriller. They're about to drop twenty million on it, and they need to believe in their decision. I explain I haven't had the chance to read it yet, but I strongly believe movies must stand their ground about social issues. "Isn't this why we all wanted into the industry?" I ask.

The woman, a homely thirty-something with a tight-curl hairdo, chortles. "I want to laugh when I go to the movies." The room goes silent, like someone farted.

"I worked with Rob Reiner on several movies. He knew the audience needed a laugh occasionally to relieve the tension of the drama."

Matthew smiles. "Great director. Made some of the best films ever. So, here's our project."

Matthew becomes a storyteller. Arms out, big smile, seriousness in his eyes as he lays out the story as he sees it. I like him, his excitement for the project. For his salesmanship. I believe his enthusiasm. He smiles like he's nailed it. I think he did.

The woman speaks up again. She's either really gutsy or really naïve. "Just so you know...our line of credit has been extended to the last half-inch. Twenty million all in is what we've got. No more." Gosh, never heard this before, I think. Are the private jets and the family travels included in the number?

I ask, "How much for the lead actress?"

Matthew speaks up. "Two million, and a generous backend."

"And if Jennifer Lawrence wants in, but at ten million, you say no?"

Matthew smiles at me. I'm a player, and he knows it. "Then we'll go shopping for more cash. Of course."

"Who made the budget?" I ask. They all look at each other. "How'd you get to twenty million?"

The man who hasn't said a word clears his throat, speaks up. He could play a Nazi collaborator or a bored trust-fund baby pretending to be a money-manager. He looks up at the ceiling as he says to me, "It's not detailed. It's what we want to spend."

I look at Matthew. He's smiling.

"So, there's no budget. It's a goal, not a real number."

Matthew smiles again. "That's why we need you."

I've been down this road before. The first number out of your mouth is the number they put on your gravestone.

"Well, let me read it and think about it, then we'll talk. But know this. It's a modest number, twenty million. That means the people behind me must have strong backbones. We want to stay on the number, we stick to our guns."

I look at Matthew. He's smiling. He knows what I just said is the truth.

GUS – LOCATION SCOUT

KC's bar in Lone Pine seems dark to me, but hell, everything gets a little blurry when you're as old as me. Christ, am I losing my eyes too? First the lungs, then the dick. I can deal with no more tobacco. I can deal with no more sex. But it'd be hard to deal with no more seeing.

This place is about thirty minutes from my house, which sometimes makes the drive home a little scary. Small town sheriffs, if you get my drift. Carrie, the bartender, is an old friend and the drinks are cheap.

I've been back in the Owens for over twenty years. I left in my early forties to follow a tall, willowy LA woman with dark fuck-me eyes and an ass as bright as a blinking road sign promising all that a lonely cock could ever want. Of course, she dumped me one drunk weekend for some guy in a VW van who owned pizza huts and chased cold beer and hot pussy up and down the California coast. I paid for my sins, whatever they were, by working in LA in the movie business as a location scout for the next five years.

Carrie hums to herself, smiling for some reason, long dark hair pulled back in a ponytail that hangs to her shoulders. She's fifty but looks forty, tall and trim. Known her since she was a cheerleader at the high school. Used to hunt with her brothers. One drunken birthday party I even got the courage to proposition her. She laughed and walked away.

14

Everyone in Lone Pine hits on her. She was married once, to the town's Big Deal Family's eldest son, but he turned out to be a depressed first son who knew he could never measure up to his dad or grandfather and killed himself driving his $60,000 Land Rover off a cliff.

I always come early, around five, because I'm a Wilson and in this valley that's like saying you're a cow puncher to a sheep fucker. People love to carry grudges. Nobody around now was alive when LA came and stole all the water, but they all know the Wilsons were the power family that opened the gate. Owned the bank, owned the third biggest ranch, got the prize choice of the river's diversion. My family is the hated family, the villain here.

But history is a bunch of bullshit. Wasn't like that and never was. Everybody took the deal. Or got pissed off when they weren't offered one. It's still a great place to live, green, prosperous, friendly (unless you're a Wilson) and small. Live here long enough and you know every house on every street from Lone Pine to Bishop.

Without the LA Department of Water and Power, Southern Californians might never have discovered Mammoth Lakes, all the hiking and fishing and skiing. The so-called rape of the water also brought the interstate highway, the great 395, and access to the Owens Valley and north on the eastern side of the Sierras. Fuck 'em, I say. Proud to be a Wilson.

As the night drops, I'll know almost every person who comes into KC's. While I sip my Miller Lite a fellow I don't recognize steps in. He's medium height, smiling like a salesman or something. Mid-forties I guess, ironed Levi's with a crease and a collared shirt. Fishing season is coming on so maybe he's a sporting goods salesman.

But to me, he smells like LA.

He sits at the bar, orders white wine, and slowly looks around. This early, we're the only ones in the room. He glances at me, smiles. I finish my beer, look to the bar hoping to catch Carrie's eye. She laughs with the stranger about something, and I see her motion toward me. He turns, looks me over again as I raise my empty bottle. She grabs a cold one and slides it toward the stranger. They share another laugh as he heads toward my table.

"Carrie tells me you used to work in the movie business," he says as he puts my beer down.

"Used to run a forklift at Home Depot too. What's your point?"

"I'm a location manager. For the movies. Might be bringing a twenty-million-dollar movie around here. Can I pick your brain?"

"You can buy me another beer. After I finish this one."

He stares at me with a smile on his face, but I know he's thinking whether my hostility is worth challenging. "Done."

"Lived in your world for five years, pal. Feel lucky to still be alive."

He nods his head, probably remembering the shit he's crawled through over the years. Locations is a bitch job. Responsible for everything, power over nothing. "The bartender told me you were a location scout," he says. "I might have a gig for you."

I smile. "Unless the production manager is someone I worked with and I can torture until he dies screaming like a baby in a house fire, I'm not interested."

He laughs. "Give me a list, I'll see what I can do."

He coughs nervously, cautiously sits down. "Look, I'll be straight with you. I need help. In a week the Designer is coming here. I gotta have great stuff to show. And probably the production manager too, so they're going to ask me where's this and where's that. I need someone who knows this area."

"Sounds exciting." I grin like the Cheshire cat. "Nothing to do with me."

"Can you recommend anybody? I need someone who can photograph. And someone who knows how things work here."

I look at him. Sincere eyes, straight mouth. A little bit of hat-hair, but he's been driving. He's got honesty spilling down the front of his shirt. A perfect Hollywood location manager. You trust these guys.

At the beginning, their quest is your quest. Their trouble, your trouble. Open mouth, insert hook. Eventually, what's at stake feels like the end of the world or something. If we don't close this highway then all is lost and we're total failures in life!

In the end, you're the dead fish baking in the sun at the bottom of the boat. This I know. You don't forget this. Still, I nibble at the hook.

"What's the project?"

He sighs, takes a sip of his drink. "A small town with a dark secret about teenage girls who want abortions but disappear instead. And the cops who finally get after the scandal. I need a cop station, a compound way out in the country, and as much of a small town as I can deliver."

"This town is too small for your project."

"This town seems perfect for this project."

"Where's everybody gonna stay? And eat? And work? In front of the camera, maybe you're right. Lone Pine's a quaint little town. But what happens behind the camera is the serious shit. You know that."

"That's not my decision."

"Trust me, you'll end up in Bishop. Aren't enough motels, restaurants, warehouses, to make it work here. You should head north tomorrow."

He's calculating; he knows I'm right. "Well, the studio sent me to Lone Pine. The Alabama Hills. Cowboy movies. Yada yada. I have to try at least until the Designer gets here. Locations are the priority; production stuff is next."

I finish my beer and wave to Carrie for another. She comes over, asks the LA guy if he is ready, and he orders another round. I wonder if I like this guy. The hook slides in a little deeper. Production is like a drug you never get over. The big puzzle is fascinating, like a jigsaw puzzle where someone hid all the corner pieces.

"Where you staying?"

"Dow Villa."

"You're at the top of the line in this town." I know I'm scaring him. He's lost control of the narrative. That's what one of my bosses in LA used to say. Don't lose control of the narrative. I smile. It's what I intended.

"Hundred bucks a day, eight hours, cash," he offers.

I answer: "One fifty, ten-day guarantee. No Sundays."

"Done."

"What's your name?"

"Rich. Yours?"

"Gus. But everyone around here calls me Fuckin' Wilson.

LARRY – PRODUCTION MANAGER

I'm trying to figure out where to hang the painting my sister sent me for my birthday, which was three months ago. She's at Dartmouth studying fine arts, specifically to become a painter. Our mother was a modestly successful artist in Seattle in her day, and my sister always wanted to follow in her footsteps. The painting isn't great, but it's good, and I'm thinking it might look good by the front entryway when the Glove calls.

He's got a small picture on location on the eastern side of the Sierras, somewhere around Lone Pine. Twenty million, but he says he has doubts about the company. It came through ICM though. The big agencies don't fuck around with small-timers. You say you want something, they get it for you, you pay for it. That's how it works. Been trying to get ICM to rep me for a year. Need one more credit.

"Is there a budget?"

"Not yet."

"Is there a script?"

"Yeah. Pretty good, actually. Can you come over and get it?"

"I'm putting in a jacuzzi next to the pool. Once the contractor gets here, I'll sort him out and drive over. Probably two hours?"

I've worked with the Glove three times. Stand-up guy. Charming. Very good with Designers, Cinematographers,

Directors. He's kind of known as a skirt-chaser, but that's not been my experience. He sees the big picture, but also sweats the details. Like everyone in production, he can wear down over the course of prep and shoot, and if he's betrayed by his bosses, he will get nasty.

Before I get in my car, I call my production coordinator, Fiona. Voicemail. I talked with her last week; she was enjoying her time off. Her husband teaches skydiving in Colorado, so she's been back and forth to Denver. We finished a shoot in Atlanta five weeks ago. We both thought there would be reshoots, but so far nothing. Atlanta is so busy, getting crew and equipment is like fighting for silver bullets in a vampire invasion. Hated the city.

I heard Truffaut once said making a movie is like taking a stagecoach ride in the old West. At first you hope for a pleasant experience, but by the end you just hope to get out alive. That's the whisper in the ear of every production manager. Just get out alive.

The Glove is not home when I ring the bell. But an envelope with my name on it rests against the door. The adventure begins. At home I read the script, which is pretty good. Strong characters, social situations, great action. I pour myself a coke and start to break down the scenes.

Next morning, I call Alison, my go-to accountant. She's in Mexico, snorkeling and drinking tequila with her young Latin girlfriend. I ask if she can do a quickie budget and she says no, she isn't back in California for three more weeks. But her new assistant can; she's bored and restless in LA.

Putting together a team is the fun, and sometimes the curse, of being a production manager. I played sports in school, and I learned team was all that mattered. But in the adult world, especially the big-boy movie business, 'team' isn't always the first thing anyone thinks about. I try to hold on to as many of my team as I can from project to project, but it's not always possible. Then you go fishing.

My doorbell rings. She's there, texting on her phone, a computer bag at her feet. She looks up, smiles. "I'm Lena. Alison's assistant."

She wears low cut Converse tennis shoes, red knee-length socks, a short summer skirt and a t-shirt that states, "My parents were hippies. What do you expect?" I'm guessing 26 years old.

"So," she says, "first things first. I've never done a budget. But I want to learn, and I'll work for free."

"I don't allow anyone to work for free. That's why it's called work."

She smiles. "Alison said she loves you, promised you'll guide me through it." She steps inside the house, lugging her bag. "She says making a budget is like follow-the-numbers at this stage. Right? Prep weeks, shoot days, budgeted work hours, how many wrap days or weeks. You'll give me the above-the-line numbers?"

She's cute, no denying it. And looks you straight in the eye.

"An architect drawing up a barn, she called it. How many stalls do you want?"

I smile, step aside as she enters, looks around. "I guess it should always be simple at the beginning," I say.

She is adorable. Tight body, bright blue glasses, pretty blue eyes. I ask her if she wants something to drink. She thinks about it. "I brought some grapefruit juice. Do you have any vodka?"

Okay. This will be interesting. But we start out with club soda.

We work tirelessly. For now, the schedule and budget are broad strokes. I show her the how and why of scheduling, always trying to hold to some sense of creative continuity in the storytelling while looking to limit the workdays of the stars, not to mention their teams -makeup, hair, costumes.

And then we hit the Movie Magic Budgeting button, and the software starts to put numbers in the slots. Lena and I discuss prep and wrap, how big the teams will be - grip, electric, transportation, stunts, ADs, accounting- and pretty soon we have something fleshed out. A start. We celebrate by putting the club soda away and bringing out the vodka. It's nearly dark by now.

The big-ticket items, construction, locations, camera package, extras, we decide to put aside. We take our drinks outside by the pool. She's smart, quick, and clearly wants to learn, to understand beyond the numbers. A second vodka and we're in the pool.

I insist she sleep in the spare bedroom. I can see her mind speeding like she's driving a race car for the first time. We deep-smile, but no kissing. Still, it's in the air. Next day she goes home. We tweak the budget over and over until it's complete. We plug in numbers for construction, locations, wardrobe, stunts, camera, and all the above-the-line.

We went high on room rates and ATL per diem. There's never enough money for the shoot, but there's always money for the star's per diem. We bumped the fringes - payroll taxes, social security, union health and pension—by 2 percent (about a $150,000 pad), budgeted fourteen-hour days and set the shoot at forty-five days. Of course, we low-ball the post-production. Someone else's problem. The number comes in at nineteen million, six hundred and thirty-three thousand. Pretty good.

I call the Glove. He's grateful for the speed and the number, and I email it all to him, expecting notes the following day. I try to sleep, but I can't get Lena out of my mind. Bobby-sox and blue eyes, vodka and grapefruit juice. There's a song there somewhere.

RICH – LOCATION MANAGER

It's exactly 8:30AM when I pay the check for breakfast at the Alabama Hills Café. If you travel like I do, there's one thing that stands out about America. It is a wall-to-wall parade of fat people. Seriously fat people. Corn bred, corn fed, corn dredged, and deep-fat fried. Come have breakfast at this iconic café-everybody on the eastern side of the Sierras knows it-and sit down to something light, like four pieces of French toast, four pieces of thick bacon, cottage cheese and tomatoes. Or three eggs over easy, four pieces of thick bacon, a pound of hash browns, and buttered toast. Meals like this just make me want to go back to bed. I can hear my arteries gasping for air.

Gus eats like he's been in prison for twenty years. He's stubborn as a mule looking at a wagon full of heavy boulders. Last night I said we'd meet at seven for breakfast. He smiled. "Eight. We'll be on the road by eight-thirty."

"I want to get an earlier start," I counter.

"Tough shit. I eat at eight. We drive at eight-thirty."

He has five years' experience in LA as a location scout. He's a member of one of the power families in the Owens Valley. Been around here most of his life. I'll cut him some slack this time. "Eight it is."

Over breakfast we discuss where to start. He says, "I read your script last night. This is really about pioneer women, right? Hard ass bitches. Don't really care about men. Can't live in towns. We need to find a complex that's in the middle of nowhere. Police station, homes, lonely roads, motels... pretty much real places. But I'm thinking the complex has to be special."

"Anything come to mind?" I ask. "An old Monastery? Government work site for the aqueduct?"

He looks at me, curious. "This used to be an unknown paradise," he mumbles while chewing. "There was no highway, no ski industry, no one ever heard of Mammoth. The Owens Valley, the eastern Sierras, the White Mountains, they were all open prairie, like an all-you-can-eat buffet for a bunch of tough old birds."

He slurps his second cup of coffee and spills a little down his chin. "My great grandpa was one. A small piece of property was twenty square miles. Water was everywhere. The mountains were covered in snow. It was nothing but potential. Like this menu," he laughs and motions to Susie to bring the check. She smiles. "This land is full of ghosts, man. We just got to go find them."

Oh no. "I prefer to go forward, not into the past," I say. "I want to see what exists NOW, not what used to be. The clock is ticking, and it'll only get faster. When it's over, I'll be delighted to sit and listen to the history of the valley. You okay with that?"

He takes a big swallow. "Totally with you, bossman. We got a job to do. I'm taking you to the heart of the matter. Right fucking now." He wipes his chin with his napkin.

I wonder what he means. "Okay. What is the heart of the matter?"

We head north on 395 toward the city of Independence. It used to be the heart of the valley, all the big ranches were there, until the twenties and the LADWP showed up and Bishop and Mammoth took over.

In twenty minutes, we turn east off the highway on Mauzorka Canyon Road, which is paved for a mile and then becomes gravel and dirt. We're heading into the White Mountains. The Sierras are behind us. Together these mountain ranges form the Owens Valley.

"Okay, most gracious leader," I ask Gus, "where are we going?"

"At one time the Mormons tried to make a dent around here. Bought a lot of land, though most locals around then would say they tried to steal a lot of land. They had one middle-of-nowhere cattle ranch, around ten thousand acres and, when none of the big families would do business with them, they closed shop, sold everything, and went back to Nevada and Utah. Mormons are a shifty tribe if you know what I mean."

"And..."

"They never sold this last parcel. The ten thousand acres. About thirty years later, around 1940, I think, someone in Salt Lake had the idea of turning the ranch into a college, for learning self-reliance, ranching, farming and community. Community is big with the Mormons."

"How many students?" I ask.

"Heard there's fifteen. One year and you get your diploma. No tuition. But you gotta work. Hard work. And study. Hard study."

"Do we know anyone to let us in?"

"My son's head of security. Department of one. But listen to me," he looks at me seriously. "They'll never let us shoot here. Mormons are weird. But as research, it's drop-your-dick-in-the-dirt-and-declare-winner." He laughs.

He cracks the window and I let him light a cigarette. I don't know why. Never let anyone do this. I don't have asthma, but cigarette smoke makes me think I might. At least he smokes American Spirit.

I'm excited. If this works, we'll have research, pictures, hopefully a prototype to search for. Isolated ranch with a dormitory. With locations, you must nail the basic logic first. Does this place make sense? Then the character of the setting, its weirdness, the beauty of the location, come into play. But first, it's got to make story sense.

He turns to me, hesitates. "You've been in the business a while now, right?"

"About twenty-five years."

"Two questions: what's the craziest thing you ever saw on location? And who's the one actress you wanted to fuck more than anything?"

I laugh. Here's this grumpy, I-have-breakfast-at-eight-in-the-morning-fuck-you old man asking me about wild times and some phantom of my dreams.

"How about you start?" I say.

He lights another Spirit. "It's a tough one. They look rough in the early morning when the location manager is the first one to greet them.'"

"Most definitely. At that hour, I think we all do."

"I was doing a TV movie in LA. Ann Margret was the lead. Her call was five-thirty, something like that. The trucks were parked, the caterer was busy, her motorhome was in place and the heat was on. And here comes her car. She was, I'm guessing, around fifty. Car stops. The back door opens before the driver can hustle out and open it for her. One leg comes out, then the other. Dancer's legs. The driver gives her a hand and she rises from the backseat. The full red hair, straight nose, dark sexy eyes. Stunning tits. Soldiers at the ready. My dick instantly gets hard. The most beautiful woman ever placed on earth. No chance for me, of course. But God..."

"Show biz."

"Glorious show biz."

We smile at each other. "And the craziest thing on location?" I ask.

But before he can answer we see the school's sign and Gus says, "Turn right here."

NINA – PRODUCTION DESIGNER

I haven't worked with the Glove in three years, so when he phones, I'm surprised. The last project ended weirdly, no one making decisions until the last minute, blaming the art department for foolish spending. But I never felt he blamed me. And the movie was a huge hit.

We had a pitcher of margaritas at the wrap party and there was a vibe of hooking up, but it never happened. Then I got the series, changed agents, and we lost touch. He's calling me about a twenty-million-dollar indie on location in eastern California, the story of a radical woman's cult fighting against abortion. I said, "Can I read it?" The email just dropped.

I'm forty-one, a youthful forty-one as my dad would say, single. I started out in set decorating lugging furniture for Amy Wells, the greatest boss and best decorator ever. I learned my shit solid and finally worked my way up to Production Designer. My break came on the Glove movie called *VALLARTA DREAMS*, a no budget movie in Mexico that made a ton of money.

I read this script and the Glove is spot on. It's about something- rare these days- and it's about women. What is the right course of action if you drink too much and your horny boyfriend gets your pants off, and BINGO! you're preggers and you're still a sophomore in high school and worrying about a kid in your belly is second to worrying about the zits on your forehead. It's in the DNA of every girl.

I try to decide. Do I want a job on location? Lately, it feels like you get a call from the Knight Templars: want to go somewhere and battle horny grips in the bars after work just so you can change the course of history? Not really.

I only want to do my job, work with good people, participate in something worthwhile. Good luck with that, the Fates always laugh. Yet, I feel this project needs female blood. The whole wrestling match over who gets to decide what a pregnant woman can do is absurd.

I am eternally grateful to all the designers I worked for, their kindness in supporting me, recommending me, but trust me on this, it's a hard road in a man's world. I call the Glove and ask, "Who's directing?" He doesn't know.

The company is in the middle of the dance with an Argentine director who made *THRILL OF THE MOUNTAINTOP* and *DARK WATER BENEATH US*. I've heard of *DARK WATER*, a lot of buzz at Sundance.

"Is there a location manager yet?"

"Rich Samuel. He's in Lone Pine now."

"I know him. A little straight, but he's great."

An awkward silence ensues. He's thinking and I'm thinking. "Let me know if you want in," he says.

"It's challenging, but it'd be great to hook up with you again." We make a date to have lunch with the money people tomorrow.

What do I wear? That's the shit about being a girl. It's ingrained. Dress for Success. I've worked for years to get rid of the worry over how they want me to look. I'm happy to be in boots and shorts hiking over a hill to see if there's a better long shot at some location. Eventually, I pick a short skirt and a white t-shirt under a forest green sweater.

The restaurant is in Santa Monica. Fine by me, since I've lived in Venice Beach for twenty years. But it's fancy: Chez Wow. Rumor is Leo and Hanks are part owners.

I'm early and so is the Glove. He orders a club soda with lime, and I do the same. He seems like the guy I used to know, tall and handsome, confident to the extreme. His hair has some grey at the temples. He's struggling with his phone, trying to text. I smile. All warriors get older. It's sexy.

"So," I say, "another project. What's your take?"

"To be honest," he says, "I don't know anymore. Everything changes at the speed of light these days. Movies are movies. Stories are stories. And on the screen, they cost. Lots. On the small screen, less."

The drinks arrive. Suddenly a hostess and a waiter swish in bringing a short, confident man to the table. He's clearly a big deal here. He introduces himself as Matthew and apologizes for being late. He smiles at me and offers his hand to the Glove. I understand he's the boss. Doesn't look it, but that's often the case.

Immediately a bottle of white wine and three glasses appear. The cork is popped, the wine poured. Matthew smiles.

He goes on to bore us with his tales of years gone past, the streets in Berlin, the town in Oregon, the plaza in Mexico.

The Glove respects him, and that's enough for me. But I've learned with movies, the past has nothing to do with the present. All the problems, all the choices, all the personalities are fresh and demanding. Every time you deal the deck, it's different.

Boldness needs to be the red blood in our veins. My job at the start is to think big, then get smaller. Spend the money, dream large, search endlessly for perfection, and then make decisions where you narrow the focus and get to the details. Rarely is this the program. Almost always, it's the opposite: start prep on the cheap and wait for panic to knock on the door. When time and money are short.

Still, I say yes. I actually love living in a motel room for months. I'm a Gypsy girl to the bone. Plus, the script is good. The movie could be major. And someone else cleans my sheets and towels, gives me new shampoo. Every day. That afternoon I'm going to start making calls for a decorator and a construction coordinator. My juices start running.

THE GLOVE – LINE PRODUCER

I feel the stress starting to strangle my nerves. Production is like doing cocaine and heroin in the same crazy dream. Faster, faster, crash, burn, faster again. My last project turned out great, but, man, it was rough. Horses, a stunt coordinator the director loved but no one else could stand, the most rain in Wyoming's history, and the local Teamsters go on strike over a pay-cut at Walmart.

How do the horses get to location, the wranglers demanded?

"Well," I said, "you're getting paid four hundred bucks a day, ride 'em out there. "

I pack my Suburban with two suitcases and two more computer/phone bags. It'll be summer and fall in the mountains. T-shirts into heavy jackets. If I need snow gear, we're way over schedule and my career is toast and the movie is screwed. That's where my head is at. Sometimes I don't know if I can do this any longer. Get my team on the roller coaster reaching for the sky, then tell my bosses I've got it under control when I feel like I've let the roller coaster go and I don't know where the ride ends.

I consider my golf clubs. Sunday on location is sacred. You must have some joy, some laughter, some exercise, some hint of friendship at the very least. It can't just be all work. I'm fifty now. Do dark clouds sneak in more easily with age? Or am I just not focused yet? For the first time in a long time, I find myself yearning for a partner. Slow days, nothing to do. Cooking, binging on all the great TV that's around. Maybe I should wait for the series.

But I'm the Glove. I'm the first one in the boat, first one on the shore. When I was young, going on location was like getting on an explorer's ship, foreign lands, connecting with human beings who never heard of a movie shooting where they live, selling the magic and power of stories. Now?

I slam the back hatch of the Suburban without the golf clubs. I go back in the house and grab two crime novels. Daniel Woodrell and William Boyle. I'll be quiet, no partying, read at night. That's what dreamers do best...lie to themselves.

The story rumbles around in my head. I believe the earth has too many people. I don't have kids. I never dealt with a hospital and having a kid. Never been involved with an abortion. Still, it doesn't seem honest that men make laws about women's choices. The final decision must be up to her, case closed.

I cruise into Lone Pine about two-thirty. Rich has booked me into the Best Western on the south side of town. Larry is playing with the budget. Going up. I text him to stop it. Steal from the stunts. Here I am again, four walls and a window looking out on a parking lot. The TV has Fox and CNN, but not MSNBC. And the movie channels are all Pay-Per-View. Around five o'clock, I start to feel hungry. I call Rich.

We meet, walk up the street to Seasons, a cozy restaurant with maybe twelve tables. Outside, it's windy and the big rigs roar up and down 395 shooting debris all over the highway.

America is one restless country. See for yourself, drive on the two-lane highways.

"So, where are you so far?" I ask. Rich is a straight shooter. USC guy. I trust him.

"This guy, Gus, he's a character, but he showed me a place a few days ago that I honestly believe gets to the heart of the matter." He takes a sip of wine. "I guess the Mormons tried to move into this valley in the early days, bought some land, cattle ranches mostly. But the old guard sheepherders didn't like them. Pretty much chased them out." He laughs, a little nervously.

"But they kept one ranch, about ten thousand acres. Something like thirty years later, an elder in Salt Lake had a vision of a ranch college, with a small dormitory."

I did a survival movie in Salt Lake ten years ago. Strange people. "Middle of nowhere with a dorm, huh?"

"The Mormons won't deal with us, but it's a vision. There are lots of remote ranches out here." I think about what he just said. Makes perfect sense to me, find a remote ranch, build a dormitory. "Why won't the Mormons deal with us?"

"There's only a three-week break between sessions."

"Okay. Makes sense."

"Then you tell me whether the numbers say we build the police station, the motel rooms. You know the art department and the cameraman will want to. If there are enough warehouses to do this. We'll find houses to shoot, no problem, and endless desolate roads. We'll go into the

Alabama Hills tomorrow." Our salads arrive. I ask our server her name. Clemencia, she says, a name as beautiful as she is.

I ask Rich, "Okay, what's the but?"

"Gus says we need to move to Bishop straight away. Between warehouses, hotel rooms, a big production office, props, stunts, and effects needing a staging area for the final shootout.... you've seen how small this town is."

Panic is not something the leaders of movie production appreciate. Nor do we fall for it. I've been in this town for four hours and I'm not running away so fast. But I hear Rich's concerns. When the egoists arrive and start complaining about bugs in their motel rooms...

Clemencia brings the entrees. My fish is delicious. So is the way she smiles at me. Okay, we have no stake in Lone Pine, I agree. Still, it's gorgeous, closer to LA than Bishop, and probably cheaper. But if you have five extra vans driving the cast and the big wig crew an hour from Bishop to locations down in Lone Pine because there aren't enough facilities in Lone Pine, you made a big mistake.

After our meal we move to the five-stool bar for a last drink. On the back of the bar is a painting of two bulls facing off in a pasture. I ask for an Irish whiskey. Rich asks for another glass of pinot.

"Well," I say to Rich, "let's stay here and dig around until Nina arrives. But, at the same time, let's send Gus up to Bishop."

Rich shakes his head. "We need Gus here. What we don't know about this valley is how hostile everyone is to LA. Gus has that poison in his veins. He can knock on doors, call in favors, at least at the start. I'll find someone who can go to Bishop, or maybe lives there, see what its got."

Suddenly, I'm staring at Clemencia. She's smiling from the stool next to me.

"My shift is over," she says. "Buy me a drink?"

"What's the number for 911?" I ask her.

She's confused.

"Joking," I say. "What would you like?"

NINA – PRODUCTION DESIGNER

I drive up to Lone Pine on Thursday. No petty cash advance, no accountant yet. On my own nickel until the cash shows up. Really irritating. Rich has been here for eight days, and the Glove for three. Can't wait to see what they've found.

I check into the Dow Villa, which seems a little dusty and tired, but I luck into a large room on the second floor in the back. The front window looks down on the pool and the parking lot, and the bathroom window looks out on a dirt field full of weeds. It's quiet and private. The TV is new and big, the weather lovely, 65 degrees with a slight breeze, clear blue skies, towering white clouds. The sound of singing birds is everywhere.

I call the boys and tell them I'm in my room. They're in the Alabama Hills, staring at amazing rock formations. They promise to come and get me for dinner. I set up my computer and spread out the research books I brought. I start to feel a little restless, so I go into the bathroom and slide open the window. A couple of tokes from the pot pipe fixes everything.

I unbutton my blouse, armpits smelly from the drive, and lay down on the bed, stretching out my legs and arms. I must admit, a margarita, a great kisser, and a nap sound pretty good right now.

I always understood this about art: our dreams, our desires, our fears all come from a shifting place behind our eyes. When art is working and it takes you away without a single thought or care, a certain part of your brain has been turned off. As much as you need to know basic math to get through life, you also need a florid imagination too.

I smile and think back to elementary school, when I played a villager in a fourth-grade production of PETER AND THE WOLF. When my brother explained the story to me, I was too terrified to go on stage, even though my mom had made my costume.

I put a pillow under my knees and prop my head on another. Red creeps into my vision. This story, Women in White, is like the Bible, angry and violent, full of the wrath of God. A child grows in your belly. Hopefully it came from a wonderful moment of love, but often not, I guess. The urge to get rid of it? Not let it in your life. Red, certainly. White? I don't know. The women who are at the center of this story are hard, moral, and vicious. I can't find white there.

I get that I'm the total opposite of them. Thank God. Must be suffocating to think nobody knows anything better than you. But as Production Designer, I have to give them my all. It's their story, after all. I must understand the why and the how of their life. What's in their brains, their hearts, in their behavior that might unlock what leads them down this path. In their youth, victims of men? Or is it just some crazy religious shit? I still see red, intense and aggressive, nothing but red.

Then it comes to me. The white is for the young girls, the victims. They're the women in white. Virgins. Lambs being led to the slaughter. My body shudders. The girls in white have no chance. Red is always the color of victory.

This is why I love pot. On my wall there's a picture of Roy Rogers on a horse in the Alabama Hills. The phone wakes me an hour later.

We meet at the rib joint across the street from the motel. It smells wonderful. I'm from Nebraska and BBQ is in my blood. Rich is exactly as I remember him, nervous and sweet and well-dressed. The Glove is always the same, handsome and alert.

"So, how'd it go today? I read the Alabama Hills are spectacular," I start. They're both drinking white wine, which in small towns is almost always crap, but when the waiter appears I order vodka rocks. Day One deserves this. Neither of them even blinks.

"It is spectacular country," the Glove says. "Low foothills, canyons that roll up into the mountains, lakes and rivers. Magnificent."

Rich just smiles. It worries me. "I came up to Mammoth about ten years ago to ski. This side of the Sierras is amazing, but Lone Pine seems pretty small."

My drink arrives. As do the menus. Pork ribs...heaven.

"Can we really do a movie here?" I wonder.

The Glove sips his wine. "I think it's definitely worth a few days checking out before we jump ship. Bishop, which is, what, an hour north, will always be there. Hotels and the backbone of a real town," he says. "We haven't landed anywhere. Let's spend a couple of days in the car, see what you think." He looks me in the eye and my toes curl.

The heart of my job is making in front of the camera seem natural and ordinary, or a little bit more than ordinary. You never want the audience to second-guess the locations or the sets. It's why we ask for research. Rich tells me about the Mormon school. I ask if I can see it. He hesitates. He's got pictures. It's complicated.

The Glove speaks up. "We'll try to get out to the Mormon compound in the next two days. Their school sessions only have a three-week break. They don't like Hollywood. It's research, that's all. But I think it's a perfect model."

The garlic bread is delicious, as are the ribs when they finally arrive. I can't seem to connect with Rich. "Are there building spaces here, warehouses, storage units?" I ask.

"Not that I've seen. That's a big problem in Lone Pine."

I turn to the Glove. "No building, no storage?"

"We may have to go to Bishop but, like I said, let's give you a couple of days to realize what you give up leaving Lone Pine."

Cool, I think. Respect. No talk of budget. This obviously isn't Disney. Things get arranged and we meet for breakfast at the famous Alabama Hills Cafe at eight o'clock the next morning. After the long drive, I sleep sound.

Gus, the local scout, is late, but when he walks in the door the waitress with big eyes for Rich has his coffee poured and on the table. He's a little guy, gray hair, red eyes. He orders scrambled eggs and crisp bacon, toast -no butter- hash browns, and orange juice. He looks me up and down as he sits.

"So, you're the art director?" he asks.

"Production Designer," the Glove intervenes. "She's your new boss."

There's definitely tension in the Glove's Suburban as we drive out to the Mormon ranch. Yet the hills are wonderful, endless ups and downs, blue flowers and streaking packs of birds. Cactus and dirt. The western mountains behind us are lined with snow.

Ten thousand acres of cattle ranch is not in anyone's imagination, at least not mine. Then we arrive at the main house, surrounded by tall green trees and a wide, welcoming porch. Gus's son is smoking a cigarette as he leans on the railing. He smiles as we pull up, puts the butt back into the pack.

"Hollywood comes to nowhere!"

He steps down off the porch, and it gives me the creeps because he has Gus's dirty smile. "Even the Mormons don't like this place."

But I do. The main house is prairie, simple from the outside, welcoming, painted in sky-blue trim, but mostly white. Seems like there's water here, the bushes are green and hardy, rare in the high desert. It's warm, desolate, and about thirty yards from the porch is an unlikely addition that is obviously the dormitory. With no gates or fences. No prisoners here. A gray color, cheap windows, AC units on the roof. Simply works. Mormon mentality.

I start taking pictures. I have no idea who will be the director or the cameraperson, so I have no idea who I'll be selling my idea of what this film should look like. All I know is this is one version of reality.

LARRY – PRODUCTION MANAGER

I never even thought about how small Lone Pine is. My breakdown has seventeen actors, at least a dozen stuntmen, and about 200-man days for extras. This town is five blocks long. The visuals and the math don't make sense to me. And I figure we're bringing at least fifty, maybe more, crew members from LA.

The terrain is spectacular, Mount Whitney towering over the whole place, but I'm thinking about housing for the actors and the drivers who take them to work, the crew that lights, films, and feeds them, the production office that pays everyone including all the per diem and motels, and the worst part of small-town shooting...how everybody gets to restaurants after work. Once in Tucson four of us took the prop truck fifteen miles to a Mexican restaurant. The rig was so big, we had to park a mile away from the food.

Feels like a big fire needs to be set here. That's my job. Be the asshole. Ask the hard questions. I'm the UPM. The Unit Production Manager. Remember the Tom Petty song? I don't either.

Before I get to Lone Pine, I'm pulled over by a sheriff. Big, gruff guy. Says I was going fifteen over the speed limit. I smile, tell him I'm bringing a big movie to the valley, and can he cut me some slack?

"From LA, huh?" the officer smiles.

45

"Yeah," I smile back.

"Well maybe I was wrong." My hopes rise. "I'll write you up for twenty over. How's that?"

As he leaves, I check his name tag: Cummings, Bryson. Asshole.

We have dinner at Seasons, a small, tasteful restaurant on 395. There's a weird vibe around Glove's relationship with our waitress, Clemencia. Glove says he's going back to LA tomorrow. The Argentine director, who he hasn't met, is flying in and the casting director is starting.

Nina says, "So there's a director?"

"Maybe," the Glove says.

I take a bite of my salad and decide to put on a scene. I just got here and he's leaving. I'm pissed. "We're trying to make a big boy movie in this tiny little town, right? Excuse me, but I say bullshit!"

The table goes quiet. Glove looks at me, calm, curious, but serious.

"With all due respect, man," I continue, "we need to be somewhere that has resources, spaces to do what we want, hotels for the crew and talent. There are seventeen speaking parts. Where the fuck does everyone stay?"

The Glove grins.

"Build sets? Or are we not going to build anything? Like some TV movie? Before you leave, let's get real."

Again, the Glove grins at me. These guys never show panic.

After dinner, Rich whisks Nina and me across the street to KCs for a nightcap. The Glove settles into the Seasons' bar with Clemencia. Outside, the wind is fresh, a little warm. Not much traffic on the interstate.

I first see her backside as she slides through a swinging door with a plastic tray of fresh-washed glasses. She sets the load down and turns to survey the room, and our eyes meet. I have, I think, successfully negotiated a life of casual relationships with women, mostly fun, occasionally crazy, twice dangerous. I cannot deny how fascinating they are. Pretty, cute, adorable, beautiful, stunning…they come in all sizes and are endlessly enchanting to me. They say life on the road is a drug. I say life on the road is full of many drugs. Strange, mysterious women are probably the best of them.

The sparkly woman who then pours me a scotch, with a light in her eye and an Irish smile on her lips, buckles my knees. Her name is Carrie.

PART TWO –
THE TALENT
ARRIVES

RODRIGO – DIRECTOR

I am waiting to leave Buenos Aires on an American Airlines super jet, sitting in first class, a first for me. I am the director of two small films that screened at international film festivals, but that and a handful of pesos won't buy me a beer even in Argentina. I'm going to LA to direct a twenty-million-dollar movie, and I'm pinching myself, when suddenly an Argentinian pop star with a blond ponytail sits next to me. I don't know her name, but I've seen her on the magazines. An older woman, probably her manager, sits across the aisle from us.

She is maybe twenty years old. She smells like she's had a drink or two already. Some people are terrified of flying. She orders a Bloody Mary. Her eyes are a little blurry, her hands a little shaky. She turns to me and says in struggling English, "Sorry if I barf on you."

"No hay problema, popstar."

She laughs and passes out, head hard against her chest. I ask the flight attendant for an extra napkin. Across the aisle, the manager stares at her, then me. Should I trade seats with her? No, I like the window.

I pull out my script. Nickel, the production company, has sent it to me in a beautiful leather notebook. Evidently this company handled North American rights for both DARK WATER and MOUNTAINTOP. Both films made money for everyone

51

except me. But now I'm getting half-a-million dollars to direct this movie. I'm the happiest guy on the planet.

I always loved American Westerns. John Wayne, James Stewart, Clint Eastwood. Hero against villain, greed and race at the heart of every story. Sometimes love, sometimes sex. I could never get enough of it. WOMEN IN WHITE feels like a Western to me. High plains kidnapping, shoot outs, the avenging angels in uniform come to wipe out the tribe that only wants to be left alone. Classic.

But I have problems. The backstory, it's very sketchy. I grew up on a cattle ranch much like the one in *DARK WATER*, miles from any city. But every few months the truck with the propane would lumber out to us, fill our tanks, and head back to the city. And every three weeks my mother would go with her team to buy supplies, rice and beans, vegetables, kitchen essentials, whatever. We were isolated, but we still belonged to a community.

In this script, there is no explanation why the town knows nothing about this compound. If the women who run it are birthing babies, where do the diapers and formula and all the stuff babies require come from? And who is the leader of the cult? What's her story? Where do they get the arms and the ammunition? I need to know all this because when actors join the team, they will have these same questions.

It's a long flight. When we land in Los Angeles I start to smile, and I can't wipe it off my face even if I want to. I always dreamed of coming to LA as the next Scorsese, gritty street movies under my belt, ready for something big, crazy, important. We taxi for twenty minutes, and I'm wondering if the plane is driving all the way to the Paramount Studios just for me. Could Hollywood have that much power?

We finally stop and de-plane. I'm still smiling. I get through customs, work permit in place. I see Victor, mi amigo, waving from a crowd of greeters and drivers with name signs for those they're here to help.

He's like a loyal dog, great in a pinch or a lonely day, but otherwise you just wish he'd go to sleep on the sofa. We embrace, and as we do, I notice the suited gentleman with the sign SANTANA, which is my last name. He probably thinks he's waiting for Carlos and doesn't even look at me.

We eat Argentine beef kabobs that Victor cooks on an electric grill on his balcony. Not as good as home, but delicious nevertheless. I'm anxious, pacing around the apartment. Once we finish eating, we decide to go for a walk. He lives in Venice, so we head for the beach three blocks away.

It's late April and the ocean breeze feels great. Palm trees dance in the wind, and lights reflect off the water from the apartments along the sand. Victor asks, "Have you met any of the people involved in this?" I shake my head, no.

"I have a few friends in the industry," Victor says. "They all say be careful. Be clear what you want, and what you expect them to provide." Then a beautiful young girl, maybe twenty, wearing a tight swimsuit, skates past us. We look at each other, burst out laughing.

"LA baby!"

My phone rings at seven o'clock the next morning. It's Matthew. "Are you alright?" he wants to know. I explain my phone died on the flight and I had no idea someone was going to pick me up. My friend was waiting for me and I stayed with him. I apologize for not returning the texts. It was a long flight, I was exhausted...blah blah.

Matthew laughs. "I just spent $400 on a beautiful suite in Century City for you! Discounted-down for me from $850."

Why would he do that, I wonder. $400 would probably buy a Sunday barbeque for the cast and the cameraman, designers, and producers. I like to do this. Crew needs to know each other deeper than work. On my first two films, I paid for these gatherings. With a twenty-million-dollar budget, I am hoping we can pay for them on the books.

The car picks me up at 9:30 and we head to Hollywood and the Paramount Studios. My smile returns. Luckily, Victor comes racing out of his building with my script before the driver pulls away. Forgetting my script the first day would be the wrong way to start.

I walk down a row of sound stages at Paramount, and my head fills with images. Where was CITIZEN KANE filmed? DOUBLE INDEMNITY? SUNSET BOULEVARD? THE GODFATHER? CHINATOWN? Always I dream of walking down a row of sound stages. What would I do? How would I feel? The place is full of whispering. I don't feel ghosts here, and I do when they're around. Growing up in the wilds of Argentina, loneliness comes with ghosts.

I find the Nickel Productions. A lovely woman sits at the reception desk. "You must be Rodrigo Santana," she says. "Did you have any problem finding the building?"

"To be honest, I dreamed of walking around a Hollywood studio all my forty-three years. Getting lost was part of the plan."

"That's so sweet," she giggles. "They're waiting for you in the conference room. Through those doors, right turn and it's the first door on your left."

But before I can visualize where I'm going a man I learn is Matthew comes bursting out the door. "Welcome! Welcome!" and he hugs me like we are long lost brothers.

I'm introduced to a tall man who is the line-producer, whatever that is. He seems friendly, confident. There's a young woman with large red glasses who is the casting director. Evie, she is called. Two executive types sit at the far end of the table. A blond woman named Trudy and a man who feels like a banker named Edwin.

It all seems friendly, sincere, yet everyone feels guarded and searching for personality clues. I see a coffee set up in the corner and pour myself a cup. I feel their eyes on me, wondering, evaluating. I'm doing the same.

We go through the expected routine, how much everyone loves the project, how much everyone is entranced (Matthew's word) with my film *DARK WATER BENEATH US.*.

"I always love the American Western. Big vistas, honest good guys," I say. "The pace is slow to begin, building toward a bloody end, whether it's Indians or banditos or sheep ranchers against cattlemen. And always about territory. The brutal taking of someone else's land."

My eyes land on the line-producer. I like him right away. The casting woman is busy going through her notebooks. Good. I was hoping we could get started immediately. But first there's one more thing I want to say.

"Matthew, can I ask you one more thing?"

"Of course, Rodrigo."

"Will I have a chance to work with the writer soon?"

Matthew seems taken aback. He looks around the room. The line-producer steps up. "Uh, she lives in Montana. That's a long way from here."

"I understand, but before we go forward, I need some backstory fleshed out."

"Can you do it on the phone?"

"No. It's a slow process with me, pull this thread and it leads to this thread, pull this one and it leads to another, so on, so on. I need to get some answers before my cast asks the same questions I have."

I look around the room. Only the line-producer meets my eyes. "This meeting will happen just once, and then, let's go. You understand what I am saying?"

"Of course," the line-producer, who is called the Glove, responds. "Let me call her and see if she's up for a visit."

"Why not bring her here?" Trudy speaks up.

"I feel it's better to go to her, where she's comfortable and maybe a little...what's the word?"

"Forthcoming," the Glove says.

And so it goes. The writer says yes; they book me a flight to Montana tomorrow morning. The Glove leads me down a corridor to Trudy's office. I'm told she handles the finances. She seems disturbed when we walk in.

"Matthew showed us *DARK WATER* the other day. Wow is all I can say. Beautiful."

The Glove steps into the conversation. "As you know, he's traveling to Montana tomorrow. We need to get him a five-hundred-dollar petty cash advance."

All the sweetness goes out of her face.

"What would that be for?" she asks.

"He's traveling on behalf of the company - Meals, taxis, hotel - who knows what happens when you're on the road?"

Trudy turns to look at Edwin, who so far has not said a word. He nods yes, and she turns back to us. "Okay, five hundred it is."

The Glove smiles. "You'll alert your bank that we'll be coming to cash it today, right? He's Argentinian. All he has is a passport."

I see her cheeks slowly turn red. Clearly not someone who likes to be ordered. The Glove seems like he's baiting her. If this was the Wild West, guns would soon be drawn.

"And while we're at it, two things: is there a payroll company handling the show? And I need a ten-thousand-dollar petty cash advance. People are working based on my assurances. They expect to get paid. And until there's a payroll company, I need a chunk of money to keep the attitude positive."

His words are met with silence. "That's the thing about production, it happens fast and not always as planned."

Trudy sits in her chair, staring up at him. "We gave Rich three thousand dollars."

"He's through that already." She is obviously not happy.

"Look," the Glove continues, an ever-growing bite in his words. "I doubt you've ever been in production, right?" She nods yes. "I've been in it for thirty years. You're probably hoping the twenty million will go out in ten checks. Makes it much easier. But it doesn't work that way. More like ten checks every half-hour. It's an Army on the move."

"But ten thousand is an outrageous amount of cash," Trudy fires back.

"You're trusting me with twenty million, and you're worried I'm gonna run away with ten grand?"

He stares at her. She turns angry red, stares back.

"Look, if you say it can't be done, fine. I'll take you at your word. Then I'm going to Matthew and say goodbye. Pull all my people from the location. If it's like this at the beginning, what's the point? It only gets worse."

From behind me, a man clears his throat. We all turn. It's Matthew. He might have heard it all. He smiles at us and says to Trudy, "Give him what he wants. Our fate is in his hands."

I look at the Glove, smile. He winks back.

She nods. Turns to her secretary to begin the paperwork. This really is like a Western. Tomorrow I'll be in Montana. Big Sky Country, they call it. Maybe they sell cowboy boots.

As they cut the checks, I leave the Glove waiting for them and head to the casting director's office.

"Hi!" Evie smiles at me like we've been working together for years. "Want to look at some pictures?"

"Any chance Frances McDormand plays the police chief and Sandra Oh the Woman in White?" Two actors I love.

"Maybe," she says. "I'll make some calls today. An Asian woman as the villain? Interesting."

THE GLOVE – LINE PRODUCER

I start the next day calling two production accountants I've worked with and trust. I prefer the company put their own accounting person on the show, but they have no one to recommend. My two are both working long term on big studio shows, so I call Larry and see if he's got someone. He does. Her name is Alison.

We meet for drinks at six o'clock in a small tapas bar in east Hollywood. She breezes in five minutes late with a big smile. She's late forties, short, curled dark hair. None of that matters, of course. She manages the money. That's all that counts.

"So, what's this project?" she asks.

I explain it's for an independent company that has money but no production experience. The budget is twenty million, the location is the Owens Valley on the eastern side of the Sierras. The director is Argentinian doing his first American movie. He's done two little independents that won prizes at Sundance and Berlin.

"You know, I grew up in the last glow of indie movies." She remembers, fondly it seems. "No studio looking over your shoulder, no second-guessing the reports. When you need money, you make the call and it's in the bank in an hour."

"I remember those days, too. But twenty million today is like ten million in the early eighties. It's going to be tight."

"And Larry's the production manager?" I nod yes.

"He's solid," she continues. "A little confrontational, but he's smart and clever. At twenty million, no stars or computer effects?"

So far, I assure her.

I want an accountant to be brave. I learned when I was a young production manager that it's so much better to confront problems, especially money problems, when they're apparent. Ignore them, sweep them under the rug, and sooner or later they become four-hundred-pound bedbugs and you're screwed. A great accountant will speak up, and loudly if they're not heard.

"So, how crewed up are you? Who's doing the payroll?" she asks.

"Waiting on bids. We have a location manager," I continue, "a local scout, production manager, production designer, director, casting director, and me. Once we pick a home base, the production coordinator and her assistant will come on and set up the office. In a few weeks, a set decorator, construction manager, maybe a costume designer."

"How soon for accounting?"

"Figure to start next Monday. I'm going back to the location, so we'll stay in touch by phone. I like to speak with people, not text short messages that hide all the sordid details."

She smiles. "I agree. Who's going to negotiate my deal?"

"Larry," I say. "I'll have him call you."

As I pay for our drinks, I think about Rodrigo. He wants to stay another day with the writer. And then spend two days in

LA with the casting director. Fine by me. But then he wants to come to us, see what we've found. That gives us four days before show-time.

Back in Lone Pine, we all have dinner at the barbeque joint again. They're exhausted from searching Bishop for facilities. Tired, but pumped. Even Gus seems happy. Rich is glowing. Larry is on his phone. And Nina sips her vodka rocks wearing a Cheshire cat smile. I invite them back to my room to watch Rodrigo's film *DARK WATER*.

We march down the street to the motel and into my room. I've set up chairs facing the flat screen computer monitor I brought from LA. There's a bottle of whiskey and one of vodka, some ice, and bottled waters, mixers, and colas on hand. Everyone pours to their heart's content.

Larry turns off the lights and I hit play on the computer. The screen comes alive, and suddenly we're all lost in another world. The film is shot in black and white, a rich, stark tone to the images. The one thing that always betrays low budget films is bad sound. The sound on this is magnificent. I make a mental note and feel Larry doing the same.

It's set on a remote ranch. The wind, the cattle, the horses, the far away business of the ranch house, beautifully mixed to set up where we are. Then there is laughing, running, two young teenagers, a girl and a boy, by a rushing river. You hear the sounds of young sex before you see it. It's Romeo and Juliet on an idyllic cattle ranch.

Juliet is the rancher's only daughter. Romeo is the ranch foreman's son. Both are strong, entitled, and helplessly in love. But then the ranch foreman catches them together and tells the rancher. He explodes, condemns the relationship, forbids his daughter to ever see her love again.

Long story short, they ride off one night on two horses. When the fathers realize what's happened, they send their best trackers to bring them back. The kids feel like they've escaped. They make love, swim in a river, laugh and show-off to each other. Then the posse gets close, and they realize they must run for their lives.

It's mostly a chase movie, but when the young lovers enter a dark and thick forest, things turn magical. The riders chasing them are close. The lovers send one of their horses off as a decoy, in a direction they will not take, so they're doubled up on the one remaining horse. The trick doesn't work. The horsemen chasing them keep getting closer.

As night falls, the two lovers hover on the ground together, coming to terms with what seems inevitable. They hear the posse approaching and climb back on their horse. As they head into the dark forest, all hope seems lost. Especially when they pass a large boulder and there is a towering black panther in their way.

But their horse seems relaxed, and the panther leads them to a hidden passage through the trees to a thick forest of ferns and an animal tunnel. The sound of the posse begins to fade. They meet other animals that speak with the horse. Eventually the posse gives up, turns back home, and the two lovers are shown over the mountains to safety in Patagonia.

When the screen goes black, I notice several sniffles. Nina for sure. And even Gus. The film is a powerful dark fantasy, told by a strong, smart filmmaker. He has a vision. It scares everyone, but in a good way. We all want to be on the team that brings his next film to light.

LARRY – PRODUCTION MANAGER

Fucking Alison wants three hundred dollars a week more than in the budget. She has two other offers but wants to do this. I need her. We go after the rest of her team. Lena's rate is in the budget, so we get into it with the size of her crew. Eventually she agrees to cut one full-time clerk and that pays for her extra three hundred dollars a week and then some.

Fiona, my production coordinator, is on the fence about going on location again. I haven't worked with anyone else in six years. I must have her as well. I bump her rate by two hundred a week and she hems and haws but eventually comes around. Two corner stones in place. I breathe freely for a moment.

The director's movie disturbs me. It's moody, atmospheric, full of rich images and very little dialogue. WOMEN IN WHITE is the exact opposite, a police procedural, lots of dialogue scenes, lots of characters. I fear this director will want someone who shoots for Tarantino or Fincher or whomever the new flavor is. He obviously loves cool shots, at the potential jeopardy of the schedule and the critical talk-talk scenes. Nevertheless, I can't downplay the beauty surrounding us in the Owens. I need to talk with the Glove.

He's not answering his phone, so I wander down to Seasons and see him through the window at the bar laughing with Clemencia. Pretty difficult to hide in Lone Pine after dark. I don't want to interrupt his dalliance, so I go across the street to KC's, hoping Carrie is working tonight.

Gus is at his usual back table nursing a beer and a shot of dark. Carrie barely smiles as I walk in, turning from behind the bar where she's prepping glasses to see who just strolled inside. Her choice, I say to myself. I sit on a stool and order a scotch neat.

I grab my drink and head over to Gus. He sees what's coming his way, blows his nose in a napkin, reaches for the Miller.

"Man, that was a great movie!" he says.

"Pretty impressive," I agree.

"Have you met him?"

"Not yet. But he'll be here in four or five days."

"When the bullets go into the chamber." He smiles.

Gus is getting a little bleary-eyed and keeps going on and on about Rodrigo's film. My imagination is running about cameramen he'll want. Low budget indies like that shoot fast and take chances. Big Hollywood cameramen take no chances and don't care how long it takes. I need to consult with the Glove, but for now I'm stuck with Gus.

"Rich tells me he senses some hostility to LA people in this valley?" I ask.

"Hostility?" Gus grumbles. "Most of them are multi-millionaires thanks to LA. A few feel they got the short end of the stick when the diversion plans were drawn up, or they refused the DWP's offer. But most went along with the program, and everybody got rich. Feeding the tourists is a monster industry that wasn't even imagined until the DWP showed up."

"So...you think we'll be able to do business around here?"

"Still got rattlesnakes in the wood pile. Got to be careful but, yeah, we can do business here." He kills his beer and waves for Carrie to bring another round.

I walk back to the motel forty-five minutes later. There is little traffic on 395 and the town is quiet. A breeze blows down from the west, off the Sierras. As I walk past the swimming pool, I notice a light in the Glove's room. I decide to take a chance.

He is clearly not pleased to see me at his door. His pants are on, but he is bare-chested. "Is this important, Lar?" he asks.

"I think it is," I respond.

He opens the door and brings me inside. The room is still set up like a screening room, chairs facing the large screen. He excuses himself and goes to the bathroom.

I pour myself a nightcap from the whiskey left on the bureau. Pull up a chair and sit. The Glove comes out buttoning his shirt, pulling the door shut. "Okay, what's up?" he asks. He pours himself a shot too.

"Just having a little bit of a panic attack about Rodrigo's movie."

"How so?"

"It's an art film. He's directing a substantial Hollywood movie now, and I just hope he doesn't demand A-Listers up and down the crew. First off, this is a crime procedural, facts and questions and conversations trying to get at the truth.

We spend three hours lighting a car coming down the road and turning into headquarters, we're dead."

"I haven't had any conversations with him about this but, believe me, I will."

"Is he represented in town?"

"Yeah, United. They got him after Berlin."

"Then he's already got their list." He nods yes.

"Oh, I want you to know I made a deal with Alison and Fiona. Alison starts Monday, she said you two talked about that. And I'd like to bring Fiona on as soon as we pick Bishop and a spot for the production offices. We saw a good one two days ago, a closed down junior high. Lots of parking, school rooms for private offices, a gym, and a cafeteria. We have a line on an IT guy who says he can do everything we need."

"Good luck on that," Glove scoffs. "He'll probably be the first one on the team to get locked up in the loony bin."

We both laugh. Suddenly the bathroom door opens and Clemencia tentatively steps out, holding her shoes.

"Sorry," she says to the Glove, "but I have to get home to my kids." The Glove jumps up, squeezes her arm and gives her a quick embrace, and she's out the door.

The Glove sits back down, smiles at me sheepishly. "I was going to read crime fiction and not go out." He shakes his head. "Fat chance, right?"

"Pretty soon we'll all be so busy there won't be time for fun. Take it while you can."

I pour myself a little more and open the door to leave. A family in a huge pickup truck is moving into the room directly beneath mine. Great.

"You feel good about Bishop?" he asks.

"We'll see what you think tomorrow. Frankly, it's a no-brainer."

The Glove sighs, looks over the mess his room is in. At the bed where...

"Don't worry, I'll call Rodrigo first thing tomorrow. What time's breakfast?"

I get to my room and look over the schedule. The casting director is whining about a day out of days—the schedule of when the characters work—so she can start checking availability of actors. The request is certainly reasonable; it's just very dangerous so early in prep when the director has not even come on a location scout. Those people involved in the process who don't ever get their hands dirty or their feet wet take the first details laid out and that is all they ever remember. Schedules, budgets, start dates, it's all the same.

RICH – LOCATION MANAGER

Big day today, everyone going to Bishop to see a potential production office complex and an art department situation. The Glove drives Larry and Nina in his SUV, I drive Gus in my Subaru. We have a date at ten with the guy who has the keys, then the art department space at eleven. The tricky part for us location managers is saving your best for last. Often the person making the decision sees the logic of the first location and wonders, since this is the first you've shown, what else is there? It's like you're offered the royal suite at the Palace in Monte Carlo, and you say, "Someone told me about this other place..."

I doubt the Glove will respond like this. But if he does, I'll remind him this isn't Atlanta or Vancouver or even Chicago or Portland. The choices are limited. And whatever we choose, it's going to take time to decide who goes where and clean up the space, furnish it and install all the communications. The army will soon be on its way. When it gets here everything needs to be perfect.

Gus's apprentice, Luanne, found this closed–down middle school about two miles outside Bishop's Main Street. The city decided to extend elementary school through seventh grade and then start high school at eighth grade, thereby cutting the middle school and saving a lot of money.

The building was constructed in the nineties. Earthquake fitted, no asbestos, twenty individual classrooms, a small auditorium, and a cafeteria with a large kitchen (caterer). Plus, tons of parking off street in two big lots. And there is a small gym for maybe wardrobe storage or stunt rehearsal. Perfect for a suite of production offices.

We pull up to the front of the building and the guy from the real estate office with the keys is waiting, a nervous man whose hair is not as grey as his pallor, smoking a cigarette and looking at his watch. Are we late? I check mine and we're ten minutes early. I park and jump out of my car.

"Are you Fred?" I ask.

"Yes sir," he answers.

The others climb out of the Glove's SUV, head toward the building.

"Thanks so much for meeting us. Hope we're not too late."

"In fact, you're early," he smiles, grinding his cigarette out on the front step. "I like early people."

I always wanted to be a writer. As a kid I read obsessively. I hated Little League and Cub Scouts, but I loved stories of adventure, strange places. Heroes. Shipwrecks and dangerous islands. So, locations felt like a perfect gig. Grind all day in the real world, dream all night in my mind's world. Get paid to work around creative storytellers. So many of us location managers start out wanting to be screenwriters. Only the young ones still do.

It's the selling part that usually puts a knot in my stomach. You've driven around for countless hours and now you're standing someplace you know is perfect, and it all turns to shit. Where the nasty bits of human nature – ego, suspicion, did I say ego? – rise and make a great location scout a bitter brawl over what works and what doesn't. Closing the deal.

This really is a no-brainer. Bishop is a city in the boonies. Robert Fortune Middle School. Wonder who he was? Empty buildings are always strange. Nature seems to have the 'after dark' keys to the doors. Leaves get bundled in the corners of the halls, spiders and rat dung cover the floors. Movie production doesn't really care about any of this. We'll clean it up and make it work for us.

Fred unlocks the front door and leads us into the main entry hall, abandoned administration offices to our left. We need space. Walls and roofs for offices and areas to prep props and wardrobe. That's all. We see the cafeteria, the auditorium, finally the gym. It's better than perfect to me. But I can't read the Glove's and Larry's reaction.

"This seems perfect. Any other choice?" the Glove asks.

"No," Larry answers. "Lots of room, private classrooms for above-the-line offices, a kitchen for the caterer, an auditorium and gym for whoever. Plenty of parking."

"Nothing else?" the Glove asks me.

"There are some warehouses, but we'd have to create offices and work areas, worry about privacy, security. And the two we've seen are both by the airport. Noisy. This is the best we've seen."

"Does the money make sense?"

Larry responds. "Waiting for you to say yes. If so, I'll make it work."

Next on the list of locations is my favorite, a closed down Lutheran church. If the closed school becomes the production offices, what we really need now is a stage for the sets we plan to build. Most of the time we end up in a warehouse, usually not ideal, but somehow we make them work.

Churches have traditionally kept the concept of a tall ship turned upside down as the space for worship. This means there aren't any center posts, poles, or supports of any kind. It's just one big empty arched space. Take away the pews and the risers and it's basically a perfect sound stage.

When the Lutherans split, they sold the pews and the risers and left the church empty. The large parking lot can accommodate all the cars and production trucks we need. Plus, they left a building that was their Sunday school, again totally blank, directly next to the church. Perfect Art Department space.

The man who reps the property waits for us. He's short, in his thirties, dressed in a white business shirt and a striped tie. We're five minutes late. As we arrive, he smiles, heads to me since I'm the one he knows.

"Hey Charles!" I call out to him. "Thanks again for meeting us."

"No problem, Rich. Long as I still get the part in the movie." He laughs. The Hollywood crew climbing out of the SUV hears this, looks at me.

"I'm afraid the only part left is the sex scene."

Charles grins, unconsciously tucks his shirt in tighter.

"I'll start practicing tonight!" He laughs.

The church is large and barren. The floor is wood, the ceiling very tall with tiny windows lined along the top part of the circumference. The Glove turns to her. "What do you think?" he asks.

"In terms of place and needs, this is absolutely..." and she hesitates, then throws her arms out wide, flashing a big smile. "Fabulous! No tin roof, no support columns, if the flooring is great all the better, but if it isn't, we'll lay a movie floor. Any idea what we're going to build?"

"Not yet. But certainly the police station. Maybe the interior compound." This gets her attention.

"The ceilings are high," she says. "Which the DP will love, and it's off the beaten path. No truck traffic noise."

"Sound will love that," Larry chimes in.

I'm smiling. I think we've got two buys on day one. And they're not just buys, they're perfect. I look over at Gus. He's staring at me, a cold look in his eye. He reaches for his cigarette pack, walks outside.

Larry asks me, "What's this cost?"

I answer, "For how long, and what are we doing here?"

He smiles at me. The game is complicated. We all stroll back to our vehicles. The Glove looks at Gus and asks, "What's the best lunch in town?"

Gus drops his scowl and thinks. Then he smiles, says, "The Mountain Rambler."

"Lead on," the Glove responds.

Larry goes inside and gets us a table. Outside, Gus lights another cigarette. I stay with him. "So," I ask, "what's going on with you? Is there something wrong you're not telling me?"

"Not at all," he mumbles, looking down the street.

"Then what is it?"

He flicks the butt of his cigarette away to the sidewalk, shakes his head. There's clearly something dark in his brain. "Don't be hiding anything. You know better."

"Now we got an office, a warehouse, you know, the invasion will be coming soon. We'll stop being a little team of friends and just turn into a cog in the big wheel. Loses something to me."

"Why you old pisser," I laugh, "you're turning sentimental!"

He gives me a hard look.

"It just shifts, that's all." I try to reassure him. "Now we're with Nina and the art department instead of the Glove and Larry. And after that we'll be partnered with the cameraman and the assistant directors. And finally, we'll be attached at the hip to the Teamsters. You know this. It's how it goes down."

Gus lights another cigarette, looks off.

"Since the director arrives on Monday, let's go knocking on doors tomorrow, so we have something to show him other than just great scenery."

"You want to pay me for a Saturday?"

"If I have to," I reply and turn back to the restaurant.

NINA – PRODUCTION DESIGNER

At lunch the Glove agrees to both the production office and the construction space, and, if Larry can make a deal, we've crossed those two big items off our list. Bishop is our new home base. The lunch is great, everyone laughing and drinking seriously cold local beer, delicious in fact.

The next morning I order the Tyrone Power Scramble for breakfast. It's delicious, but very spicy. Not the gift I want to send my stomach before a long day inside a car on bouncy gravel roads. All the rich food lately has started a mini rebellion in my gut. Oh well. I'm not above shitting behind the car in the desert.

I ask Gus where we're going. He gets this look in his eyes, puts down his knife and fork. "Before I turned twelve, I was totally afraid of girls. They were all like my sisters and mother. Pure evil. But Rosemary Silvera, who was in my sixth-grade class, invited some of my friends and me to her 12th birthday party." I catch Rich looking away, a slight smile cracking his lips.

"Her father was the biggest sheep rancher in the valley, and his best friend controlled a large part of the Owens River. There was about twelve of us, in three boats, and we went up the river to try and catch our dinner. But the girls had a plan, you see.

"Twenty minutes out from the dock they took off their shirts and pants and all that was left were these bathing suits.

Man, me and my friends freaked out. Never seen a bikini before. Sometimes I think my dick's been hard ever since."

Rich laughs. "You wish."

I don't know what to say. "So, she's the owner of one of the ranches we're seeing this morning?" I ask.

"First one." Gus grins. "Haven't seen her in twenty-five years."

Oh great, I think. Is this going to turn into 'What Ever Happened to Baby Jane?' You get in the scout car, you never know. Just another example of the glamor of show business.

We pile into Rich's Subaru, and he offers us bottled water. "Gonna be warm today."

"Let's keep them in the cooler until we get thirsty," Gus says. Rich agrees, puts them back in his little camper cooler.

We head north on 395. I ask Gus how many acres this Rosemary owns. "She said around four thousand. At the height of her Daddy's reign it was about twenty thousand. She don't run sheep anymore. Leases out the place to outsiders."

"Still sheep?" Rich asks.

"Far as I know."

Forty minutes later, we're in Big Pine. The road is busy with pickup trucks and big rigs. It's Saturday and everyone is on the move. To the right are the White Mountains. We turn off 395 on Hwy. 168 and head east into the morning sun.

This highway has been cut through some tough volcanic rock. We wind around the two-lane road for about twenty minutes, steadily climbing into the mountains. I try to imagine the 1920's and 30's, when things were bustling around here, trains shipping livestock from the ranches and minerals from the mines to the south or north, LA or Reno.

I realize, if I wanted to hide while I carried out some crazy shit to end abortion, this desolate country is perfect. I read in one of the research books that it all started to change about the time the LA DWP came snooping around. There were bigger ranches and more product north of here, Oregon, Washington, Idaho, Wyoming. Roads were getting built so trucks could bring their goods to market. Though the ranches in the Owens weren't small, they ended up not being able to compete. Slowly the rail lines faded into the desert dust as the highways replaced them.

The desolation is also perfect for something else. Taking a crap by the side of the road. Which needs to happen right now. My bowels don't listen to reason. Maybe yours do. I ask Rich to pull over. Then I plead with him. Then I scream my fucking head off.

Fortunately, Rich has a box of Kleenex in his car. Once that's over, squatting in the sand, I get back in the car, grateful for the download. They're smiling at me. "Fuck off," I say. "Better out there than here."

In minutes, Gus motions for Rich to turn left off Westgard on White Valley Road, another two-lane paved road. Gus is alert, checking notes he's scribbled on a cocktail napkin. He spots a small sign on a fence post by a gate that reads 'Silvera' and motions for Rich to turn left up to the gate.

He jumps out and unhooks the latch and swings the gate open. We're here. Rich drives through and Gus closes the gate and climbs back into the car. "Twenty-five years, huh?" Rich smiles. "Nervous?"

"She asked me if I still looked the same. I said I do if you do. She laughed."

The road down into the valley is gravel and bumpy, but we descend into an arroyo where I catch sight of grazing sheep and a couple of men on horseback. It really is isolated and really beautiful. No power lines, no phone lines.

We drive for a mile until we come around a bend and there is the ranch house. It's nestled in the foothills with a creek beside it, and the working innards of ranch life spread out to the north. A bunch of dogs come running to see who is here. If you were going to raid this place, coming from above with a magnificent background is pretty much perfect, at least cinematically.

Gus is looking at me in the rearview mirror. He winks.

'Course the old girl don't disappoint. When we was in high school she set me up with her best girlfriend at some dance. Both lost our cherry out back of the boys' gym. I figured Rosie was put on earth to show me not all women were like the ones in my family. She never came close to me, but she was the sister I never had.

Rich parks and we get out. The dogs are jumping on us and, in Rich's case, slobbering all over his pressed khakis. This unravels him. Nobody has pressed seams in the country.

The place feels familiar but different somehow. The house used to be painted brown; now it's white. Trim was green. Now it's dark blue. I don't remember the rose bushes along the pathway. There's a tall trellis that blocks the view of the Sierras off the left side of the front of the house. Still, nothing's really changed all that much in the past thirty or so years.

Front door opens and the dogs go quiet. She's thin, silver gray hair, in jeans and boots. She stares straight at me, and I instantly feel guilty about something. Same old, same old.

"Rose?" I ask.

"Gus," she answers, smiling.

"My God, you're still beautiful," I stutter.

She offers her hand, business–like. "It's been much too long."

I introduce Rich and Nina. This ain't your typical social call if you live in the White Mountains. Rose is charming yet guarded. She brings us inside, toward the back patio where there's cold lemonade and a tray of butter cookies.

Back when her dad was alive and the ranch was jumping, it wasn't weird to see boots and rifles laying around the living room. Now it's a fancy sitting room, and there ain't no clutter.

Rose pours drinks all around. "Well, welcome to my family's home. We've been here for over a hundred years."

Nina clears her throat. "It's magnificent, Rose."

"Yeah, really is," Rich agrees, trying his best to be the leader full of smiles. LA people never get it. People like Rose don't give a shit about that stuff.

Rose turns to me. "So, how can I help you, Gus?"

"Well," I answer, wondering if Rich has already put her off. "We're making a movie about a small town in the Owens Valley, and we need an isolated ranch to film at."

"Really? What's the story?" Rose asks, smiling innocently. "Been a long time since Hollywood has come calling around here." I look at Rich, and he looks at Nina. Where's the Glove when we need him? Rich clears his throat. We're dead, I think.

"Well, in this small town there's a one-woman clinic, a three person police team, two schools, first through seventh, eighth through graduation. And there's this weird thing that's been happening. Teenage girls get pregnant and go to the clinic, asking about abortions, then they disappear. Months later they're found wandering in the hills with no idea what happened to them. And no longer pregnant."

Rose is confused. Clearly turning suspicious. She looks at me, gives me a severe look. But Nina speaks up. "The story is about a cult surviving in the middle of the central issue in women's lives today. Have your baby and give up your own freedom to it. Or abort it and continue on your path, wherever it leads you."

I sit back and watch as Rose starts to think. Keep my trap shut.

"These are not easy choices," Nina continues. "And the police chief, a strong woman with a teenage daughter, is fed up with the town's men telling her to go back to ticketing big rigs and drunk fishermen and forget about the young girls who end up without a memory of the most important months of their lives."

Rose leans forward.

"As this policewoman scratches the surface of this, all kinds of evil come out. Including a compound in the middle of nowhere where older women kidnap these girls, nourish them until they give birth, then brainwash them and set them free, wandering without a memory."

Nina looks to Rich, who nods to continue.

"At this compound, the Women in White raise the babies as anti-abortion warriors. When the cops finally come, they end up fighting these fierce women and girls with automatic weapons."

I'm ready to go. Nobody in the Owens Valley is going for this. What was I thinking? But Rose looks directly at Nina. "And my ranch would be the compound?"

"That's what we're here for," Nina continues. "We're looking for a setting that is stunning in its beauty and tricky in its terrain. If these radical women are to be dealt with, they need to be formidable. They need to be isolated. And the setting needs to be powerful."

Man, I need a drink right now. Make it five.

Rose is solemn, looking slowly to each of us. My Dad always told me her father had the longest slow burn in the county. Nina drops her head, convinced she's blown the whole deal.

Rose stands. "Well, if this ranch is in contention, shall we go look at it?" She looks at me curiosity. She seems to be slightly intrigued. We head outside. Rose asks me if I want to ride a horse or the ATV?

"You don't have a helicopter?" I ask. She laughs.

We explore the property in ATVs. Gullies and streams, hills and dips. It's beautiful. I've spent my life running around hills like this, but to the fresh eyes, it's a little slice of Heaven. Nina smiles like a kid at the beach. Rich even takes his shades off.

The last stop on our tour are the pond cabins. As the ATVs come around a stand of pinon pines, we see a large still–water pond surrounded with tall green reeds. Sitting on the water like a royal family are five mallard ducks.

Up the surrounding hillside are eight cottages, old twenties' structures with front porches and clothes lines, stone chimneys and water wells with pumps and buckets, raised bed vegetable gardens, horse corrals, nobody around but clearly the feeling that somebody lives here.

"Dad always moved the herd to this meadow in the late spring, after the snow melted," Rose explains. "In the old days we ran five or six hundred head of sheep, and usually it took ten shepherds to drive them here from the valley. He built these cabins for their families. Drilled into the marsh to create this lake, stocked it with trout. And that's how it's been for over half a century."

"Could we build a two-story house here?" Nina asks Rose. "Probably have to cut a road. Or even better, ship in three cargo containers and create our own compound."

"My. All that for a movie?" Rose wonders. "There is a pickup truck road, out behind the cabins." She clearly likes Nina.

Rich steps up. "I don't know if Gus explained the process, but we're the first wave, then the director comes and sees the place, then plans are created and changed over and over, then a decision is made."

"Would the shepherd families have to leave?" Rose asks.

"Probably," Nina says forcefully.

"But we'd pay them for the inconvenience," Rich adds.

Rose looks at me. "Everybody gets paid in Hollywood," I say.

Nina takes off with her camera and spends a half hour photographing the compound. She's briefly chased by an aggressive rooster, but the noise brings out an angry old Mexican crone from the nearest cabin waving a cast iron skillet. The rooster knows he'll lose this match and retreats.

Rose takes me aside. "Is this really real?" she asks.

"It is. This is the process, Rose. You need to understand yours is the first place we've looked at, and we haven't even met the director yet. He gets the final say."

"So, this may all be a waste of my time?"

"Got to see me for the first time in twenty-five years." I smile.

"Better than drinking a pot of coffee and listening to Rush Limbaugh."

"Tell me that's a joke."

Rich wanders over, having taken his own five billion pictures. "I've been doing this a long time, but this might be the most beautiful location I've ever seen. Your father had quite a vision."

Rose smiles. "My father was a tough man in a tough business during a tough time. But he always said you take care of your workers, just like your family. Otherwise, you've got nothing and you're building on nothing."

Nina bounds back, all smiles and heavy breathing. "What's the altitude here?" she asks.

Rose answers, "About thirty-five hundred feet."

"Man, I can feel it." Rose assures her you get used to it.

We're finished here and we climb back in the ATVs. Rich and I can see Rose and Nina talking and laughing as we make our way back to the main house. Rich tells Rose we're going to want to come back some time Tuesday.

"Make it morning," Rose says. "I've got church duty Tuesday afternoon."

With that we drive away. First stop, home run. Always weird to leave a location full of positive energy knowing the next place may be even better. Especially when the person you're hustling got you laid the first time.

LUANNE – LOCATION ASSISTANT

Gus owns an old two-bedroom house off the highway in Independence. I've rented the back bedroom from him for the past year while I take on-line courses in screenwriting. That's what I want to do, write movie scripts.

Gus worked in LA in the film business, so we hit it off at the jump. He's got fantastic stories about Hollywood greats he never met. Especially after a few beers and a hit of pot. Last week he told me about this movie project he's working on. Wondered if I wanted to earn some money as a location scout. You live in the Owens, you never turn down money.

First, he wants me to find some large place for offices in Bishop. No problem. I guess Bishop is like most small towns these days; the booming eighties are gone, the civic buildings mostly abandoned, everything is for sale or rent or whatever.

My mom's friend lost her job as a teacher when the city closed the middle school. I call her, get a number, go and see the empty school. I take some pictures, and, like throwing your first cast into a lake you've never been to, there's a strike and you land a ten pounder.

Next, he wants me to find a large empty space with tall ceilings and lots of parking. My church, or rather my grandma's church before she became a Baptist, just closed its doors. Country Christians watch TV on Sunday mornings now. The mega-churches rake it in from the TV and the internet.

I check out the closed church. It's what was described, high ceilings and empty as a day-old sushi joint. Hit number two. I guess the powers that be loved my pictures. To Gus I'm now a rock star. But next up is the big challenge. The primary location in the movie.

I ask if I can read the script. After all, it's what I want to do with my life. I'm blown away. It's a war between good and evil, each side determined and armed. It calls for a compound that's protected from any prying eyes, doesn't need any 'Keep Out' signs. And run by a nasty bitch who cuts slack for no one. Fits my grandma perfectly.

That's why I'm waiting on her porch looking for a Subaru to come down the two-mile straight-line dirt driveway to her house. The house was built in 1890 when her great-grandfather ran a cattle ranch west of the town of Benton. About thirty miles north of Bishop. You had to take a wagon from the ranch to Bishop, and Bishop was like Paris to his kids - a Woolworth's and a gun shop, oh my. It's on a long, water-rich valley where they still grow alfalfa and run some cattle, but now grandma leases out the grazing to California corporate ranchers and their Mexican foremen.

A wide porch surrounds the front and sides of the house, and inside there's an entry parlor that leads to a large living room. Upstairs there's six big bedrooms, three with balconies. The kitchen hasn't changed since grandma was a little girl, large pantry and a washing and scrubbing room that leads outside.

I grew up visiting this place. I learned to ride a pony here, shoot a gun, kill a chicken, even helped birth calves and puppy dogs. We made apple and cherry pies in the same kitchen as it is now. Always with the dark shadow of Grandma hovering over everything.

At first, Grandma was not remotely interested in a movie coming around, but then I told her how much it could help me and how much money she would make if they liked it. She's a tough old bird, early-sixties with the attitude of a twenty-year-old devout Baptist, and she doesn't like anything about the culture since before Elvis showed his pelvis. But she does like money.

Right on cue, she steps out the front door as I see the dust plume of a car pulling off Highway 120. Like an arrow, this road has nowhere to go except straight to this porch. I look at my grandma. She's small, lean, probably a beauty in her day, her eyes like blue flint. She sees the 'incoming', looks at me.

"What kind of money we talking here?"

"Don't know. They're shopping right now. If they like it, and I think they will, they'll be back in a few days with the guy who makes the final decision. Least that's what Gus says."

"And this Gus, he's your landlord?"

"He's a Wilson. He's honest. Been around, but you know…"

"He's a Wilson, he's a snake," Grandma says.

I smile at her. "We all know that."

The dust trail keeps getting closer. Feels like two trains about to collide.

"What's this story about?" Grandma asks.

"It's about hard ass women fighting for God's way against abortion and coming to a confrontation with the government that don't agree with God's way," I answer, hoping this will cool her down. "It's just a movie, but it raises some questions in your mind."

She chews on this for a while. "You make a child, you make a commitment to God. That's all there is to it," she announces.

The dust trail is almost halfway here. Can I suggest my grandma get cast? I shake my head, rethink what I just said. And in an instant, they're here.

NINA – PRODUCTION DESIGNER

As we drive to the next ranch I sit back and go through the pictures on my camera. Rose's place is intriguing; a hidden beauty, hilly, rolling with gullies and steep canyons. If we shoot here, I know the sun's position will be critical. Bright sunshine and dark, shadowed hideaways. Evil and danger always need a visual mood. This could be scary. Bright, lush Heaven and dark, shadowy Hell in the same frame.

While I'm dreaming about this, Rich turns off the highway and we enter a narrow agricultural valley. It looks like where they shot *The Waltons*. I keep this observation to myself, but I can't help but laugh. We've gone from sheepherding on rocky mountains to cattle ranching on lush pastures. I wonder: Does this have the same dangerous quality as Rose's?

Rich heads down a driveway that looks to be at least two miles straight as an arrow. To the right and left scruffy desert stretches, no buildings, no nada. But in the distance, there is green. Civilization. Irrigation. (Are they the same?)

Like I said, the driveway is long, very long. Dust kicks up as we head toward the end, where a stand of tall trees suggests a home, a base of operation... a lonely place in the middle of nowhere. My antenna perks up. I start to forget Rose's place. It's creepy.

None of us have been here. It's all on Luanne, the hero of the office complex and the construction space. The place is strange, quiet. The colors are green, drab green, which would be great in Pasadena but here feels guarded, unwelcoming. And then there are the two women on the porch, standing and staring.

I hop out feeling a little nervous. The gray-haired lady on the porch radiates hostility. I've met Luanne before, briefly, and I smile at her. She smiles back. The older woman's eyes are narrow, like a cat on the prowl. She doesn't see me or Rich; she's staring down Gus. He stays by the car, silent. Like a frightened puppy.

I see the shot. Both directions, cop cars coming down a long dirt driveway kicking up dust, charging the bad guys with an attitude that says, 'we're coming, and you can't stop us'. It's a classic Western movie location.

Rich and I walk over to Luanne, greet her. She turns and says, "Grandma, this is Rich. He's the location manager and my boss. And this is Nina, the production designer who puts the pieces together to make how the movie looks."

Grandma somehow snaps out of her mood and gives us the most disingenuous smile I've ever seen. Says, "Well, welcome. Luanne has told me a little about your project."

Rich tries to spread the scent of adventure and money in front of her, see if he can get her curious enough to get a rope around her without her feeling it. I'm always amazed anyone would let a bunch of strangers into their home. At first, it's a few people, a dance of seduction. Wows, movie stories, a thousand pictures. Next there's a dozen of us, measuring and talking quietly together in a corner about the stairway your father built twenty years ago and the color your mother painted it. It can get heartbreaking.

If it goes full-term, when the cameras and the actors arrive at your private space, there's over a hundred of us. Complete invasion. Every single day. No one knows who you are, cares what you think, and it's better to start drinking early while you wait for your money.

I once shot at a home outside Atlanta for six days, six days of nightmare, double-heads in the roof, carefully planted flower beds stomped to the ground by electricians pulling cable, a neighbor's dog hit by a van taking a load of actors back to the hotel at night, and in the end the sequence got cut from the movie. Heartbreaking.

Luanne has her grandma arm in arm as she shows us inside. I wish it wasn't so; Rose is so nice and trusting, her ranch so beautiful. But this property is perfect. Isolated. Dark. Ominous. I can see a small army of fierce women here, cooking and cleaning and planning for the apocalypse. Red bleeding through white.

It reeks of scary haunted house. It even has a basement, dark and musty and full of soundless noise. The living room has the bones to become the Women in White nerve center. There's been talk of building this as a set, but holy cow! It'd be fun to watch this old lady's sitting room transform into a sophisticated war room as they sense the jaws of the law closing around them. Sideboards flip into computer workspaces. The Evil Empire rallies its outside forces. The huge windows to the sunshine beyond become cold, aggressive mirrors.

I'm thinking we shoot it all right here, build no sets to match this location. Then I shudder. This should be a set. I know this. But it's so perfect. And sets that play inside to a real outside are tricky. Yet, the space is large. It could work.

We go outside and I notice Gus come hesitantly around the corner from the front yard. With a cold eye, Grandma spots him. He smiles, lights a cigarette, and turns back toward the front. We used to have a big dog back in Nebraska who just did not like one of the ranch-hands, and that dog could put a bead of sweat on that man's forehead from a hundred yards. Grandma and Gus remind me of this.

Rich smiles. "You good?"

"Very," I say.

"So how much do I make?" Grandma wants to know.

"Well, it's all a process, ma'am. Next step, we bring the director here. Hopefully that'll be on Tuesday. If he likes it, usually he'll want to think about it, maybe come back again, plus we've got one other place to show him... say maybe by the end of next week we'll have a decision."

"I got to wait that long?" Grandma groans. "What other place are you showing him?"

"I think her name's Rosa Salinas," Rich says.

"Silvera," Luanne chimes in.

"This ranch is perfect for our story," I speak up, trying to keep everything positive. "It's isolated, obviously it's built so solid you could lift it up fifty feet in the air and drop it and the tablecloth wouldn't move. Bet it comes alive with wild animals when the sun goes down."

"Oh, you bet. When I was a little girl, I used to swear I saw a white buffalo up on that ridge behind us. Right at sundown. But you're not wanting to drop this house to the ground from fifty feet, are you?"

I smile. "No, I just said it because it seems so strong."

"My granddaughter thinks you folks are honest," she says, looking at Luanne, who nods yes. "So I guess I'll go along. Let Luanne know when you want to come back. But don't wait too long. I'm old and feeling restless about things these days."

"Oh, Grandma!" Luanne laughs, "You've got a year's worth of yarn in there to keep you busy."

As we drive away, I lean forward and put my head between Rich and Gus. I'm like a teenager now. "Oh my god! That place is so weird!" I squeal.

"But you know what's really weird? It's perfect! Middle of nowhere! Feels old and tired like nothing's going on. Perfect camouflage. And you can just feel the resistance, can't you? Don't come around here, nothing good will come of it."

"Probably right about that," Gus mumbles.

We finally get to the end of the driveway. As we turn on the two-lane highway, we all look back. This could be our home away from home for the next three months. "Hey Gus, what's the weather like around here, summer through early Fall?" I ask.

"Snow nine days out of ten," he grumbles. "And on the tenth day hell freezes over."

Rich and I laugh. Can't wait to hear what it is about this place bothers him.

"You go out with her too?" I ask.

"Wouldn't touch that with Rich's dick," Gus growls back. We all laugh.

Okay, so far so good. We have two solid choices for the compound. I'm wondering if Luanne should keep looking. If we had one crappy choice we could show first, then the other two would shine even brighter. Admittedly, it's bush league, but at the end of the day selling property is what the location department does. Plus, I haven't sat down with either owner. Bound to be some surprises.

It's just after three when we roll into Bishop. We're looking for a place to get a beer and some food. Gus points to a driveway leading into a city parking lot. There's a neon sign for a place called Rusty's Saloon, food, drinks, and dancing.

We enter a hallway through the back door. Immediately hillbilly fiddler music fills the joint. I look over at Nina. Her eyes are wide, her smile even wider. She's got crazy on her face. I know she feels, in her own words, we 'fucking nailed it' today.

We turn out of the hallway to a dance floor and a small stage full of drums, amps, guitar stands, mics, the usual set-up for a bar band in the boonies. At present, though, two fiddlers in blue jeans and Western shirts are wailing away.

Nina immediately starts dancing. Out of nowhere, she's joined by a tipsy old gent who's actually pretty good. She looks at me, laughing, and motions she needs a drink. Vodka rocks, no doubt. I nod and join Gus at the small table he's grabbed for us.

A thin, older waitress comes over. Gus orders a double whiskey with a beer chaser. I order a shot of whiskey and a beer, plus a double-vodka rocks for Nina. We settle in, check out the scene. It's afternoon, but the stools at the bar are almost full.

The front door rattles open as a big rig rumbles outside, and a tall American Indian man, maybe forty years old, steps inside. His hair is jet black and tied in a ponytail that falls down his back. He's wearing black jeans, a black long-sleeve shirt, and a black formal Stetson. Dapper. He surveys the room and steps toward the music and the dance floor. Nina and her partner are still laughing and twirling away.

Gus watches him like a hawk.

"What?" I ask.

"I say we drink up and move on."

"What are you talking about?"

"This is Saturday in Bishop. Fighting day around here."

"I'm starving. Can we at least get some barbeque before we leave?"

Gus doesn't even hear me. He's looking at Nina as she leaves the dance floor. The Indian introduces himself. She smiles, shakes his hand, motions she's with us. He looks over, sees Gus. Understands he's being watched. This is all too Starsky and Hutch for me.

Nina slides into her chair as the drinks arrive. "Wow! That was fun," she beams. "That old guy can still pick 'em up."

Gus turns back to us after staring at the man in black. He picks up his whiskey and takes a healthy gulp. "You want food, gotta go next door to order it. They'll bring it here once it's done."

"But first," Nina interrupts, a sexy smile spreading over her face, "you have to tell us what's up with Grandma and that place."

Gus takes a pull on his beer, sets it down. Takes another sip of whiskey.

"The old bird is a Dieter by birth. Her great grandfather and mine had beef over a piece of land out by Rock Creek, where the hunting lodge was and the pack horse stables are now. About thirty acres with river and lake fronts. Worth, guessing—five million now. Gramps Wilson won in court."

Gus looks us in the eyes.

"The Dieters thought Gramps bought off the judge. Been war ever since." Maybe this is Starsky and Hutch.

Gus stands. "I'll order some ribs, how 'bout it? I'll have to pay. You got a card or something I can put down?"

"I'll go with you," I say.

He looks over to the bar where the Indian has claimed one of the stools and is enjoying a beer in a bottle. "No. You stay here." There's something sinister in his eyes.

I reach into my wallet, hand him my MasterCard. "Do you want my ID?"

"They know me. Don't worry. Pork, right?"

"Absolutely," Nina says, then chugs the rest of her drink. As Gus goes next door to order food, Nina heads to the bar. "One more for the road!" she laughs.

As she leaves, I realize I haven't taken a piss in three hours, and half a beer turns me into a longhorn looking for a flat rock. I get up and wander toward the back where the toilets are. There's grease on my trousers I need to deal with ASAP.

When I finish pissing and scrubbing, I find there aren't any paper towels in the dispenser. Okay. I try the toilet paper but it's thin and breaks up in my hands. Why don't restaurants buy good toilet paper? How expensive can it be? I need paper towels. I go outside and realize I have to wait for someone to enter or exit the ladies' restroom.

In about two minutes a woman comes out. I explain my situation. She looks me up and down, sees the water spot on my pants, thinks, and turns and goes back inside. She returns with a couple of paper towels. I thank her as she walks back to the bar.

When I return to the table, there's no Nina. Not on the dance floor. Not at the bar. And where'd the Indian go? Our waitress comes over, wondering if we want another round. "Yes. Did you see where my friend, the woman with short dark hair, went?"

"Oh, she said to tell you she went off with Cody and she'd see you tomorrow back at the hotel."

"Cody?"

"He's the one dressed in black. Great dancer." She smiles, hustles back for our drinks as Gus returns to the table.

"Where's Nina?" he asks.

"I went to the head and she left with somebody named Cody. Said she'd see us tomorrow back in Lone Pine."

Gus turns ashen, then red with anger. "God damn it, that guy is bad news."

"I don't know what to say. Did she just get kidnapped?" I feel horrible, and I don't know why.

"Around here people think he's a shaman. You know what that means?"

"Do I want to?"

"I don't fucking know! Jesus, Rich, I told you this isn't Studio City! There's serious danger around here. Why would she do this?"

Our drinks arrive and Gus chugs his whiskey. I can see the wheels turning in his head. "There must be something... what should we do?" I ask. I pull out my cell phone and dial. It rings and rings, then goes to voicemail.

"Nina, it's Rich. Please come back to Rusty's. We're worried about you."

Gus stares at me. "She's on the rez by now. Out of our hands." The food arrives and we eat hurriedly, in silence. Then leave. I drop Gus at his house in Independence. He'll get Luanne to bring him down to Lone Pine tomorrow for his car. I tell him I want her to keep looking for another compound, preferably a little less perfect than the two we saw today.

I'm numb about Nina. If this was San Francisco or Portland and she hooked up with some guy on her day off, no biggie.

But Gus has put the fear of God in me. "Don't worry about her," I say to him, pretending it's okay. "She's a big girl."

He grunts and opens the car door. "Hope you're right, Pal-o-mine. Also hope you learn a lesson."

And off he walks to his house. Funny little man with all his suspicious energy. I call out to him. "Did your great grandpa pay off the judge?"

He stops, turns around. "What do you think?"

As I drive back to Lone Pine I continue to worry. What if this is bad shit? Should I call Larry and tell him what happened? Saturday on location is for two things: relaxation or adventure. 'What happens in Bishop stays in Bishop' kinda thing. Still, if she's in danger, can I live with my silence?

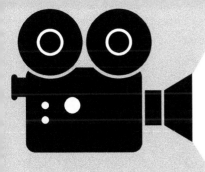

PART THREE – PREPARE FOR BATTLE

LARRY – PRODUCTION MANAGER

First day with the director and I'm on edge. No one saw or talked to Nina all day Sunday. Then Sunday night she calls me, confused by the dozen phone messages from me and Rich and Gus. She met a quiet man and a great dancer who took her to the Paiute reservation for some kind of ceremonial dance, and she ended up staying the night and most of Sunday, and nothing happened and she's fine so if I would please tell Rich she's okay and tell Gus to fuck off, she's a big girl and there aren't goblins or monsters alive in the hills or on the rez, and if there was, she's not afraid of them either.

I'm in the Creekside Inn in Bishop in a conference room the hotel comped for a lunch meeting with the director, who's on his way from LA with the Glove. I was restless, didn't bring my golf clubs from home, so I went to the Bishop golf course and rented some. At the driving range I met a young kid and asked if he wanted to help on a movie that's coming to town. On payroll. He enthusiastically said yes.

Now he's at Mountain Rambler waiting for a take-out order of lunch for 8, though I ordered for 12, in case choices are needed. I'm looking at my clipboard, my list of things to deal with today. I made deals at the Creekside for the above-the-line and the Cielo Hotel next door for the key below-the-line crew. Everyone else is going into the Best Western down the block, at least until they run out of rooms.

In LA, Alison is working on a bank account and getting checks printed with a local Bishop bank. By Thursday, we'll need to write checks. My credit card, and Rich's, are maxed out. Fiona and her assistant, tall Liz, will be here tomorrow setting up the offices, along with the two in accounting.

My Teamster captain arrives tonight with a twelve-passenger maxi van, and I need one more office PA by the end of the week to bird-dog the communications guy and the furniture company in Reno. The IT guy is meeting Fiona in the afternoon tomorrow, and she'll give him the details.

The Glove texts me. Should be here in thirty minutes. I call down to the front desk. Start bringing up the beverages and ice buckets. Still no word from Arlo, the golfer PA. Damn me, I forgot to get his phone number so I can't text him. I can text Nina, making sure the flowers are in the director's suite. He's on the creek side with a balcony looking out on the water.

Suddenly, the door opens and Arlo, Rich, and Gus scurry inside, each carrying a medium tray, one with sandwiches, one with pasta, and one with salads. Check! Then Boyzie hustles in from the hotel, two large plastic bins loaded with iced beverages riding on a dolly. He and Rich hoist them up on the table.

"Be right back with the coffee," he says. He told me this morning he's from Boise, Idaho, the only Black man to escape Idaho in a hundred years. Pretty sure he's joking.

Nina sneaks in as Boyzie leaves. She's in denim shorts, a black-striped blouse with short sleeves. With her reading glasses, she could easily pass for an eighth grade English teacher. She carries her laptop and several reference books.

Rich is looking out the window. He turns, catches my eye. "Eagle has landed." I take a count. Me, Nina, Rich, Gus, Arlo, the Glove coming in, the team so far. And now the ship's captain and his assistant will be with us. Eight. Check.

They say the director is the one who answers a hundred questions a day. Compared to the UPM, that's nothing. The director can say what he wants or sees, and that's the end of the conversation. The UPM must argue his side until the other gives up. Money. Crew size. Prep time. Equipment rentals. Location costs, props and set decoration and wardrobe rentals, extras count, caterer crew size. It never stops. That, my friends, is what the UPM deals with every hour of every day. Sword fighting fourteen hours a day for the next five months

Right now, I just hope Rodrigo likes the food. They march in, first the Glove, smiling and confident. Then Rodrigo, slight and grinning. And bringing up the rear, Rodrigo's assistant, Victor, the one I will have to deal with. There is lots of sincerity, hugging and the like.

The Glove insists everyone get something to eat and drink, mostly because he's starving. We all settle at the conference table. Rodrigo and Victor are checking us out, as we are checking them out. All seems pretty open, friendly.

Rodrigo speaks. "I just want to say how grateful I am for your support and energy. When you do little films, the prep is slow. There's no ticking clock." He laughs. "But this, I am told, and I believe, is very different. First thing I understand is we are starting a race, so I'm thankful for all of you coming aboard and getting right to it." He smiles again as we smile back. "But there's one thing I always do with my close-to-the-heart crew. I ask them to say what their three favorite movies are. It helps me get a feeling."

Gus clears his throat, pipes up. "Shouldn't you start?"

"Exactly what I want to avoid."

We all look at the Glove. He sits, a buddha smiling quietly. "I'd say, *GODFATHER II, DANCES WITH WOLVES* and...*SHAMPOO*." I swallow my laugh; can't believe he's stoned this early. *SHAMPOO*? But Rodrigo grins. "Love *SHAMPOO*. Good choices."

We go around the table. Nina's are *AMADEUS, BLADE RUNNER*, and *FATAL ATTRACTION*. Because the sex is so great. Rodrigo smiles. "Three great American movies," he agrees.

Gus catches my eye, taps his pinkie finger. I look over at Nina. On her left-hand pinkie is a small ring with a silver feather attached. She catches me looking and smiles.

Gus starts his turn with a question. "Pornos don't count, right?" We all laugh. His choices are *BACK TO BATAAN, CHARADE*, and *BABE*, about the pig on the farm.

Rodrigo chuckles. "I love *BABE*. Good choices, Gus." He turns to Arlo, who's cramming potato chips into his mouth. "And who might you be?" Rodrigo asks.

Arlo panics, looking to me. "He's our production assistant. He's from around here, knows the local lay-out." He looks around the room, nervously stretches his long fingers involuntarily. He's a good-looking kid, around six feet, short, sandy-blonde hair. Athletic. Can hit a golf ball on a line for miles.

Rodrigo smiles. "Welcome, virgin."

Arlo turns rigid. I laugh. "Come on Arlo, what's your three favorite flicks of all time?"

He thinks. "Umm...I guess the first *JURASSIC PARK*. Man, that flick blew my mind. *8 MILE*. That is one dope movie. And my grandpa's favorite, *LONELY ARE THE BRAVE* I think it was called. Must have watched it ten times with him. This loser dude on his horse in the mountains running from the Feds. Sad."

We're all a little mind blown. Arlo steps up! Rodrigo smiles. "You're right about *8 MILE*. Great movie. And *LONELY ARE THE BRAVE*? Classic." And so it goes around the group. Rodrigo's picks are *THE GODFATHER*, *Z*, and John Ford's *STAGECOACH*.

"So, we do have some changes to share with you," the Glove says between bites. "Rodrigo spent three days with the writer, mostly, and forgive me if I'm wrong about this, working on the back stories, who the characters are, where they come from. Not a lot of changes, but one fairly big one."

He looks to Rodrigo, to see if he wants to take over the conversation. Gus gets up, goes to the food table. I'm surprised the Three Stooges weren't on his list. Gus gets a text. Rodrigo clears his throat, takes a sip of Diet Coke.

The Glove says, "Well, the story now takes place on the planet Carlothian."

Victor laughs, and that cues the rest of us.

"Actually, the changes seem minor to me," Rodrigo starts. "The woman sheriff served in the army in Iraq, where she was raped and impregnated and came back from active duty determined to have the baby. And her daughter is now sixteen and herself pregnant. And adamant on having her baby, which her mother is totally against. Count on the Sheriff's house with more scenes than before."

"Do you see it as a set, on stage?" Nina asks.

Rodrigo laughs. "Tell me, pretty lady, what's a set?"

The Glove speaks up. "There's one more major change."

"Yes," Rodrigo agrees. "The Women in White. They're not just isolated predators. They are part of a western-states network. They steal young girls from the three surrounding... what did you call them?"

"Counties," the Glove answers.

"Yes, counties. They belong to a national organization. It's how they pay for the hiding places, the food, electricity, water, weapons. The Network generates lots of dark money. They are as sophisticated as the survivalists you see on TV. In bits and pieces, I'd want to see this network, feel its anger and its power."

"When do you think we'll get the new pages?" I ask. The Glove and Victor speak up. The Glove lets Victor continue. "Hopefully by next week," he says. Rodrigo nods his head.

"So tomorrow," I say to Rodrigo, "we want to take you to the Alabama Hills back in Lone Pine, and then two choices for the Women in White compound. A long day, but we'll see how we do."

Rodrigo looks at Nina. She nods. "They're great locations. It's amazing around here."

With that, the meeting is over. I look at Rich and Nina. One big change, but if that's all there is, we can handle it. The Glove grabs his bag as I slide over and whisper, "Did you get a chance to talk about cameramen with him?"

He groans. "The town is already on to us. Rodrigo wants lunch dates with Bob Richardson and Chivo. And some new guy, up and coming Mexican, named Xavier."

"I hear he's great. Fast and funny. We can't afford Richardson or Lubezki. We'll double the schedule and the crew."

"I know, I know. But let's not go to war on day one. Let me play this out. You work on AD, Props, which is going to be big because of all the weapons. Call Craig, see if he's available. And the Effects team. I'll handle cameraman and editor and stunts."

"Okay. I'd like to meet tomorrow for breakfast, say 8AM? Can you pass that along to Rodrigo? And Victor, I guess."

The Glove nods, turns and leaves for the front desk. He's staying at the Creekside too. Nina comes over. "Just wondering if there's any chance I can stay at this hotel. It would be great to be near the director."

"Can't right now. All the hotels are jumping, especially toward the fall. I guess this is a new LA destination to see the trees changing. I want to hold all the rooms I have for the key actors."

"And the cameraman, probably," she sighs.

"No, he or she is next door, too. At least until Rodrigo goes to the Glove."

Before Nina can move away, Rich and Gus surround us. "We've got a problem," Rich says.

"What?" I ask.

"Rose Silvera just texted that she heard from Luanne's grandma, and now she doesn't know if she wants to get involved with us."

"What did Luanne's grandma say?" Nina demands, puffing up.

Gus speaks up. "Apparently, she and Rose's family also have beef, and understand, Rose is a delicate flower. Scream at her and she goes away."

Nina is furious. "Look, I can't go over there now. I want to get with the director. You two go over there. Fix it. This is production! We need both ranches!"

Arlo has been packing up leftovers, but he's been listening, and speaks up.

"You talking about Rose Silvera, in Big Pine?"

"You know Rose?" Gus asks. "What's your last name?" Arlo answers, and Gus says, "He's coming with us. Now!"

Boyzie sticks his head in the door. I nod, say, "We're finished here. It's all yours. Thanks a million."

"Oh, I won't charge you that much...yet." He smiles.

Rich slides up to me. "You coming with us?"

"Can't. Go fix this yourself."

Rich asks about money in the budget. I calculate. "Let's say six weeks prep, first and second unit, two weeks shoot first unit, one week shoot second unit, and a week wrap. Ten weeks. Thirty thousand dollars, no more than fifty. I'd love to end up south of thirty."

Rich nods. "Got it. Let's see what happens."

ALISON – PRODUCTION ACCOUNTANT

Lena and I are waiting in line for a table at Paramount's executive commissary. We just met with the rookies at Nickel Productions. I'm daydreaming back to my first day in the business. 1987. We thought it was heaven in '87. The Pretenders. David Byrne. Madonna.

I was living with my boyfriend in an apartment over The Poet Lariat bar in Marfa, Texas. He was an artist, a painter, supported by his grandmother who thought he was learning to paint cowboy pictures to sell to hotels. Mostly he was smoking weed and drinking beer, which I learned was how a lot of young artists get ready to face the starting line.

I was the accounts clerk for the local paper. Two hours a day and all the instant coffee I could stomach. Waiting in line to eat lunch at Chez Que in Marfa, I listened in on a conversation between two older women also in line. They were going on about finding someone in town who could add a column of numbers. I could, for Christ's sake.

I gleaned they were the first wave in on a movie shoot that was coming to town, and instantly became curious. The last movie production around here split with two girls pregnant. Folks were pissed.

There were no open tables when I got to the head of the line, so I settled for a seat at the counter. Two minutes later the same two ladies sat down next to me. I smiled. They asked me what was good here. I said the orzo salad and the filet stir fry were the only things to consider. Unless you loved beef ribs, which I didn't at the time. And, of course, the lemon meringue pie.

They ordered both the salad and the stir fry to split, with pie as dessert. We started talking. The job consisted of three weeks of filming at a cattle ranch outside town, with some bar/restaurant scenes sprinkled in late in the week. The production was looking for local people who could fill in at the second-tier positions. Simple accounting. Copy makers and runners. Assistants to drive some of the bigshots to and from location.

I told them I could do accounting, and as for the rest of the locals, Marfa was full of people who would love to get paid for making copies and driving stars. The woman who turned out to be my boss, smiled and hired me on the spot. Eight-week guarantee, five-hundred dollars a week (some six-day weeks), and can I start tomorrow? Five hundred a week for eight weeks? That's four-grand in the bank. Four more than I ever had. I got the bug right away.

Now, I'm next in line at Paramount with my adorable assistant. We're ushered to our table. In the corner a producer I know, sexy little girl, Elisabeth Seldes, is surrounded by young assistants fawning over the incredible opening weekend for her film, *HOBERMAN'S DILEMMA*. A Christian movie from Disney about a man who cannot set foot in an elevator, any elevator, because of a phobia so powerful he wouldn't do it to save his life. And now that he's dead from a heart attack, he must take the elevator to Heaven or remain here in Hell, working at Disney.

We sit and order lemonades. I get right to it. "Okay, tomorrow we see Larry. What's to be expected?"

"I told you this already," Lena moans. "I got to his house around ten, he opened his computer, showed me the schedule. He was serious about me understanding it, because he said everything else comes from that, why actors are scheduled this way, why night work slides toward Friday, moving in and out of locations for first and second units, always trying to compress the time we take up in real people's lives."

"And..." I ask.

She smiles, shrugs. "We worked really hard, concentrated on the details, not wanting a computer error to poison the number. By the time it was seven PM, we'd pretty much gone through a first pass at a budget.

"We head for the pool, and he orders Chinese delivery. I like him. He's intense, all about the business, but sweet. Seems to love to play the victim. UPMs are like that. You told me that."

"And that was Monday? And you got home Tuesday?"

She looks at me like a sister who's about to admit screwing the gardener.

"I went online last night. There are some great rentals around Bishop and Mammoth. You want to share one, save some money?"

"What's in the budget for crew hotels?"

"Originally it was $140 a night, but we bumped it up to $175."

"That'd be $350 a night for the two of us. $2,450 a week. $9,800 a month." Sounds evil.

"We could have the greatest party house ever!"

That might not be a plus, I think.

ARLO – KEY PRODUCTION ASSISTANT

I'm in the back of Rich's Subaru and he's driving fast. Gus asks me, "How well do you know Rose?"

"Well," I say, "my Pops started working for her about fifteen years ago. Her husband had just died."

"And?" Gus keeps going.

"I remember she cried a lot. The sheep were in the valley and the upper ranch was real quiet, just her and her daughter and a bunch of dogs. Sometimes my dad would go out and make sure the tractors and the three-wheelers were running and check the plumbing in the house too. That's when I was there. First time I ended up in the pond, I didn't realize she was in too."

"Must have been cold as hell."

"I stepped in dog shit by the cabins and wanted to clean my boots, so I went down to the water. The edge was so slick I just slid right in, clothes and all. But the thing was, she wasn't wearing any clothes. Swam right up to me out of nowhere and pulled me to the dirt. Naked as a blue jay."

"And?" Gus asks.

"I remember the veins around her nipples were blue," I answer. I feel embarrassed, but it's something I've never forgotten. "Never seen a naked woman before."

"Dad didn't have Playboys in the bathroom?" Gus asks.

"Was she still friendly after that?" Rich asks, pressing the point.

"My Pops calls her a saint. Always gives us a whole butchered lamb for Christmas."

"Answer Rich's question!" Gus growls. "How does she get along with you now?"

"Oh, we're fine. Nothing happened, and neither of us ever mentioned it again."

Gus coughs. "Can you help us persuade her to stay in the process?"

"Are you going to say her ranch is it?" I ask. "So she can stop listening to Luanne's grandma? That woman's a witch."

"You know Luanne, too?" Rich asks.

"She used to date this guy who had the best weed in the valley. We're still laughing about some jokes that no one will ever remember."

We turn on 168 and head east. We pull up to the old house and the dogs come running out to meet us. Always trust a home that has a bunch of dogs. The front door opens and Mrs. Silvera steps out. She's smiling, but I feel it's a fake smile.

"Oh my God, is that Arlo?" she asks, beaming at me.

"Hi, Mrs. Silvera!" I answer. "It is indeed Arlo. From many moons ago. I'm working on this movie. How's the day going for you?"

"Well," she says, looking at Gus, "I'm a little confused..." and she waves her hands in the air like she's trying to get rid of a swarm of biters. "To be honest with you, Arlo, I don't know if I've been invited into a pond of hungry alligators."

"Well," I say, "I know these people, and there isn't any alligators. I'm sure we can work this out. There's definitely money involved. I guess there's some history with you and Grandma Dieter."

"There's more than that." She drops her head, shakes it sadly. "She's crazy, but crazy like a snake. Somehow, she knew our ranches were competing for the job, and she called me out of the blue and started screaming about how the Silveras were not going to screw the Dieters one more time!"

She struggles to catch her breath. "I'm old, I don't like conflict. And I especially don't like Mrs. Dieter. I don't even know what she's talking about anymore." She squints at us. "Where's Nina?"

Three days ago I was lofting seven irons 160 yards straight down the middle of the driving range. Now I'm speaking for the location department on a major Hollywood production. What wormhole did I fall into?

Gus steps up to her. "Can we have some cold water and sit on the patio for a bit?" A light like friendship switches on in her eyes. "Of course," she says.

We settle in on the back patio. Mrs. Silvera brings a pitcher of cold water and some glasses. "I've got stronger if anyone wants," she says. Rich jumps in. "This'll be fine, Mrs. Silvera." Gus frowns, reaches for his pack of cigarettes.

"I do wish you wouldn't smoke around the house," Rose says. "Too much temptation for a forty-year addict, I'm afraid."

"Mrs. Silvera," Rich says.

"Please, call me Rose. All of you."

Rich smiles. "Okay, Rose. Thank you. I obviously don't know what Mrs. Dieter said to you, but like Arlo said, all of us think your ranch is one of the most beautiful locations we've ever seen. I've been in this business for almost three decades. Your place is simply incredible."

Rose blushes, sneaks a peek at Gus, then me. Rich continues.

"Unfortunately, where we shoot the movie isn't up to me, or Gus, or Nina. It's the director's choice. Our job is to present him with wonderful choices. And your ranch is at the top of our list."

"Yes, I understand all this, Rich. It is Rich, right?" He nods; she continues. "But once your business is over and you've all gone away, I still live here. And I'm feeling this is much more... impactful in the grand scheme than just a little movie filming at my ranch."

"But it's really not. Whatever location we pick is like an enclosed bubble. We only deal with the local community when we buy materials and hire crew members who live here. All anyone sees is a good thing in the neighborhood. We don't bring our own hardware, lumber, heavy equipment, whatever. We buy it or hire it locally."

She looks at Gus. "Stay in the race, Rose," he says softly. "If it's you, I'll personally take care of you and your ranch."

Rose pours another round of cold water from the pitcher. I can see her wheels spinning.

Rich leans in. "Just so you have all the information, we're thinking about a month of preparation around the cabins and the pond, a month of filming between main unit and second unit, and another two weeks to wrap. Ten weeks, three thousand dollars a week."

Wow. Thirty grand and all the shit goes down a mile away from the house. Seems pretty sweet to me.

Rose sits back, thinks. "And Nina is here all the time?" she asks.

"Absolutely," Rich lies.

"Well, I was thinking more like five thousand a week, to be honest with you."

"Based on what?" Gus leans forward, almost growling.

"Based on what I want for all the distraction. And there's one more thing. I understand most of the activity will happen a mile from my home, but friends in Los Angeles have told me there's a never-ending stream of questions. So, I want Arlo here at this house with me every day your company is on my land."

Rich looks at me. Gus looks at me. I didn't do nothing! Far as I know, I'm Larry's guy. Rich answers, "Fine. Arlo's yours. Does this mean we can show the ranch tomorrow to the director? Has to be in the afternoon though."

"Already it starts. I said in the morning, I have something with the church in the afternoon."

Gus pipes up. "You don't need to be here. I will. This is just the first step. Broad strokes, as they say."

Rose stands. "Well, I don't know how I feel about this at all, but okay, let's take the next step. With friendship and trust in our hearts. And if it's this ranch, you'll take care of Mrs. Dieter before her cross-eyed kin come round and burn me out?"

Rich and I laugh. Gus doesn't.

"Of course," Rich says, standing. He shakes Rose's hand, and we head for the front. Victory secure, so far.

"But," Rose says before we leave the patio, "let's get the money straight. Gus can tell you my grandpa and dad were all about the money. And so am I." Everyone freezes.

"Thirty grand is what I have in the budget, not fifty. But maybe we can split the difference?"

"That's forty thousand dollars, Rose," Gus chimes in.

"I took the same math class you did, Gus. Even went to it," she says. "Okay, if my place is the choice, we have a deal."

FIONA – PRODUCTION OFFICE COORDINATOR

There's an old saying: Shit flows downhill. It's not Irish, but it should be. I'm the production office coordinator, I run the mothership. The home base for all that is production. War is always about protecting the home base.

I crack the whip, try to make sense of it all, the changes, the personalities. The team behind the camera are my babies. The ones in front? We'll see. Probably just babies. On the Mothership, we women always protect our babies.

And we do that through organization. Logistics is our sword. See the need, find the answer, make it happen. Murder is not out of the question. The crew knows if they want something, a prescription or a room change, a piece of equipment from New York, a plane ticket for a loved one or a weekend snog, a production deal on a weekend car rental, it all comes through me. And the crew is typically seventy or more people. Rarely do I turn a blind eye to any request. I like helping babies. I'm Irish. I've known my share.

Tall Liz is my right-hand woman. We've slogged through five projects together, three with Larry and two with people who shall remain nameless. In my early days in the business, just come from Toronto where I worked as a production assistant on some LA-based TV crap, I was working as an assistant to a TV producer.

He and I once sat in a smelly retirement hotel in downtown watching our production trucks come from a cemetery in East LA where the day's work began, to a parking lot across the street from the hotel on skid row. It was five o'clock on the Wednesday before Thanksgiving.

The effects crew was rigging rain towers along the street, a second effects team was planting the explosives that would blow up a storefront and key the stunt chase, the pre-rig electricians were lining the gutters with electric cable and scaffolding for lights, and the stunt team was going through the big explosion/car crash that was to be filmed that evening, hopefully before midnight when all the labor rates went into triple time because of the holiday.

My boss turned to me like he'd just had a religious experience. "It's like war, a fucking war," he realized. "It gets prepped, the soldiers arrive, what's going to happen is talked out until language is not even relevant, and then some idiot yells ACTION! and it all blows up! And the same idiot asks, can we go one more time?"

I understood completely. In war, survival is the only thing that matters. You outlive your enemy, you win.

All that said, Liz and I drive to Bishop on Tuesday morning. We have an eleven AM meeting with the assistant, Luanne, who found the closed-down school which might become our home base, and the realtor representing the building. Sometime after lunch we meet a communications guy from Bishop.

125

I pick up Liz at 5:30AM and we head north. We both have large, insulated coffee mugs and the car heater is blasting. It's cold this early in the morning. There's barely enough room for our bags in my Toyota minivan.

She's got the longest legs in history, and she's wrestling with the passenger seat to move it as far back as possible. "Please don't break my seat," I beg her.

"I'm surprised you didn't rent a Mini Cooper for this trip," she growls back.

We smile at each other. Been through a lot together over the years. Her father died four days before we started shooting BLUE RIDGE RHAPSODY in Virginia. We were dealing with a schedule change because a freak early storm destroyed an exterior set in the mountains, and we were trying to change travel dates for nine different actors, some coming later, some earlier.

It was just her and me and a couple of locals who answered phones. She knew he was sick, but not this sick. She tried to work through it, but after losing her for two half days to tears and exhaustion, I told her to go home, be with her mother and sisters and brother, not to worry about me or what's happening here.

She thought it over that night and showed up at the office at 7AM with a suitcase in hand. We both knew how fucked this was, but we didn't say anything, just hugged and waited for the teamster to take her to the airport.

"See you in four or five days," I said as I kissed her. Two days later she was back at her desk. Family is family, but the team is the team.

We arrive at the location ten minutes early. Luanne, young, pretty, around twenty-two, with a face full of concentration and intent, is on her cell phone by the school's main entrance. I park and sit watching her for a minute. I'm hungry. Thought about the McDonald's we just passed. Can't give in to junk food this early.

At first, it's like house shopping. A production office needs a roof, floor, rooms, entrance, large rooms for departments, security, parking. Mostly parking. Then comes the furniture count, desks and chairs and tables and sofas and VIP furniture.

Liz is my shadow. I walk the floor, see the scheme, walk it again and change the scheme. I get one chance. She keeps count. Number of desks, chairs, tables, sofas, file cabinets. I've heard there's a fast, efficient furniture rental place in Reno. Liz keeps a tight count on what furniture I'm riffing on. I like to go sparse. Make them come begging for a floor lamp or a soft chair.

I spot Luanne stepping out of the space that was the school's cafeteria. She's staring at her phone, reading a text while trying to get at an itch above her right knee with her left one. Her brow is creased, jaw set with determination. Liz leans over to me, smiles.

"If her hair was red, that could be you ten years ago."

I look at Liz. "In her dreams," I say.

TIM – TRANSPORTATION CAPTAIN

I'm waiting in the driver's seat of a twelve-passenger maxi van in the parking lot of Jack's Restaurant on 395 in Bishop. The survey crew is finishing breakfast inside. I ate there two hours ago. Then I drove around Bishop, getting the lay of the land, where the crew hotels are. I topped up the van with gas, washed all the windows, filled the ice chest with bottled water.

Larry steps outside, waves. He's good people. Been with him four times. They all file into the van, the Line guy standing by the shotgun door, holding it for the director. The director tries to climb into the back where the bench seats are. The Line guy stops him, tells him in the US all directors are given the shotgun seat.

"So, I fire at the robbers first," Rodrigo laughs. "Where's the shotgun?" Little does he know it is broken down in a case under the seat where he plops his ass.

Transportation is basically the heart of production. Something goes wrong, anything, it all comes to the office. The UPM is straight up, the girls in the office flirt back, we handle the problems of production. Pick this up. Go get this. Bring her here. When you think of it, that's what production is, handling the shit. Drivers are the army of production.

In the beginning I try to observe the key players. Their emergencies will be mine. The director, who knows? He's working in America for the first time. The Production Designer is hot. Dark hair, friendly smile, nice rack. Drivers know everything. Don't go into film production without understanding this. We see everything. I understand Fiona and Liz are in the office this time. All-Star team. Solid paperwork, truthful answers, and legs. Bless you, Liz.

We head south to the Alabama Hills. It's an hour drive but the line producer and Larry think it's the best way to start out seeing the valley. Show him the jewels and get his heart rocking. To our right are the tall Sierras, in the late spring their granite peaks still dusted with snow, Mt. Whitney towering over everything.

Rodrigo is excited. He wants to go where no one else ever has, where no camera has ever been. Bad instinct. Picking locations at a place where the trucks can't go? What's that? Inside a whore house with no money.

Rich, the location manager, sits next to the Designer, his maps and a notebook full of diagrams and scribbles spread across his lap. He tells me to turn right after we cross the creek, on a little dirt and rock road. The van is mine, and it's riding on heavy duty shocks and springs. After ten minutes of bumpy road, he tells me to pull over and park. He flips open the side door and everyone piles out.

Rich leads, followed by Rodrigo and Nina, then the Glove and Larry. The director's assistant and Gus guard the rear. Off they go on a trail toward what looks like a cliff area overlooking the valley. I go the other way around the van and take a long piss.

It's my job to think about where the trucks park if we shoot here, and where base camp gets set up. Trucks, talent trailers, catering, all the worksites. What vehicles do we need to run actors and equipment back and forth to the shooting site, probably around that huge rock and down into the valley. Narrow hiking trails with small hard rocks all over the place.

I learned a long time ago that shooting in the desert, high or low, is dangerous for transpo. To fight for the impossibly beautiful location, the creatives swear they'll need the bare minimum on set, and they'll understand and be patient with the logistics.

Then we're shooting and it's six thirty AM on set and 35 degrees out and everybody's shivering and blowing hot breath on their hands, and the ADs are on the walkies to me asking if craft service-hot coffee-can come closer, and if there's any chance the talent trailers can also, especially the director's?

Or even worse, the director promises we're shooting this direction only so I can park all the trucks close to camera, because it's the desert and there's no place to hide the rolling stock without creative cooperation. Then the DP gets to set. He takes the director on a long walk, and they come back and whisper to the First AD, "Sun has changed. All the trucks have to move."

To where, they don't know or care. There have been some historic fistfights over moving all the trucks, who's to blame, what takes so long? Pros work hard to avoid this. I smile, think back to the two hours at night that asshole rigging grip spent stranded high up in a condor in the snow on *REDTAIL HAWK*. How the dogshit must have tasted when he finally apologized.

ARLO – KEY PRODUCTION ASSISTANT

There's a good-size roach in my ashtray when I get to Rose's, and I'm early so I park along the driveway and finish it off. I have no idea what's going to happen today. The big boys are coming to figure out if they want to film here. Gus told me now it's only about getting decisions from the top.

As I'm about to knock, Rose opens the front door.

"I thought you had a church thing this afternoon," I say.

"Oh, just another gossip session about raising money. I told them to go ahead."

Rose smells the weed on my breath, but I detect a little sherry on hers. Touché! She's anxious, wonders if I've heard anything from the group. Then my phone rings. It's Gus. They're just turning off 395.

Rose grabs her vest and says, "Let's go! Meet them at the pond."

I wasn't prepared for this. Gus told me to make sure Rose wasn't there and then head for the cabins and the pond. But she's here and seems a little rattled. I say, "Not sure that's what they want, Rose. Gus told me they like to look around by themselves."

"Oh, I don't care! I need to meet them. My friends in LA told me always remember, it's my choice, not theirs." And with that, we hurry out of the house and into my car.

We arrive first at the pond, coming up on a dozen sheep watering on the far side. Chickens peck over the dirt in front of the cabins. An abuela and two ninas laugh on a porch. As we arrive, they hurry inside. We barely have time to park when the van bumps down the dirt road into view.

Tim, the Transportation Captain, is driving. Be friends with him, Gus told me, and life gets much easier. The gang piles out and Rose and I smile and greet them. Nina is all huggy and smiley. She introduces Rodrigo and then the Glove. Gus glances at Rose, then glares at me. I shrug back at him... she didn't go to church.

The group spreads out. Rodrigo and Nina huddle together as she describes her vision of the set. Larry and the Glove go over papers Larry's brought with him. I know the office is being set up today, and the accountants are arriving, so this is a busy day. Rich joins Nina and the director. It's calm, everyone taking in the sights and thinking about how this place fits in their vision of the movie. Rose drags me and Gus toward Nina and the director. Gus rolls his eyes.

"So, what do you think?" Rose asks.

Rodrigo turns away, but Nina smiles and takes her arm. "I'm sure you're sick of being told this is all a process, but, unfortunately, it is."

Rose nods her head, but she doesn't understand

"The director sees the cabins as where the young children are raised, and I'm working on describing how four cargo containers can be turned into a modular command center, but we may have to build an exterior house here and then match it on stage with a set."

This goes right through Rose's ears. "Well, if he wants a house why don't you show him mine?" she asks.

"Because it needs to be a compound, Rose, all the buildings together."

Rose looks over at Rodrigo, who is standing by the water with his assistant and Rich. Suddenly she marches toward them. Nina and Gus try to grab her, but she's on a mission.

"Excuse me!" she says. They turn toward her. "I'm just wondering what you're thinking. It's a big deal for me so if you're doubtful I'd like to just get it over with. I have some friends in LA, so I know a little about your business."

Rodrigo smiles, and Rose starts to melt into the homecoming queen being charmed by the football captain. "I'm just taking my time," he says. "It's the second most important decision I make on the film. I too come from a large ranch, in Argentina. These old cabins say a history of family."

Rose nods her head, thinking about what he said. "So, this seems like it might be the one?" she asks.

"I just have to see the guts, what Americans always call 'the war room'. The story is about bad people determined to spread their sickness. And keep it hidden from all eyes." He gives her his most sincere smile. "It is a serious decision."

Rose turns and looks at Gus. Gus takes her arm, leads her away, but she breaks free and goes right back to Rodrigo. His face changes. He's irritated now.

"I know it's a process," she says. "Your team has made that abundantly clear. But I'm just asking what you think, since I guess it's up to you."

Rodrigo smiles, again tries to calm her. "I understand," he says. "But quick decisions in production are almost always poison. Please, give me some time. I love your land. You are so fortunate."

Rose relaxes. She turns back to Gus, relieved. But I watch Rodrigo lean toward Rich and whisper, "Let's get out of here. She's crazy."

The magic is gone. In fifteen minutes, everyone is back in the van and Gus and Rose and I stand on the dirt road, watching them leave. I smile because they think they're running away from craziness.

Gus and I know better.

LUANNE – LOCATION ASSISTANT

If I wake up one morning and there's an angel on my chest asking how she can make my life better, my answer would be to never see my grandma again. Said angel hasn't arrived yet, so I'm standing on the porch of Grandma's house waiting for the van with the bigshots to arrive, fielding constant texts from the production office about the IT guy whose car broke down on his way from Mammoth to Bishop.

I just want to be a screenwriter! Movies take me away like books never did. Let me daydream in my pajamas and write stories! Not this shit. I see the dust trail coming down the long drive. "Game on," Gus told me last night. The van arrives and all the men, plus Nina, climb out.

I look at my grandma and she is smiling. She's been eating men her whole life. It's a trap, and Hollywood is stepping right into it. Evil always overpowers kind. Rich is out first and up the front steps. He greets Grandma. "Mrs. Dieter, how are you today?"

Grandma squints at him, spits off the porch. "Depends how this goes, don't it?" she replies. Rich ignores the spit, smiles, and introduces the team. Director, Producer, Production Manager. She knows Nina.

And then, almost like ghosts, they spread out and walk around the property and all through the house, whispering to each other. The director and Nina are tied at the hip.

Grandma watches the teamster survey the driveway and backyard, sensing in her own way the reality of the potential encampment.

But the real invasion happens inside the house. The director is enchanted with the bones of the old place. Hundred-year-old hardwood flooring, tall ceilings, wallpaper from the 1920s, furniture and pictures from the early century.

Nina comes alive. She tells him we could shoot all the scenes practical, right here, save the cost of building sets. The house is so spacious. She's thought about the sun's travel during the day, when the light is strong in the front windows, how the upstairs bedrooms could become the private quarters of the evil empire.

To me, it feels like a box of cockroaches has just exploded on the property. But Grandma's eyes are alive. She's got the winner, and somehow, she knows it. Fifty grand, she told me. There's a look in her eye I've never seen before.

The Glove steps up to the director. "It's pretty isolated," he says. "But it's not hidden in the mountains. Do you believe no one has ever questioned what is going on here?"

Grandma steps in. "This is a working ranch, mister. We buy seed, propane, service farm vehicles. Pay our water bills. But no one cares what happens inside our fences."

Rodrigo, the director, smiles. He agrees. "Hide in plain sight," his assistant says.

Out back there's just fields and a stream cutting through rolling hills, nothing to bring the community, or the cops, into play. Perfect place to train survivalists. I think I'm watching evil connect with evil.

The transpo guy huddles with Larry. He's waving his arms as they talk about where to hide the trucks, make a basecamp as Gus explains to me. Production is unrelenting. All the planning must be made early and correctly, and all the brains that go into every decision must agree.

"If base camp is in the wrong place," Gus says, "you could lose half-day of filming. Lots of money. The days are long, the pressure to get the scheduled work intense. You gotta have all your resources close at hand."

When my grandma gets excited, she starts to rock on her toes. When us kids were little, we'd come for Christmas. After the undercooked turkey and the dried-out dressing, we'd open her presents for us. A small bag of walnuts! A new Farmer's Almanac! Socks that we'd given her last year! We never knew if she was excited about putting one over on us, or nervous we'd figure it out. Some movie, I forget which, called that 'the tell'. She's rocking on her toes right now.

The energy is expanding everywhere. Arms are raised, fingers pointing to the fields and the rolling hills behind the house, hands raised framing views like what'd you see through a camera. I spot Rich, hustling to keep up with the director and Nina, making notes. He's got a grin on his face like he just sold the White House to the Russians.

In the end, the director, the Glove, Nina, and Rich stand in front of the house. They're looking at it, but I sense they're really looking at what's behind it. The long straight dirt driveway, almost two miles, where the righteous world with guns and sirens comes charging down to show the heathens their way is wrong. Kinda Biblical to me.

ALISON – PRODUCTION ACCOUNTANT

Okay, where the fuck is he? He texted he'd be at the hotel in ten minutes, and it's been forty. Lena and I were over at the school and picked our offices, but there's no internet/phones/toilet paper in the bathrooms. Or heat, and since it's coming on summer, no AC either.

So okay, it's day two and the building has been shut down for a year, but still. I feel bad I got in Fiona's face, but like a zombie invasion, there's going to be a line of crew at my door in forty blinks asking for money and I don't even have a desk yet. Two safes? A secure check printer? And I'm hungry.

There's a knock at the door. A cute boy smiles at me, a platter of cold cuts and fresh bread in his hands. "Are you Alison?" he asks.

"Are you Johnny Wad?" I answer.

He doesn't get it. "No, I'm Arlo," he says. "I work for Larry. He's just parking the car." He puts the platter on the desk and as he steps toward the door he remembers, turns and grins. From his back pocket he pulls a pint of chilled Grey Goose vodka. "Larry wanted to share this with you."

This will be our third movie together. He's good with numbers, the schedules always stay current—thank you, Fiona and Liz—but he's kind of like Captain Hook on the end of the plank. Bullshit and bluster; if it works, great; if not, into the deep end. The sliced turkey on rye is delicious.

There's another knock at the door. And there he is! All smiles and welcoming vibes.

I reach for the Grey Goose. At the Best Western, there's only Styrofoam cups. No biggie. I'm staying in a hotel and getting a paycheck and I don't have to think about LA or its ridiculous traffic. Pinch me, please.

We spread the food out across the bed, sharing the bottle without cups. Delicious. He acts apologetic. He should. His hair has gotten a little grayer, but he's still trim and bright in his eyes. It's funny about history in production. When the show's over, the show's over. No looking back, no nostalgia. Then you run into someone and you laugh, remember, and you realize that was your life. Not that you watched your kids grow up on that block in the valley, when you bought your first Chevy, when the fire burnt down the high school. It was when you were in some tiny motel room in Bumfuck USA using bedspreads for charcoal at Sunday BBQs.

"How much cash is in your bag right now?" he asks.

I never lie. "Five grand."

He's probably got five grand in receipts in his bag. "Look, we've been here a little more than a week. We got a production office, a stage space, a primary location, in a week!

"And a local bank account that's funded," I add. He gives me a tired, 'welcome back girlfriend' smile.

"What about Lena?" I ask.

"Look." He gets all embarrassed. "She's a bombshell and she was in her swimsuit, and I had a couple of vodkas and she climbed out of the pool staring at me. Down there. Said she heard Jewish guys have huge cocks and pulled my shorts down." This is shocking even me.

"It was the greatest shiksa blowjob of my life. And I've had a few great ones."

"You are such a pig." I start to stand up.

He grabs my hand. "You know I'm not a pig."

"If you talk like one and smell like one, you are one." I smile. He loves to kid, but I'm so much better at it than he is.

"That didn't really happen."

"And Jesus didn't walk on water either."

"Glad we got both of those things sorted."

"Look," I tell him as I hit the Goose again, "that office isn't going to be up and running for a week. This place is fine if all I'm doing is sleeping, but I heard the hotel up the street has huge rooms and Lena and I could spread out, set up shop for a few days."

He knows it's his job to fend off all the department heads who want to stay in the talent hotel. He sighs.

"And how would you feel if we took the room rate for both of us and rented a house in town? Sunday barbeques in the summertime?"

"There's no elevator at that hotel, actually there isn't one anywhere in this town. But I'll get people to help you move in. Look for a place but give me a week to make sure this is all real. Then, of course. Have a ball."

He takes a pull on the Goose and the connecting door to my room opens. Lena strides in, gym shorts and bra and not

142

much else. "I'm hungry," she exclaims. Then sees Larry. "Oh, hey! How are you?"

"There's food here," he indicates to the platter, "and a little bit of vodka left."

She sweeps the pint from his hand and drains it.

"Wanna have dinner tonight?" she asks, smiling. "I hear the bowling alley up the street is a blast!"

RODRIGO – DIRECTOR

I'm feeling good as the Glove and I drive down to LA to interview cameramen and editors and continue the casting. We have a solid team so far, production design, two great locations. Now, as the Glove says, comes the details.

I see the land where we'll shoot. I like it. Strong, dramatic, yet ordinary. Mountains and small neighborhoods, busy highway and lonely roads. Friendly people, and murderers with secrets under their smiles. These are words. Movies are images. We're going to meet people who might be the eyes of the picture. The cinematographer.

I like the Glove. He's calm, decisive. Then his phone rings. Because he's driving, he puts the call on speaker. It's Bob Richardson's agent, canceling this afternoon's meeting.

"What's going on?" the Glove asks.

"Well, to be honest, Bob wants to take a three-week commercial in the Swiss alps shooting for BMW. That would cover his nut for the summer, and then he's circling a Mitch Marcus project about the Beat poets featuring Allen Ginsburg. He's slowing down, only wants to pick and choose according to his heart. He said to tell you both he loves the script and wishes you nothing but a great shoot and a big success."

I look at the Glove. He's seething. "We're driving from Bishop to LA today to meet him. Why are you calling me now?"

"Look, I know it's fucked up, but I know you and you've done your homework. He's like that. He loves every great project that swims his way. And then, as the clock gets closer to midnight, he gets real. He got real late this time."

"It's fucked up and you know it."

"Can I give you some other names?"

"We have other choices." And he hangs up.

I like his style. Then, thirty minutes later, we get the same call from Chivo's agent. Inarritu just got a green light on the Crazy Horse biopic and his client is going to wait for it.

"Shall we get off the freeway and take the side streets?" the Glove laughs.

I don't know what he means.

"This is not starting off good. Maybe if we drive slow the bad luck can't find us."

Which leads us to a little Mexican restaurant in downtown LA called Angel y Diablo. Xavier, who the Glove says is being talked about as the next great Mexican cameraman, waits for us in a back booth. It's early, but we have editors in the afternoon and casting starting at four PM. He rises when he sees us, big smile on his face.

He thanks us for coming to him. He lives in downtown LA and needs to be around this afternoon for a carpenter who's doing some work on his loft. In Spanish he says, "Welcome to LA. This place has the most delicious Mexican food in the city."

We sit and immediately a large older woman with a big smile comes over. Xavier is sipping a coke. I ask for the same. Glove orders a coke and three shots of tequila. Here we go.

"So," I say, "you've read the script?"

"Por supuesto. Very powerful, very strange. Are you Catholic?" he asks.

I roll my eyes. "Born that way, but hardly anymore."

He smiles. "Yo tambien. But this whole matter of abortion. How do you feel about it?"

The drinks come and I reach for the tequila. Sip. "I think our mother earth is in danger, tremendous danger, and the key to saving it starts with fewer people."

The Glove downs his tequila.

Xavier slurps his coke. "Couldn't agree more."

The three of us smile, glad that part of the interview is over.

I continue. "So, I see this as a classic American Western. The quiet hero, trying to do her job, only to be pissed off and finally forced to action by the town that doesn't care about what's happening to its young girls. What's the one about the clock, you know, ALTA MEDIODIA?

"*HIGH NOON*," the Glove answers.

"Exactly. Gary Cooper is forced to act when no one else will. What do you think?"

Xavier smiles, thinks. The Glove and I exchange a glance. "Yes, I agree, but one thing jumped out at me when I read it. This is about two dying cultures." He gives us a look.

"A town and a religion that will soon be dust in the wind. So as such," and he drops down to the dark tile floor with his hands out as though the lens of a camera, "I think it's more of a Mexican Western, few high shots, even fewer big vistas,

146

a land of death, shot low and wide where both sides, good and evil are just...what? Cousins."

He tips over a chair, slides around it as if to shoot through it. "Lots of foreground rot, skulls and broken fences that go nowhere." As he slides around the chair to the other side. "Train tracks leading into sand and cactus."

I look at the Glove. He's motioning to the woman to bring more tequila. Xavier gets up off the floor, looks at me. "What do you think? Am I crazy?"

"Probably," I laugh. He laughs too. Even Glove cracks a smile. But what I really think is: Did I find my cameraman?

"There doesn't seem to be a lot of night work," Xavier says. "Is that going to stay the same?"

I look at the Glove. He's non-committal.

"I like the script the way it is. Maybe some tweaks, but mostly it is what I want."

"So the raid on the compound isn't going to turn into night?"

"Hmmm. Had not thought of that. Why?"

Xavier looks at the Glove. "Just asking about any plans to change what's day in the script to night. Mainly the raid on the compound. Makes a big difference."

"Look," the Glove says, "we have enough money to make a great small movie. It's as simple as one-two-three. Make a huge change like that, lots of things go on the table. There's no studio behind this, no deep pockets. Add a lot, lose a lot. That's how it is."

Xavier nods. He wants in. I know I found my cameraman.

NINA – PRODUCTION DESIGNER

Rich calls the local sheriff and asks if we can come over to get an idea of what a real sheriff's station in Bishop looks like. We've all seen a thousand police stations on TV and in the movies, but I want to have as much research as I can. This set is the primary one in the film.

I figured it would be a metal-sided industrial complex structure outside of town, but it turns out to be an old government building that got turned into the sheriff's station sometime in the 1950s. Gray stone on the outside, linoleum flooring, bars on the windows, a typical entrance with glass barriers protecting the working innards from anyone in the public who isn't allowed past the sergeant at the front.

Sheriff Conrad is a kindly man with the worry-lines of a boss who has made too many tough calls, probably some that involved life or death. He greets us with a smile and shakes Rich's hand. This is the kind of situation that Rich excels at, being sincere, grateful, trustworthy. When you're asking the world to help us with our play-date business, genuineness goes a long way.

He ushers us into a large open bullpen with eight desks, four against the corners of the walls, and four in a square in the middle. No one is here. Nobody at any of these desks. And they're large, business-like, and most of them have nothing personal on them, no papers, pictures, nothing.

One has a trophy for hunting, one a framed picture of a boy in a football uniform. Bulletin boards line the walls, notices about changes in law, changes in speed-limits, new construction from Lone Pine to Mammoth. There is a gallery of locals with warrants on them, businesses that were closing or had been closed, that kind of thing.

But the one thing I'm hoping to see, get a feel for, understand – the personal effects of the men and women who work here—is nowhere to be seen. I ask the Sheriff about the lack of personal touches, and as he starts to answer he is called over the PA system. There's an urgent call in his office.

"Sorry, but I'm going to have to get this. Be right back."

As Rich and I start taking pictures of what is here, a uniformed officer and a tall teenage blonde girl enter. They're laughing about something until they see us. Rich immediately goes into action.

"Hi, we're from a film that's going to shoot around here in three months, and Sheriff Conrad said we could come over today and get some research photos. It's a story about a sheriff's office and we want to be as accurate as can be. I'm Rich, the Location Manager."

The officer looks him over like he's a drug-smuggler from Mars. Then he looks at me, like he's deciding who goes into the cuffs first. He turns back to Rich, smirks. But the girl beats him to the punch.

"Are there any jobs on the movie?" she asks.

The officer gives her a stern glance.

"Because I'm looking for work," she continues. "I'm going to Fresno State in the fall, but I need to make some money this summer. Hopefully not waiting tables. Working on a movie...I don't know, sounds kinda fun."

"So, what are you looking for here today," the officer asks.

I step up. He's one of those guys that looks you in the chest first, then the eyes. "It's weird to me, there doesn't seem to be any human touch here. No family pictures. No phone chargers even. Do humans actually work here?" I thought this was a joke, but this guy doesn't seem to get jokes.

"I work here, and I'm human. Though most of you LA people don't seem to think cops are human." He leans toward me. "Until you're drunk, that is, and get into an accident. Or your boyfriend ODs tripping in the mountains."

"Wow." I say.

"Daddy..." the girl says.

He ignores her. "But here's the truth. We're squad car cowboys around here. Our desks are our dashboards. We only come here to deal with the fucking paperwork. I don't care what the Sheriff says, that's the way it is. This is the west, lady. Our home is on the road."

Rich tries to step in. "Yeah, but you do spend time here, right? I mean, there's eight desks. Something must go on?"

The officer gives him that smirk again, then rotates it to me. "You really want to see where we show our colors?"

"Daddy," she says again. He ignores her.

"Come with me."

Reluctantly the three of us follow him – into the men's room down the hall. I must admit I've never been in one before, and it smells just like all girls imagine. Urine. He leads us to the first of two stalls. Rich and I are looking at each other. The officer opens the stall door. Motions us inside. A toilet. Okay. Then he points to the stall wall. In fancy graffiti is inked "Jews are living proof that Arabs fuck camels."

I don't know what to say. I turn to leave.

"Know what it says next door?" He motions to the next stall.

Gives me a big smile. "Sicilians are direct descendants of niggers," he laughs.

"Any Jews or Italians work here?" I ask.

"Haven't the faintest," he says.

I stare at him. "Doesn't seem like it, does it?"

"Doesn't seem like what?" he asks.

"Nobody but white bigots work here." His face turns dark. Rich grabs my arm and leads me away.

"I ain't no bigot, lady. I hate just about everybody. You learn that as a cop!"

As we leave Sheriff Conrad catches up with us. "Did you get what you wanted?" he asks. All we want to do is get the fuck out of here.

"What's that officer's name?" Rich asks.

Sheriff Conrad shakes his head. Understands. "Cummings. Braylon Cummings."

THE GLOVE – LINE PRODUCER

We have a fantastic casting session. Evie and her assistant set up a steady stream of readings, good actors for the various parts including one incredible young woman for the part of the girl who starts the story, wandering in the mountains, lost and confused about what happened to her for the past eight months.

The last appointment is the best. Toni Collette comes in to meet only, not read, but she is radiant. Real, sincere, humble. And curious about Rodrigo's take on the material. He starts out asking if she's ever known a young woman who's gotten pregnant and was completely lost dealing with it. Toni thinks, nods her head. "We all know girls."

She's younger on screen, but she has a wise tone that translates to a woman with a sixteen-year-old daughter. And she carries herself like she's gone through the training to be a cop—looks you in the eye, shoulders square, no confusion.

She and Rodrigo talk about the dilemma of women waging war on other women. Is this a story of victims pressing their anger at other victims? Rodrigo says this is the tragedy of the story. The church and the laws and basically all the social power is in the hands of men, and all the victims are women.

She's deep. Thoughtful. In the end that translates as wonderful and powerful. If we can work a deal, I think she's our leading lady. Rodrigo and I leave the office stunned.

Neither of us was prepared for such a sharp, compassionate mind to challenge the story.

I take him to Musso's for dinner, where he has his first Martini, and we sit pretty much in silence. He finally gets around to the editors we met earlier. Didn't really respond to any of them. I tell him in my experience editors give the worst interviews. They're reactive not proactive; they deal with what they're given. By nature, they're cautious. In the editing room, caution and consideration are big pluses. Hurry up is a virus.

But in a room with someone you don't know, wondering how your energy will match theirs, caution is not a plus. I agree to go to the union and see if I can get a waiver to bring his Argentinian editor to work on the film.

I drop him off at his hotel, and as I drive home my phone rings. It's Matthew.

"So, how'd the day go?" he asks.

"We found a cameraman we love, and we met with Toni Colette, who blew us away. So yeah, it went pretty well."

"I got a call from Bob Richardson's agent. He's pretty upset."

"He played us. Then tried to offer some other clients like this project was his to staff. All I want from anyone is straight talk, and I don't think he gave us that, end of story."

"Fair enough. So, what else is going on?"

"Honestly, I think if we can close with the DP and Collette, we can establish we're ten weeks out. That puts the start of shooting after the Fourth of July and wrap the end of September, something like that."

"Can't start any sooner?" he asks.

It always gets around to this. "If we can, we will. That I promise."

"Okay, Glove. I trust you; you know that."

Things start to go fast now. Time to make lists in the morning: I need to get this and this and this done today. The long march to the start of filming. Time to find out who is a real soldier and who is a pretend one. When the going gets weird, the weird start laughing. No one's laughing yet.

FRANKIE – FIRST ASSISTANT DIRECTOR

My Grandpa built a cabin up the road from Bishop in 1955, just south of Lee Vining. My bros and I used to spend summers there, fishing and swimming and later, smoking weed and riding motorcycles. Mono Lake is one of the strangest places I've ever been. If there are aliens, Mono is where they hang out in summer.

So I'm smiling as I drive up the Owens Valley. I met the director in LA on one of his casting trips, and we seemed to hit it off pretty good. I like working with Larry and the Glove. I check in at the hotel, and when I enter my room, I realize for the first time what's different. Gabby isn't here.

Normally she'd come on location, especially during prep when the hours aren't so long. But she decided to stay back in LA and keep working. She's half-owner in a boutique business called Celebrity Arrangement, catering to visiting bigshots by providing elaborate floral arrangements for the houses and hotel suites where they stay.

Fiona and Liz greet me at the production office with big smiles. After hugs, I reach into my bag and pull out two pastrami sandwiches from Langer's that I brought. I get kisses of joy. Already they're bored with lunch choices in town.

I knock on Larry's door. He yells "Come in!" and I enter. We settle around his desk. "Just wondering if you talked to Glove about the credit?" I ask.

"Haven't. Busy getting everything set up. But let's go in there now, see what he thinks."

Both my dad and my grandpa taught me one thing about the business. Nothing gets offered. You always have to fight for it. I love being a first assistant director, but it's not the end of the trail for me. I want to produce. My grandpa was one of the first to establish the modern film industry. Producing is in my blood. Having a walkie talkie on your hip is not exactly a key into the club.

The Glove smiles when we enter. We laugh about getting the team back together, and Larry speaks up. "I promised I'd talk to you about Frankie getting an associate producer credit on this. He agreed to take the job if this could be worked out. What do you think?"

The Glove seems taken aback. I've heard the excuse before. Credit goes to those who do the job. Otherwise, everyone's credit is tainted. I just got off a studio picture where there were more executive producers than grips. I told Larry I'd only do this if I got associate producer credit. The Glove smiles, sits back in his chair.

"Let me talk to Matthew," he says. "But if I do this for you, Frankie, then I have to do this for you, Larry. So it's two new credits."

"You won't be disappointed." I tell him. "I want to learn. Larry said he'd give me a copy of the budget. I want to look a little closer at the schedule. I want to be a part of the brain trust."

Larry laughs. "Using the word 'brain' in this room might be considered a stretch."

I'm shown to my office. Two desks, for when the second assistant director comes. I settle in, plug in the small stereo I always bring, put on some jazz, open my computer. By the end of the day, I've gone over the schedule and made a few changes. UPMs make schedules based on chunks. Usually they are paranoid about actor carries, stars length of schedule, moving in and out of a location.

I change things the way I believe is best for the director. Continuity, even if it means going in and out of a location, even if it means carrying a small part three additional weeks. I finish and give it to Fiona to print.

An hour later, I see our accountant go into Larry's office with my paperwork in hand. Hmm. In five minutes Larry comes out of his office and into mine. He closes the door.

"Frankie, you added a day to the schedule. You can't do that."

"Even if it's right?"

"Even if it's right! Our job is not to inflate the budget, which I know everyone thinks I'm just bullshitting about. This isn't Fox or even Searchlight! There's no going over budget."

"I just want to be on record, I think this shoot needs another day."

"I know. But you want to be a producer? Right? That means getting a strong commitment from the money people first and foremost. It doesn't include raising the budget without a reason."

"Yeah, but don't we want to be straight up with everybody?"

"It doesn't always mean straight up with the numbers. That's their Achilles' heel. They remember the first number. They guard that with their life. Money is life to them."

Some things never change.

"You know what else happened when you messed with everything?"

"What?"

"The villain, Sandra Oh's part, went from three weeks to seven! And she's only available in a tiny window of time. This—" he holds up my schedul—"this takes her out of the movie. She's not available. We can't do that to the director."

I look at him. He's serious, a little angry, but I know he's smiling inside.

I'm always the court jester. I shrug. "Oops."

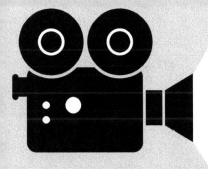

PART FOUR –
TRAIN
LEAVES
STATION

TIM – TRANSPORTATION CAPTAIN

It's almost eight o'clock on Day Two of shooting and me and Captain Eddie are sitting in the director's Explorer, watching the crew set up the first shot of the day. Yesterday was bitchin', out in the Alabama Hills for the first scene in the film. Granted, we only got five shots, but the Glove said they were great and well worth the day. All us drivers agree the nineteen-year-old playing the lost girl is smokin' hot.

As I start to take a bite into my second bean/egg/sausage burrito of the morning—I've been up since four—Captain Eddie reaches over and squeezes my hands. Beans and eggs and salsa spill all over my crotch. He laughs at me like I shit myself.

All this goes down as we watch the cutest butt in the history of Hollywood sprint across the parking lot with a paint bucket in one hand and a brush in the other. Antoinette, the on-set painter, fixing a flare in a window with fuller's earth.

Next comes the real surprise, a local called Carrie who runs KC's Bar in Lone Pine but is staying with her daughter in Bishop after she got hired as the camera PA. Man, oh man, she's tall, lean, black-gray hair down to her shoulders, athletic. This show is starting off right.

She stretches up tall, holding the slate, her tee shirt pulling loose from her jeans. The rig on the dolly raises up, camera is rolled, and Carrie claps the sticks. The sheriff's car comes forward. Day Two begins.

Toni Collette is a good driver. She pulls the sheriff's Suburban into the parking slot as the camera dollies into the driver's side door. She opens it and stares out across the vista to the mountains, a troubled look on her face.

It's the first time we see her in the film. Seems like everyone likes the shot, but we do it again. Downtown JB backs the Suburban into its starting position. The actress gets in the driver's seat. Carrie runs out with the slate. Suddenly, the cameraman, an energetic Mexican, jumps up and stops everything.

We're adding a second camera, long lens, low, stationary, getting cuts of the license plate and the tires as the vehicle comes forward. The first and second camera assistants hustle out on the driveway and quickly get focus marks. Carrie puts tape down on the asphalt to mark the distance. The camera crew is ready in under ten minutes. Captain Eddie is impressed. Me too.

After twenty-five years in the business, I'm still amazed how much pride a team takes in being a precision unit. Watching movies is like swimming underwater; but making them is a military march. On take two Toni misses her mark slightly, and when she opens the door, it hits the camera on the dolly.

Two hours later we give up and move to the next shot. My friend Reno always said, 'Beware of optimism.' Take one, perfect. Two hours later, moving on with the taste in your mouth you just never got the shot.

Quick assessment of the crew: ADs are solid. Frankie's a character. Wardrobe is still a mystery, uniforms and ranch clothes until we get to the Compound. Prop master I've worked with before, jolly and fun and pretty crazy after wrap. I had to bail him out ten years ago in New Orleans on the vampire movie when he started squirting fake blood all over the Mardi Gras Ball.

The dangerous ones are the stunt puppies. Rooster, the stunt coordinator and second unit director, who I've worked with six times, showed up at the production office with a twenty-two-year-old hottie wearing a leather-fringed short skirt, high leather boots, a tight tee-shirt and not much else. Rooster is at least sixty-five years old. But he's still got the smile of a twenty-year old. He doesn't want our help yet, but Luanne and them have been out at Grandma's the past week. God knows what's being planned.

As drivers, we're watching the cameraman and the director. They're always the wild cards. So far, they seem solid. No 'move the trucks' moment yet. We know Larry and the Glove are solid. But we also know when the storm hits, that's when you find out who is really the captain.

One thing bothers me. We brought Captain Eddie's kid, Junior, on the payroll as a permit to get him in the union. Town's busy, we're into permits. He's nineteen. The actress who worked yesterday is nineteen. We put her in Junior's van at the end of the day to drive her back to Bishop. No one has heard from either of them since. Neither are answering phone calls or texts. She doesn't work again for three days. He may never work again.

I hear brisket is for lunch. First week is always the best for the caterers.

NINA – PRODUCTION DESIGNER

I got my period on Sunday night before we started shooting. It was a rough one. Like I was a teenager again. Put me in a foul mood, even though Cody and I had hiked around Lake Sabrina during the day, and he showed me all the different birds living in the mountains. It was a wonderful day with a shit ending. Now we're shooting. Most of the sets are designed and approved. The ones for weather cover are standing inside the church—hallways, police offices, a bedroom. The church is a perfect stage.

This is one of those days that seems easy for everyone except transpo and props. We're outside the Middle School where the production office is, now dressed as the exterior local sheriff's office. We've added large stanchion lights on either side of the front door, a great weathered sign stating the county sheriff's office, anchored parking designation signs on poles for the VIPs and visitors. It looks and feels like a sheriff's headquarters.

We're shooting all the comings and goings of cop cars in the movie. The front end of the schedule is loaded with exterior scenes because even if we're in summer, you can never rest easy with weather in the mountains.

The two young prop assistants have been humping all morning getting license plates and decals on the right vehicles, guns in the holsters of the extras playing cops. In the afternoon, we'll do it all over again for the other counties that in the story join the search.

I've come to really like Craig, the prop master. I heard a lot of stories about the crazy days when he was a young fireball who loved coke, beer, and girls. Not necessarily in that order. I feel a little cranky, so I gravitate toward him. He's always good for a smile. As I show him the police decals for the afternoon, he starts laughing. At first, I wonder if he's laughing at me, my seriousness over something we've gone over a dozen times.

"I figure this is something like my fifteenth feature as a master." he says. "Each one is a test. Stay focused, try to keep ahead of whatever changes the "creative" team dreams up. Then after wrap, it's another kind of test. Try not to turn into a rich twat. Per diem!" He has a big, deep laugh. "Was always lousy keeping it, always lousy keeping out of trouble spending it. Coins from hell."

Now this adorable camera PA is running up to us. "The director asked Frankie if it's possible to have rain in this drive-up?" she blurts out, like she's delivering the final peace offering to end World War Two. We both look to the sky. Blue as her eyes.

"Well," Craig says, "the effects guys are all out at the compound with Rooster, so there's no rain towers or even a water truck to make rain. I guess we could do it digitally, but it's pretty sunny to pull that off. I'd say reschedule it or get everyone drunk on mescal and imagine it." He winks at me.

She looks at us like he just spoke some ancient language. I turn away not to laugh.

"No, darling, there's no way to create rain right now."

And as he says this, a massive cloudbank covers the sun, the air turns cold, the sky dark. God hates prop masters. Everyone knows this. Now she does too. We follow her to the camera, where the director and the cameraman and the AD are huddled. They all look at Craig.

"Well," I say, speaking up, "if the cloud cover holds, we could do a big wide shot and add rain digitally."

Frankie, the AD, asks Craig, "How much hose do you have?" Figured this was coming.

"About a hundred and twenty feet," he answers. "There's a spigot on the lawn, I've got a gentle rain attachment for the lens, but there's no way we can wet down a large area."

Xavier, the cameraman, who I really like, turns to the director. "Let's lay about eighty feet of dolly track, wet the truck and use the windshield wipers, tight on Toni, and dolly with the rain hose over the lens. Get that shot, strike the track and get up on the camera truck. Hopefully it's still overcast, and we get the wide establishing shot and add rain digitally."

The director thinks for a moment. "Close, wide, then jump into the interior. Love it."

The Glove walks up. "Gotta plan?" he asks. Frankie explains and Craig is on the walkie to his guys. "Pull out the hose and the spray attachment, all of it, and bring it to camera."

I call the construction warehouse to see if we have any hose there. I tell the foreman to send two guys to help the prop boys with the rig. The second AD is on his walkie to the makeup trailer. "We're making rain for scene 54, get her ready."

It takes about forty anxious minutes to lay the dolly track and rig the hose over the lens. The clouds hold. The grips rig the spray attachment and work out the camera move while keeping the hose out of the shot. My guys stand by to help.

Props wets down the picture car. We get two rehearsals and we're shooting. It all goes perfectly. The gray sky holds. Two takes and we strike the dolly track and bring the camera up on the truck for the wide shot. And, low and behold, as we're about to shoot, a light rain begins to fall. I look over at Carrie. She stares at Craig like he's a god. That's what production offers, I think: occasionally a chance to be a fake god.

As we wrap, one EFX guy shows up. I tell him they must rain the windows on the interior scenes, which are scheduled in a week, but could come up in days, depending on weather. We all smell the brisket, look at our watches. Almost six hours into the day and we're hungry.

My team is solid. The set dressers are mostly gay, and I'm too old for the carpenters. Thank God for Cody. No more on-location racing around, smiling, ducking and dodging. Grandma's place has turned into the epicenter of our universe. Every other day she throws us out, quitting the deal, raging at the intrusion, and Rich and Luanne talk her down from the rooftop.

My decorator, Bryce, and I have spent hours imagining what the movie reality of the compound is. Is it CIA? Is it secret-cult religion weirdness? Does the wallpaper have to go? Does the whole paint scheme need to change? When I bring these questions to the director, he wants to have dinner and try to kiss me.

And then there's Cody...quiet, soft-spoken, the sexiest man I've ever known. He dances me through life. I'm five-years-old in his arms, then fifteen-years-old, twenty-five-years-old, eighty-years-old. He makes me feel like I'm in the middle of a Leonard Cohen song.

It's the thing about production. You pull up the rudder and you're skipping on the wind.

The accountants rented a four-bedroom, two-story house outside town and they throw a BBQ party every Sunday. It's fantastic. I love how women are taking power in the business. Crap restaurants? Make your own. Afraid of serious decisions? Chick up. Can't commit to a creative decision? We will.

We're getting muscle mass slowly but surely. Men's vision of warriors and conquest is over. It's boring. The race needs to embrace kindness, consciousness, an honest look at what is real out there. Men want alcohol, pussy, and killing. We want something else. Starts with compassion, ends with vegetables.

RICH – LOCATION MANAGER

What did I ever do to deserve Luanne's grandma? She's batshit crazy. Quiet, somber, then exploding with rage over nothing. We agreed on a deal; I offered $35K, we settled at $50K. It's now up to $58K and we're still in prep. Larry is furious. He wants to pull out of the deal. The Glove won't let him. A day of second unit gets cut to pay for the extra location fee.

We're shooting at the sheriff's house location in Bishop. Mr. and Mrs. Barton have lived in this two-story home for many years. They raised three boys here, and five years ago he retired from the post office. She was a substitute teacher at the elementary school and retired when her husband did. Really nice people.

It's a quiet street, the houses built mostly after the second world war. They have large lots, usually two-stories, with a detached garage. Probably the same builder. It feels safe. It's quiet, slow-moving. A place where you'd want to raise your daughter if your job required strapping a gun to your hip every morning.

We start with the windows blacked out (rigged yesterday), all the interior night scenes. Then as the grips take the black-out fabric down, we switch to day scenes. It's going smoothly. The DP runs an energetic, happy crew. Hopefully, we'll get outside for the daylight sequences before the sky turns gray. Weather here changes on a dime.

I leave Gus and Arlo to deal with whatever comes up, including the next-door neighbor who smokes elk for a local restaurant and has a karaoke machine outside that he uses to sing Steven Tyler songs while he's working. Gus has a better voice than him. But three fifties speak louder than karaoke. The elk does smell good though.

I get to Grandma's location at eleven o'clock. Beautiful, hot summer day. Hardly any traffic on the roads, just ranchers pulling hay wagons and livestock trailers. The movie truck traffic is starting to rip up the hardpack dirt drive, which is okay because every vehicle that comes toward the house announces itself with a dust cloud.

Luanne is on the porch, on her phone. Reception out here is sketchy. I need to fix that. Some sort of relay station. The construction crew is dragging rusted farm equipment toward the barn. Carpenters are framing what will become the living quarters for the young warrior girls. It feels organized, productive.

I step on the porch and into the house, like a character in a scary movie. And there's Grandma, in the sitting room with a drink in her hand, laughing, and Rooster, who's just punched his joke. He's got a drink too. They both look up at me.

Rooster says, "Look what the cat dragged in!"

I smile.

Grandma takes a while to recognize me, even though a week ago she pointed a shotgun at my balls. That's when I agreed to 58K.

"How's it going here?" I ask.

They look at each other, burst out laughing.

I notice she's barefoot. Her hair is loose. Rooster's in tight jeans, big cowboy belt buckle, a form-fitting black tee-shirt. Something's going on.

"I was just hearing about Burt Reynolds' movies in Mexico back in the seventies," she chuckles. "Sounds like them were the days."

Rooster grins. "No bras, no AIDS. Them were the days."

I look at Rooster. "So, what do you think about this location?" I ask.

"Pretty straight forward," Rooster says. "But we do need a Sunday rehearsal with the director and the cameraman. And I'll need all my hands on-deck for a couple of days before that. I got some ideas I want the freedom to present."

My phone beeps. A 911 call from Arlo. I excuse myself, run into Luanne. She's pale, panicked. "Arlo just called. The generator surged and set the house on fire!"

By the time I get back to Bishop, the fire department is leaving and we're back filming inside. A faulty junction box exploded in the attic and the sparks set the dust up there into flames. Arlo greets me.

"Gus is going to the hospital," he says.

"Why?"

"He called the electric best boy a horse's ass for cabling through the attic and not telling us, and the guy swung on him with some cable and hit him in the face. Knocked two teeth right through his cheek."

Oh shit. I see the ambulance off to the side. Hurry over to it. A crowd of crew, mostly drivers and electricians, are standing by. Suddenly the crowd parts, and like a bull let into the ring, Captain Eddie charges the electric best boy. He pulls a tire iron from behind his back and with his massive arms whacks him in the knee. The guy goes down like he's been shot.

The electrician crew – five burly guys with bad attitudes and steel-toe boots - surround Eddie, who stands brandishing the iron, snarling "Payback is a bitch, huh fellows?"

Tim and the other drivers step in. There's a stand-off. The electrician writhes on the ground. Quickly Larry is in the middle of it. The gaffer, who was inside with Xavier, comes running out. The electricians are vocal, some saying they should just walk off right now. The teamsters are quiet, staring them down.

Nobody leaves, nobody quits, no one's equipment gets returned home without the drivers. Slowly, calm returns. The best boy is loaded on another stretcher and goes toward the ambulance. Everyone goes back to work.

I turn to Arlo. "Anything else I should know about?"

"The actress who ran off with Captain Eddie's son came back. She said they went to Reno and almost got married. Slept in the van the first night by Convict Lake, drank tequila and had sex all night. He's back in LA in the doghouse. Captain Eddie's in a foul mood."

At that moment, the second assistant director, the one who is the chief mechanic on the production team, comes hurrying up. His nickname is Rainman. "The question is if we don't get outside for the day exterior shots, do we start here tomorrow? Or can we come back some other time? In other words, is the location friendly or not?"

"You don't think you'll finish here today?"

"We just lost an hour to firetrucks and ambulances. And they're re-cabling the house. And the Glove wants a crew meeting about being on a team."

I think. The Bartons are staying at their sons' house in Mammoth. Tomorrow we're scheduled to shoot at a church in Bishop not too far away. Not a heavy day. The UPM just left for the hospital with two crew members.

I reach for my phone. "Let me get on it."

THE GLOVE – LINE PRODUCER

When you start filming, it's like you step off the cliff and hope you soar. You've prepared for everything, but suddenly it feels like you've prepared for nothing. In-production panic hits actors, cameramen, directors. All of us. You're Wiley E. Coyote and you got conned off the edge again. You adjust, change, keep going forward.

The business is freelance. You don't get a job for life. Even if you're in a union, the future is not secure. It's job to job. Those who can handle this are those who aren't afraid of the future. This is what production is all about. Getting strong people to see a common vision and play like a team. Today, the team broke down.

I love Gus. He tells these incredible stories about the Owens Valley, from the land-grabbing to the monster bass pulled out of alpine lakes. It breaks my heart he's at the center of the first crack. But he left LA for a reason. He's not a team player. He didn't have to confront the best boy about the cabling that set the house on fire. Especially if the guy is twenty-seven and a bodybuilder.

And then the Transpo co-captain kneecaps the best boy. What do I do? It's schoolyard retaliation. I understand this. But now I've got a situation where everyone connected to the camera fears everyone connected to the trucks. It's like the initial virus on a cruise ship.

First, we have a days' work to finish before the light fades, and a backup plan to establish in case we don't. And we're looking for a new best boy. I don't know what the insurance deductible is if we must file a claim. Probably $100,000. I call Alison, ask her to find out and start a quick, prelim cost of crew costs per day. She's already heard the news, has the answers—she's good.

She asks about concerns over lawsuits coming from the best boy and Gus. Hadn't thought about that. Every action is a potential court case these days The director and cameraman have stayed calm throughout. The actress, Toni, is loose and energetic, focused. Making the day is the mantra of production. But for the artists, greatness is the quest.

Rich tells me Rooster wants a rehearsal on Sunday next, with his three top stunt guys, a basic effects crew, and the director, DP, and myself. Behind his eyes I see concern. I ask what's bugging him. He's inarticulate, stumbles. Finally, he lets out there's something weird between Rooster and Grandma. He doesn't know what, just that it's weird.

But first, let's make our schedule. I huddle with Xavier and Rodrigo and explain the give and take of not making the day, starting back here tomorrow and then packing up the trucks and moving to the church location and starting fresh. Not impossible, but with the moving out and moving in you lose time for performance. In the end, we go outside and get the day-exterior scene and then go back inside and light the day-interior scene we didn't finish. We make our day. Stay on schedule.

Fiona calls from the office. Gus has a hairline fracture of his jawbone and a gash that required eighteen stitches. The electrician has a busted knee cap. The replacement best boy is traveling today. Warren Zevon is in my head: send lawyers guns and money, the shit has hit the fan. She asks if we send flowers to Gus. I laugh. "He'll probably be in jail after he murders the best boy."

FIONA – PRODUCTION COORDINATOR

I'm looking at a man in a sheriff's uniform, staring at me from the chair in front of my desk. Sheriff Conrad. He's here about the incident at the set this morning. He wants to know where Edward Rowell is. Captain Eddie.

Well, as my Da would say, by the Christ indeed we made it through prep and no one got killed. Now we're filming and two of our crew are in hospital, one with a busted jaw and stitches, the other with a broken kneecap. So much for 'teamwork makes the dream work.'

The sheriff tells me the teamster captain said he sent Eddie on a run to Reno for some equipment. Is that true? "Yes," I lie. "We had some gels for electric and more grip clamps sent to the airport, and four more nail guns for construction."

"Where does he stay at night?"

"The drivers are in the Starlight Motel on Mission Avenue." I click on my computer. "He's in room 109."

"What time do you expect him back here?"

Right now, he's in my room at the Best Western. Alison and Lena are on the phone trying to get some legal advice about what went down. We all love Captain Eddie. The best boy was a prick to us in the office. Fuck him.

"No idea," I tell the sheriff. He looks at me, wondering if I'm lying.

As I said earlier, this is war.

We have a wonderful girl, Etta, newly graduated from high school, as our runner. Gets lunch. Goes to the set with tomorrow's call sheet and waits for its approval. She answers phones when the ringing never stops, and even files for Alison and Lena when they're swamped. She's saving her money to go to New York City and get into movie makeup. She seems pretty meek to dream of NYC.

After Sheriff Conrad leaves the internet goes down. I call Janni. The call goes to voicemail. Alison is freaking out. The cost-to-date has to get to LA today. It's the end of week one shooting and the money people need some idea of how we did. I have several travel plans pending with actors that need to get finalized. The motels have sent their weekly billings. All the department heads want their petty cash envelopes cashed out today for the weekend shopping. We need digital power.

Janni finally calls me back. There was a blackout just south of Mammoth, and it blew the whole system. Just unplug the main tie-in, he tells me, wait ten minutes, plug it back in. It should all be good. I do, and everything comes back online. Thank you, God.

Captain Eddie comes sneaking into the production office. He wants his per diem and wonders if we can rent him a room at the Best Western and cancel his other room. Alison is quick. No. That puts us in the law's vision of hiding a fugitive. Eddie understands. Just thought he'd ask. Cash in hand, he slides out of the building. Weekend can't come soon enough.

And then there's Rooster. He wants to book rooms for three stuntmen for next weekend. Have you cleared it with Larry,

I ask? Who's Larry? he challenges back. My boss, I answer. Oh yeah, he answers. The UPM. Well, the message has been sent. Let's see what they say. But book the rooms anyway.

Nobody likes him. But I find some rooms and book them. Always a juggling act in a small town with a year-round tourist season. Rainman calls from the set. They're going to make the day, so Monday's call sheet should run as is. Etta is on it, and within a half hour she's on her way with a hundred copies for distribution. We made our week.

ARLO - KEY PRODUCTION ASSISTANT

On Saturday morning my phone rings. Tim needs a favor. His construction driver heard about a mobile whorehouse setting up on the Nevada side of the border, out near Benton, where Grandma's compound is. A few of his drivers want to go there tonight, drink whiskey and see what the scene is. He wonders if I'd be the designated driver, meaning not drunk.

"Do I get paid?"

"Two hundred cash."

"Where and when?" He tells me be at the motel where the drivers are staying around six o'clock.

A mobile chicken ranch? What will they think up next? They started me at $100 a day, then pumped it to $150 because I knew lots of folks around here, and so I'm making $750 a week and now $200 cash for Saturday. I'm thinking new golf clubs. Or maybe a better car.

I get to the motel five minutes before six. The white van is there. Tim is standing outside his room with a glass of brown liquid on ice. We meet at the van. He puts the key in the ignition and turns it. Honks the horn. Slowly drivers stumble out of their rooms. Roughly cleaned up, smelling of after shave, red-eyed, smiling.

This is definitely a journey to the dark side, and everyone knows it. A local cab screeches up and Captain Eddie steps out. He's smiling, with a half-full bottle of Jack Daniels in his hand. Everyone laughs.

Tim is the boss, but Eddie is the spark plug of this group. Now he's a fugitive. The police have been around the office, this motel. Everyone protects him. No one knows where he is. Except now. He's in the van I'm driving, laughing like a girl from high school who just chugged her first Jägermeister.

I follow the GPS to a county road in the flatlands where they grow alfalfa. In the far distance I see a big red barn down a dirt road, all lighted up. Must be the place. Eddie is telling a story about driving a motorhome for Jeff Bridges in Hawaii. The cops come and search the premises for weed but, thankfully, Eddie's eaten the half-ounce in the kitchen-drawer, and no one is arrested. Three hours later his buddies found him by a waterfall talking to an old lady with no teeth.

The van is rocking. Glad I'm not drinking; glad I have a doobie in my pocket when this kit goes inside. And inside they charge. Eight large bodies each with cash in his pocket. Credence and Skynyrd blasting out the doors.

It's a slick setup. The barn seems like where the party happens, where I'm guessing the girls and the rooms are. As people file in loud music explodes from inside. Do you have to be deaf to get in there or just figure you will be when you leave? Two identical catering-like trailers are set up next to the barn. This is the bar. You start your night here. A big line waits patiently. There's a sign says NO OUTSIDE ALCOHOL ALLOWED. Haven't seen any girls yet.

Pickups start coming down the driveway, over the cattle guard. They park in front of the barn, mostly ranch hands, farmers, a few Mexicans, even a few couples. Pretty soon, there's maybe twenty pickups out front. I reach in my pocket.

I'm about halfway down the doob when the doors open and my crew stumbles out. It's a little after nine o'clock. They head over to the van and climb inside. One's missing. Guess. Then the barn doors open and three security guys, big hay-throwers, toss Captain Eddie out the door. He's naked as a blue jay except for the rubber on his extended penis. He's laughing and dancing and singing 'Little Deuce Coupe.'

The bouncers toss his clothes in the dirt. Tim groans, climbs out of the van and tries to collect him. But Eddie sees a truck entering the compound and breaks away, racing toward it. He stops it from getting close. I roll down the window and hear him say to the other driver,

"Don't go in there, don't go in there, they charge $40 bucks for a blowjob. I'll give you one for $20!"

The drivers hear this and explode with laughter. Tim finally drags Captain Eddie to the van and the others pull him inside. Everybody's shitfaced. Eddie immediately passes out on the backbench. Nobody mentions the fact he's still naked and we don't know where he's staying.

We roll back into Bishop. For five miles I sweat the headlights following me, convincing myself it's the cops about to make a move. But eventually whoever is behind me turns off. We make it to the motel.

All the guys try to wake Eddie, but he's out cold, so they pull him out of the van, start dragging him to Tim's room. That's when the red and blue lights flick on. The Sheriffs have been waiting. Three men in uniform drag Eddie to their squad car, toss his clothes in on top of him, and away they go. The Captain's going to jail.

Tim hangs his head. Spits in the dirt. "This is fucked up," he says as he opens his door. The others all go into their rooms. Tim turns back to me and opens his hands. Keys? I lock the van, walk over to him and hand them over. He gives me two hundies.

LENA – ASSISTANT PRODUCTION ACCOUNTANT

When Larry and I first met at his house four months ago, we both ended up a little confused. After finishing the budget, I had too much to drink and I couldn't drive home, so I stayed at his place that night. We started in his bed, even kissed for a while, but I could feel he was freaked out. I'd never been in a guy's bed where he wasn't all over me, so it freaked me out a little too. I ended up in the spare bedroom.

It's been a slow dance since I showed up on location - flirt, step back, flirt some more. He can't keep his eyes off me when we're in a room together, but he's afraid to get near me when we're alone. It bugs the shit out of Alison.

We came close two weeks ago at Whiskey Creek, sharing a ribeye-stuffed potato with horseradish and chives and a bottle of wine. He walked me to my car. I was ready to go back to his hotel. Horny and ready. After a knee-buckling long kiss, he walked back to his hotel, and I drove back to the house.

Last weekend Alison invited the office staff over for Chinese take-out and some good gossip, and Larry and I just looked at each other and giggled, like we were pretending to be in junior high. It was impossible to keep our hands off each other. So, we didn't. We went up to my room, sweet and easy together, laughing and giggling, slowly undressing each other. We've been together each night since.

It's Sunday morning and I wake to the sound of the caterer helpers in the backyard. Yesterday the caterer decided to roast a pig to celebrate our first week. His guys brought the smoker into the backyard last night with a load of hardwood they set on fire. Around ten, when our wine ran out, these same guys came back with the pig. The wood had burned down so they put the animal on the coals. Larry brought out a bottle of tequila and I put Miles Davis on the CD player.

The helpers stayed for two hours, drinking beer and smoking weed, laughing on the back lawn. Fortunately, our neighbors split for the summer, so no one gets upset with any noise.

It's nine AM and I'm awake now, wandering in my PJs and robe. I need coffee. The smell of roast pork is all over the world. The same helpers are setting up long tables and covering them with white stretchy tablecloths. Then they lug in the folding chairs.

I brew coffee, pour a cup, adding a little tequila to it, and step out on the patio with my phone. Even on Sundays, production can turn into a war zone in a flash. I hear Larry come hurrying down the stairs a few minutes later. He's on his phone, quickly pours a cup of coffee, and jams out the front door. Doesn't kiss me or say goodbye. Something's up.

I get on my computer and start reading emails. Pour more coffee and languish in the smell of slow-roasted pork over wood coals. If something happens and they need me,

I'll put in for the day, too. Get paid to do this on Sunday? Millionaire's stuff.

The three-week tradition is the Sunday party kicks off around one o'clock. At eleven, four teamsters show up with huge metal containers. They put them at the end of the tables and pile bottled beer into each one. The final touch is to cover the bottles with ice. There's at least sixty beers chilling in the cool, but sunny Bishop air.

A little later, the girls from wardrobe arrive, carrying stainless-steel caterer's bowls filled with guacamole and salad. Of the four that arrive, two are from LA, two are from Bishop. All are Latin, and I know from the last two parties their food kicks ass.

The young assistant props guys, both from LA, both always smiling and wanting to help in any way, arrive with a ten pound bag of tortilla chips which goes next to the guacamole, and a covered tray of what turns out to be pot brownies – bought from a local gal who grows in her garage, evidently has no income visible to the world except her inheritance, and is rumored to have $300,000 in cash buried in her backyard. She sells to the LA music scene and mostly travels in private jets. I had a taste last weekend. Enough said.

Around noon the sound guy shows up with his speakers and a mixer. DJ Roger. He enters the backyard, surveys the setup, grabs a brownie and starts to work. In thirty minutes, Marvin Gaye is asking 'What's Going On?' and his voice floats through the neighborhood. Alison finally makes an appearance.

She pours coffee, which is cold by now, and starts to make another pot. As it brews, she sips a tiny taste of the remaining tequila. She steps out on the patio, surveys the scene. It's almost noon. She takes in the smells. The pork, still over the coals, dominates the air. She smiles.

"What was Larry so anxious about this morning?" she asks.

"He just called. Captain Eddie got picked up by the cops last night," I answer.

She picks up her phone, dials Fiona. "I just heard Eddie Rowell is in jail. Do you know anything about this?"

I look up and the craft service team arrives with armloads of coleslaw and potato salad, which go right on the serving table. They go back for the plastic knives and forks and the thick paper plates, and finally they come with the trash barrels. It's getting there.

Alison's and my contribution arrives next. The liquor store guy hauls in a case of wine, some tequila, vodka, whiskey, tonic and soda. He too has an enormous ice chest, filled to the top with cubed ice. And plastic glasses. We both step out on the lawn to greet him.

He smiles, hands me an invoice. I look at it carefully, then reach into my robe pocket and take out a roll of cash. We contribute from our per diem for this, our treat. He's paid off and leaves happy.

Just as the clock strikes one, Carrie from camera arrives with her daughter, each carrying a large clay pot of homemade chili. I stroll over to greet her, grab a plastic fork on the way. Carrie smiles at me, smoking hot for fifty years old, and takes a lid off one of the clay pots. I dig in with the fork and take a big bite. It's blue-ribbon quality.

It's time to get dressed, and I head inside. This will clearly be a feast. As I walk toward the house, I spot Nina, leading a troop of four people I don't know. They look Native American, three women and a tall, handsome man dressed in black. They all carry something.

I'm worried about Larry. This has been a stressful week. Twelve-hour shoots, two hours after in the office with the paperwork, up at 5:30 the next morning. He needs to relax, have some fun. Not worry about some crazy driver. But that's who he is. His team is his family.

RODRIGO – DIRECTOR

Victor and I get into the car at one-thirty. I'm hungry and anxious to get to the party. It's one of the things I dreamed of, all of us getting together on Sunday, eating and drinking, getting to know each other. We've missed the first two Sundays because we were in LA for casting, so today's the day. I heard there's roast pig and homemade tortillas.

It is my impression the Glove has put together a first-rate team. I love the designer, Nina, who gets the gritty reality of lonely rural life. The designs and the sets I've seen are rich with small town touches whispering of hope and sadness, lust and violence.

Xavier, my cameraman, is a gem. Happy, thoughtful, never misses a thing—a smudge on an office window, no depth in the lighting in the long hallway in the Sheriff's home. A soft light on a framed picture in the background, quietly sitting alone, full of answers. He's painting. And we agree on the colors: brown, dark green, and silver. Sort of eco-evil. Like our story. I ask Victor how much longer 'til we get there? We arrive. He smiles.

It's like walking into a movie party scene. We stroll into a soft jazz tune, George Benson I think, and I chuckle and start to glide. I smell the pork, see the natives pressing tortillas. There are the wardrobe girls, cute and Latin, serving their salads.

Victor heads for the brownies. He's heard they're great. He returns munching half of one. He offers me the other half. I take it, put it in my pocket, and head for the bar. I see tequila and ice. Never drink during shooting. We're not shooting today.

At the bar, I step up next to the Glove. We hug, congratulate each other on a crazy, but great, first week. Then he gets serious. "Rooster wants to have a rehearsal next Sunday at the compound, in the morning before the party."

"Grandma's?" I ask. "What's this about?

"Don't know. He's been working for a week on the attack with the special-effects guys, and he wants to show us something real. I know him, he's clever and inventive, but he likes to keep secrets. 'Fresh eyes,' he always says."

I look at him. It's not just about hours worked with him, page count, numbers of extras, like a few people warned me. I look up and Nina's dancing with Cody, the native dressed in black, and it's like *DIRTY DANCING*, and she's beautiful and they flow together like water over rocks, and I can't take my eyes off them.

Rooster and Grandma come through the gate. He looks like he's being brought to the gallows. She looks nervous about entering a dragon's lair. Her hair is trimmed, she's wearing makeup, tight stretchy pants, and some fancy blue heels.

The Glove smiles at me.

Rooster comes right up to me, reminds me who he is, and tells me how much he loved my movies. People stories. I ask him what he thought about the gas station scene in *DARK*

WATER, and he smiles and praises it. There is no gas station scene in either of my movies. This is what everyone told me about Hollywood. Mostly bullshit.

I ask about the rehearsal next weekend. He gives a quick look to Grandma, flicks her a quick wink. She smiles. "Well, we've been working on the attack sequence. Depending on the numbers, which Larry ain't got to me yet, I think I've got a pretty dynamic vision of the attack.

"We'll do a full speed rehearsal of the beginning, the cops charging the compound, then go by the numbers of the battle. That's when you and me and the DP can work out the individual beats, what's first unit and what's second unit. How's that sound to you?"

Luanne strolls into the yard with Arlo, the young man who seems to be everywhere. Grandma sees her and leaves to say hello. Luanne does a double-take on what her grandma is wearing. Rooster watches her walk away, a lecherous smile on his lips. When he turns back to me, he knows I busted him.

"When you're working in Indian territory, always helps to have the Indians on your side. Know what I'm saying?"

I don't. I wonder if all the rich, older women around here are loco en la cabeza. "I hope there will be as little second unit as possible. I want you to get the actors ready to do their own warfare. And remember, I direct the actors."

"Absolutely, Chief!" Rooster crows. "As few doubles as possible always been my motto."

"Good. Now let's get some food and have some fun." I smile at him.

I turn and catch Glove watching us. Frowning. It feels like palace intrigue. But then Nina is by my side, Bossa Nova is on the speakers, and she's dragging me to the dance floor.

LENA – ASSISTANT PRODUCTION ACCUNTANT

I went to a private high school in Santa Barbara and then to a Catholic university in Washington state. Man, did they rock! NOT. Both had zip community spirit, or any kind of spirit for that matter. There were organized dances in high school and church festivities at university. Obviously, nothing stuck to me.

I'm dancing to Brazilian samba with the two young prop assistants, trying not to spill my drink, and laughing as the director's assistant bangs into everyone on the dance floor, stoned on a brownie and dancing furiously with himself.

I know this is a business, and some little voice in the back of my head tells me I should show some restraint. I'm in accounting, after all. The buck stops here, bullshit bullshit. But for fuck's sake, we work under such stress, I think it's fine to let it rip on the weekend. Fuck 'em if they can't take a joke.

Just because I'm drinking and dancing with the crew doesn't mean I won't challenge their timecards or their petty cash envelopes. I'm a pro, as are all of us. Suddenly everyone goes quiet. Heads turn toward the open gate as Larry enters with...Captain Eddie!

The crew rushes him, smiling and clapping him on the back, hugs and kisses from the girls, a big ole shit-eating grin spread across his wide face. The Beatles' *ALL YOU NEED IS LOVE* blasts from the speakers. Roger the DJ is on his game. Larry finds me, takes my cup and drains my drink.

"The Best Boy declined to press charges. It's all over." He hugs me, kisses me quickly on the cheek.

I look over where the camera guys and the electricians are sitting, joking and drinking beer. They don't drop everything and go to Eddie, but they don't have to. Eddie gets a serious look on his face and heads for them. I wander over to hear.

"Look," Eddie says, sincerely. "It was the heat of the battle, I lost my mind for a minute, did a stupid thing. I'm really sorry. If I could take it back, I would. We got a long road ahead, let's be friends."

The DP, Xavier, nods his head and reaches out his hand. "It's the past now. The kid started it, and the company has promised to take care of him. So it's all good. You're right, we've got a lot of work to go." With that, the assembled camera and electric crew members all stand and shake Eddie's hand.

Larry comes up behind me, hands me a refill. He has a bowl of chili and I take a big bite. I wonder if my mouth will ever have so much good stuff put into it on any other movie I work on. Suddenly the music shifts to Motown and the Isley Brothers are crooning This old heart of mine/been broke a thousand times... and the crowd charges the dance floor.

I notice Alison and Carrie dancing together until the prop boys cut in. Even Alison is laughing, shaking her booty like a twenty-year-old. She's such a great boss. Brilliant, anticipates everything, a dagger-like sarcasm. It's great to see her laughing like she's got nothing in the whole freakin' world to worry about.

THE GLOVE – LINE PRODUCER

I wander away from a conversation Rodrigo is having with Xavier and the gaffer, a tall fifty-year-old man with a red beard down to his breastbone, Brian Tomsett. Been around as long as I can remember. Lit some of the biggest movies in the past twenty years. He and Xavier are like brothers, laughing at each other's jokes before they're even finished.

Yesterday I got a call from Matthew. He heard about the fire and the fight and wondered if everything was okay. I told him we had a great first week, the cast and crew seem top rate, the fire was an accident that we dealt with and still made our day, and the fight was simply tempers flashing, and all had been resolved.

I didn't tell him I agreed to keep the best boy on a forty-hour-week salary through the shoot, including health and welfare and pension, which made any talk of a lawsuit go away. I also told him that next Sunday it looked like there would be a stunt rehearsal for the raid on the compound. If he was thinking about coming for a visit, that might be a good time.

He said he was in Chicago through Friday, but he'd try to get up to Bishop on Saturday. He might be coming with one of his Russian investors, so I told him I'd book two suites on Saturday.

I spent yesterday with Clemencia. She cooked and I played with her two little boys in the backyard; then we drove up into the hills and hiked along a bustling stream with the kids, throwing rocks in the water. We ended back at her place for an old-fashioned Mexican feast.

Being single, I don't carry any troubled thoughts about dating a woman. But being in the middle of someone's family is kind of weird. By the end of the day, I turned restless. Kids and TV and beers on the back porch started to feel like a chore, and honestly, a bore. She's a great, easy, beautiful woman. We come together like young lovers in bed, but the domesticity has really started feeling like a pillow over my mouth.

On Sunday morning, I left early, telling her I had work at the office to finish before the crew got together for a BBQ celebrating the end of the first week. I knew she was hoping I'd invite her, but I couldn't. Didn't. She smiled and gave me a big hug in front of her boys.

When I got out on the highway, I noticed a banged-up white pickup truck behind me. It would aggressively come up and then fade back a few car lengths. Clemencia told me about her ex, how he was jealous to the point of violence. I wondered if he was following me.

I pulled into the gas station in Independence and the truck did too. I went inside to pay for gas and get some water, and when I came back the truck was parked off to the side and the man in the driver's seat was staring at me. I looked at him, waved my hands at him like 'what the fuck?', and proceeded to pump my gas.

When I finished, I got in the car and drove north toward Bishop. The white truck pulled out but headed south back toward Lone Pine. I called Clemencia, told her what happened. She was sorry. Now she had to gather her kids in case he came back to her house. She probably would spend the day with her mom. He was afraid of her mom. She had 911 on her speed dial.

At the BBQ, I pick up another taco, meet the ladies from the nation who are making fresh tortillas like a factory line, and wander over to Larry and Lena, who are sitting on the house patio.

"Well," I sigh, "one week down." I look over the crowd and see Rooster and Grandma dancing. "What do you think is going on there?" I ask Larry.

"God only knows," he laughs. "You worked with him a couple of times, what do you think?"

"Seems weird."

Lena stands, draining her glass. "Seems weird to me too. Like Rooster's fucking Grandma. Try and explain that one." She heads off toward the bar. Larry holds up his empty glass and she grabs it. Explain that one, indeed.

Later, I grab a road beer as I head back to the hotel. I wave goodbye to Rodrigo, who is dancing with one of the local wardrobe girls. He grins, waves. Xavier stops me on the way out. "Listen, Glove, I just want to say thanks for the leadership this week. Could have been a lot of anger over what happened. The team trusts you." I hug him, tell him I'm very impressed with his work and his style.

I'm almost on the highway when the phone rings. It's Toni. We've worked the schedule to give her tomorrow off so she can go to some performance by her kid in LA. She's calling to ask if we can work it out to give her Tuesday as well.

Off the top of my head, I don't know. Probably. I hesitate before saying, "I'll call you back after I talk with the AD and the director." She tells me she loves Frankie. Matter of fact, all the cast love him. I hang up, dial Frankie. "You'll never guess who I just talked to."

"She called me first. I told her to call you."

"So, what do you think?"

"I've been going over it with Rainman. Let me talk with Locations, but I think we can do it. But this is the last time. She's in just about everything else 'til the end of the schedule."

"Okay, get back to me when it's set. Call Larry too. I'll call her after you confirm it with me. Missed a great party today, where were you?"

"My Dad went into the hospital Thursday, so I went back to LA."

"Nothing serious, I hope."

"Lung cancer. Fifty years of two packs a day."

"Jesus."

"I tried to ask him if it all seemed worth it now, since I've been trying to get him to stop for the last million years... but he started swearing at me and then coughing his lungs out, then spitting up blood and yellow puss and the nurses kicked me out."

I don't know what to say.

"But the show must go on, right?" he continues. I hear ice clink in his glass.

"Yeah, the show must go on," I agree. The show always goes on.

LENA – ASSISTANT PRODUCTION ACCOUNTANT

The party's over and almost everyone has left. Just those cleaning and packing up are still here. Carrie's daughter brings me a bowl with the last of the chili. I eagerly take it. Dinner for the next two nights. Then one of the wardrobe girls brings me a pile of left-over guacamole, which I also eagerly accept.

I put them both on a tray and head for the kitchen. I awkwardly grab a bag of chips and gently put them on top of the guacamole. Inside it's quiet, kind of nice for a change. Then I sense voices from the kitchen. I step toward the open door and hear two people, a man and a woman.

Before I step inside, I stay back, out of sight, to hear what's going on. The pretty young actress, Josie something, who plays the young girl who goes missing at the beginning of the story, is drunk. She's telling the hottie stand-in, Jimmy, about the first day of shooting.

"You don't understand what I'm saying," she whines, "The camera was two hundred yards from the base camp, and my starting point was another hundred beyond that. It was like a million miles to me."

I quietly set my tray down on the dining room table and plop into a chair in the dark room. I can see into the kitchen, with all the lights on, and hear what they're saying, but they can't see me.

"And all the shots are with these lenses," she goes on, "so a million focus marks and actor marks, where I should stagger over rocks, where I should stop, bend over and catch my breath. Where to fucking look up to the heavens and ask what the hell happened to me. Which is exactly what I was thinking! What the fuck is happening to me?"

They're at the kitchen table, Jimmy's got an empty beer bottle in front of him, she's got a half-full glass of something clear in front of her. "I wish I was there," he says, all sympathetic and sickening. He's a flirt, but a really cute one. When I come to set with the crew per diem, he watches me like a hawk. Creepy but kind of exciting, to be honest.

"That's what we did all morning. No dialogue. Takes, one after another. The director running at me after each take. Try desperate at the beginning, less after the look to heaven. Okay, let's swap that. Just plain weary at the start, desperate after looking to heaven. Great. Now, a little slower. Now, a little faster. The first fucking day on my first big movie and I'm praying I don't pass out in front of everybody."

She gulps the rest of her drink, lets out a big burp. They both laugh. "Sorry," she says. He reaches over, takes her hand. She continues, "After the lunch break, I didn't know what the character was, who I was, why we were out in this desert doing the same thing over and over. On the first take

203

in the afternoon, I heard the director say to the cameraman, 'Now we start the day's work.' Start? What the fuck?"

"But you made it, and everyone says you were great."

"I ended up screaming at them. They kept telling me to trip at that rock, stop at this one. I screamed 'You're a hundred yards away, what fucking difference does it make which rock!' They looked at each other. Xavier the cameraman comes running to me."

"Long lens focus marks," Jimmy says as he pets her cheek. She nods yes, smiles. What is this, I think, an episode of Friends? It's making me gag.

She squints at him, trying to stay in the conversation. "Where was I? Oh yeah. So, on the way back to the hotel, I realized what the director did. Can you believe this? He got me in the perfect place my character was supposed to be. Angry and exhausted. Confused. I got so excited about this insight! I understood the director's process! Never even thought about this before." Jimmy pets her again.

"So I asked the driver to stop at the gas station/liquor store and buy me some tequila. He said he wasn't twenty-one, so I said no sweat and hopped out of the van. But he jumped out and told me to stay there, he'd be right back. And sure enough, the only tequila they had was a fifth of Cuervo. He also bought a bag of ice. Things got a little weird after that. I was on hold for the next three days, after all." She gives him a cutesy-pie smile of innocence.

I've had enough of this bullshit and pick up the tray of leftovers, stride into the kitchen. Jimmy's eyes light up when he sees me. "Lena!"

"You know, most companies would have fired your ass for doing that," I say to her. "Some of the nasty ones would have made sure you never work again. You better wise up, sister. You never know when that one fuckup ends your career. Like maybe what just happened to that driver. Just nineteen years old, starting out."

Jimmy looks at me. "I think she's learned her lesson," he says, trying to make peace.

"She's an actress and a spoiled brat. That combination never learns lessons. Unless someone starts cutting off fingers."

Josie tries to stand up but struggles with her balance. Jimmy reaches for her, helps her to her feet. As she grabs her glass she says, "You don't know anything about me!"

I can't help but smile. "We all know everything about you."

She staggers, and I reach to steady her. Jimmy leans in. We get her legs back underneath her. I'm angry because that kid, a really nice boy, might be finished in the industry. But my anger melts when I look into Jimmy's eyes. He feels my fire, knows by instinct I fight for the little guys. Foolishly, I pet his cheek with my hand. Jimmy blows me a kiss as he helps Josie out of the kitchen. I'm not even sure what just happened.

Passing them as they leave, Alison steps in. "Wow. What the hell was that about?"

"Rookies in the big leagues, I think, is your term."

She looks at me. "You're no rookie," she says. "May I remind you."

"What does that mean?" I ask.

She gives me a look like a nun who knows but can't prove anything.

PART FIVE –
REVEILLE

LARRY – PRODUCTION MANAGER

I'm watching Frankie organize the shot. He is a solid first AD, tells funny jokes, never quits until all the questions are answered when the director, cameraman, and he make the plan for the day's work. He knows the rhythm of the set, sees the way some directors hide, maybe from the number of shots, length of a dolly track, number of extras, the light in the sky, whatever.

Yet sometimes he's too smart for his own good. He sees complications where there are none. He makes small changes to the schedule that don't need to be made. Creates a paper storm of new information. Even his team gets confused, especially his Mexican 2nd AD, swapping the order of the scenes in a location to the point that we bring in most of the actors working that day early because no one has faith in the order of shooting on the call sheet, the bible for each day of production. You read it, you know the order of the scenes to be filmed, you get a feel for when each piece might come up in the day. Constantly changing the call sheet is like constantly changing the meds on the crazy ward.

This morning, Day Six, Monday, Frankie is depressed. Far away. His father is in the hospital and he thinks Death is about to knock on his door. It's an easy day; the character Claire is in the Women's clinic getting the news she's pregnant. There's a nurse, the lady doctor, three extras, and the villain desk nurse, who tells the names of any teenage girls testing positive to the Women in White. We're on our stage at the church for the first time, and though it's rigged for lights, there's a long time for adjustments after the full cast rehearsal.

Frankie whispers to Rainman to take the floor. His real name is Renan, but Frankie calls him Rainman. Frankie sits off to the side, a gloomy, no-energy veil hanging over him. The cast and the crew are worried. People come, asking if he's alright. Everyone loves Frankie.

The Directors Guild fought and fought against bringing Renan from Mexico, but they finally gave up when Frankie persisted. His grandfather founded the DGA. He told me once that it's the force of will that always wins on a movie. He won this one.

As the 2nd AD, Rainman's main responsibility is getting the talent through wardrobe and makeup and to the set. Once that happens, he sets the background action with the 1st. When we roll the camera, he cues the extras. Go here, laugh with her, sit and order a coffee. And he supervises all the paperwork. Call sheets, production reports, schedule changes, you name it.

Now as the 1st AD, it's about getting the energy of camera, grips, electric, background, props, actors, and the director into synch, ready at the same time. Everyone does their separate work, and it all comes together ready for action when the talent arrives on set. One part of the sequence is late, people ready to shoot are left waiting? All eyes are on the 1st.

As I reassure Rainman he can handle the job this morning, I don't see Frankie slip away. Rainman has to remember to call for 'last looks,' make sure it's all perfect before we roll the camera. He must remember to roll the camera. This is all instinct with a 1st, but not if it's your first-time calling rolling.

We all figure it's Frankie's Dad. He's Sicilian, so family is very important. The director comes to the camera. Carrie is ready with the slate. Rainman calls for first positions. The actors are in place. He double checks with the camera operator, who nods he's ready.

"And...we're rolling!"

ROLLING! echoes through the stage. The sound mixer calls speed. Carrie IDs the scene, claps the slate. The director softly says "Action," and Rainman's first shot as a 1st AD begins.

The take is good, but there are a few technical problems. The director steps in with the actors while the cameraman and the key grip adjust the timing on the dolly move. They decide to shift the position of the dolly track.

I look over to Rainman, who is trying to control his face from bursting into a wide grin. It may seem like a little thing, but the first time rolling the camera is exciting and terrifying. I slide out the stage door, looking for my friend. I find him in his office, packing up.

"Your Dad?" I ask.

"Fuck no. It's Gabby. She doesn't want to get married now. I'll be back in a couple of days." I hurry back to the stage to tell the DGA team what's happening.

"Have you heard from Frankie?" Rainman asks.

"I have," I say.

"His Dad?"

"They're Sicilian. Death is like not serving pasta for dinner. Makes no never-mind. But women...? Gabby told him she was calling off the wedding. Not because she didn't love him, she does. But because she's still married. Catholics...Anyway, he's leaving for a while."

Rainman thinks for a moment, then bursts out laughing. Quickly, he tries to cover it up. "In Mexico, the Catholic church is more important than the government, but it is a tiger with no teeth," he says. "We pray, but we don't pay attention."

"He's going back to LA and sort this out. He's never left a show for any amount of time, for any reason. But this? He's a mess."

We look at each other, wondering what this means. The DGA will go crazy if this guy assumes the 1st AD role. I look over at the cameraman, who is signaling that he's five minutes from being ready. Rainman tells his team to give the five-minute warning to actors and the director. I can't help but smile. I think he can step up to this.

LUANNE – PRODUCTION ASSISTANT

I've been stuck here at Grandma's for the past week and a half. If I didn't hate men before, I sure do now. Cocky young guys with saws and hammers and big white pickup trucks. They have no idea they're already a cliché.

Then there's Special Effects space cadets, wandering around measuring walls and searching for places to run wires for God knows what. Asking me to find out where the gas line runs, any other underground cable, that kinda thing.

And Rooster, who struts around the place like he's the king of the swinging dicks, taking in every twist and turn of the land, wondering if he can use it in some dramatic, thrilling stunt. Yada yada.

Before he got hurt, Gus told me the carpenters and the stunt guys are the testosterone cowboys on a movie set. Maybe the grips too, but I haven't met them yet. Swinging dicks, Gus called them. No shit. I've been asked out six times and they've only been here a little more than a week.

Nina shows up, checking on her construction crew and the dorms they're building, if they're on pace, having any problems, does it look good, fit naturally into the landscape? If the plasterers and the painters are scheduled and ready?

From what I can tell, everybody's got a list of fifty things to remember. Daily. That's every single person on the production. Probably a hundred. Gus told me making movies wasn't rocket science, but it seems to me it's at least high school homework. Getting ready for tomorrow, next week, in a month, today, right now. Maybe that much day-to-day stress is why there's so much partying.

Inevitably, Nina falls into conversation with Rooster. He grins like she's his best friend. "What do you think if we do...? If I wanted to blow that wall, could you build me three fake ones? Can you build one of the dorms to set on fire?" That's all I can hear. The usual, as Nina described it to me.

"That's why this rehearsal on Saturday is the real deal," he confides to her, putting his arm over her shoulder as she walks back toward the house "We get some hard answers, we're ready to roll."

She quickly removes his arm, turns to him. "I thought it was Sunday morning?"

"I gotta talk to that UPM. If it's Sunday, that blows everybody's Saturday night. I been around this track enough to know that's not how you treat your crew. Boys need to party." Nina walks away, shaking her head.

I'm having trouble getting my mind straight about how my grandma is behaving. I mean, she's a piece of work, always has been. A force of nature, I guess you could say. And lately, she's a force of a nature I don't recognize. For instance, right now she's up on the roof of the house with a camera Rooster gave her. "Photographing all the land we own," she says. "Roo thinks we could do a god-damn series out here."

This is not my grandma, in blue jeans and work boots, swearing up on the roof looking for movie locations. She's got a grin on her like a sixteen-year-old. Rooster looks up on the roof.

"See anything interesting?"

"You ever seen that TV series, Big Valley?" she answers. "Damn if you're not right, Roo, we could do another Big Valley right here."

"One step at a time, Janie." Rooster laughs. "Let's get this one done first."

Janie? My Grandma's name is Mary Jane, and I faintly remember growing up she was known as Janie. No one in this century has seen her in blue jeans and boots or called her Janie. Much less talking about creating a TV series.

She jumps off the ladder three rungs from the bottom into Rooster's arms. They're laughing like teenagers. I never had that much fun when I was a teenager. Rooster's phone rings and he answers, motions to Grandma he's got to take this, shouting "Who's this? Can't hear you!"

Grandma looks over at me on the porch. "How's your day going, Luanne?"

"Not too bad," I say. "I am confused about one thing, though."

"What's that?"

"Where my grandma went."

She gives me a hard, righteous look. For a second, I see my old grandma. But then she smiles, waves me off as she heads for the back door. "This is all just a game, I know that.

But it's entertaining! I read somewhere that even people from your generation like to have fun sometimes. That true?"

I must admit, I like Janie. There's no Repent or Go to Hell! coming off her like old Grandma. She flipped the page, said 'fuck off' to bitterness, 'howdy' to groovy. I still can't shake the rumors from Sunday's party. The smug smiles, rolling eyes, the focus everyone had on them. Grandma's fucking Rooster. I try to force myself to not think about it. But it's so bizarre and so clear. She might be fucking that old bastard.

But what's in it for him? Gus also told me it's always a battle for power. She owns the big location. Can it be that obvious? It's feeling like a Bette Davis movie. Evil. Dangerous. Love Bette Davis movies.

Last Sunday at the BBQ I ate about a quarter ton of chili while I sat with Kenny, the Special Effects coordinator. He's tall and lanky with fists that look like he fought a long war barehanded. Chili and a couple of beers. Free. Something better?

Kenny has worked with Rooster two other times. They don't like each other, but they respect each other, and count on each other to speak the truth. "The thing about Rooster," he explains, "he's a coward with a determined heart." I don't understand.

"He doesn't trust himself, so he works like a snake-oil salesman getting everybody believing in him, supporting him." I still look at him blankly. "If he fucks up, we all fuck up. Pass the blame around so it doesn't stick to anybody. You understand now?"

"He's not a leader?"

"Oh, he is. Just the worst kind."

"What's that?"

"A finger-pointing chicken shit."

LARRY – PRODUCTION MANAGER

I'm feeling pretty good. Day eight and we're on schedule, under on hours, and no explosions from any of the departments about going over budget. And another interesting thing: I'm falling in love with Lena. Okay, call me an idiot.

I love her temper, but it's her kindness and consideration that really gets me. We're both single, so there's no hiding anything. I'm the production manager, true, but that doesn't mean we can't be a couple. As in the 'couple' the crew is inherently suspicious of. Accounting and production. The evil empire.

The Owens Valley is quiet when you get away from the interstate. We're filming in a neighborhood in Big Pine, fifteen miles south of Bishop. Our sheriff is staking out the suspected snitch's house. The actress who plays the nasty little tattletale is really a stand-up comedian and she's hilarious. The crew calls her "Knick," because her character always has her knickers in a bunch.

It's a half-day of little pieces, comings and goings of good guys and bad guys, that string together the bigger scenes and propel the story forward. Kind of a waste of a day, but we must shoot the bits and pieces. Still no word from Frankie. 'Knick' was his idea.

We finish the location efficiently. Glad I rolled the dice and sent the caterer to the next location to set up for lunch. We move to a gun shop in Bishop, next to a big empty parking lot for base camp. The wardrobe and makeup/hair trailers were moved early. The equipment trucks, props, the director and cast trailers all march in line. Tim directs each vehicle to its landing spot. It's precision, an army on the move.

Rodrigo, Xavier, and Rainman get there first, go inside and work out the staging, then try and make a shot list. If we're lucky, maybe get a cast rehearsal, and then lunch. Perfect time for me to go to the office, check the cost numbers with Alison, what's being reported and what's being fudged, go over the logistics of the rest of this week with Fiona.

I enter the building and run smack into Lucille, the drama teacher at Bishop High and the woman we hired to cast the extras. Her assistant, Katie, a senior at the school and the musical star of the drama department, hurries up behind her. When I look at Katie, I can't help seeing her in whiskers singing 'Moonlight, say hello to the moonlight...'

Lucille is calm, smiling, reminds me of a quiet assassin in a Hong Kong martial arts movie. Katie is ready to explode. "What's going on, ladies? You look like you just saw a ghost."

Lucille begins. "We just talked with Alison, and she was very emphatic about not inviting the stand-ins anymore to the Sunday BBQ. They're part of the crew, aren't they, Lar? In Jimmy's case, he turned down construction work in Mammoth all summer to take a hundred dollar a day gig with us. That's a ton of money he walked away from."

He's the one who's hot for Lena.

"And Wendy, don't forget," Katie chimes in. Wendy is Toni's stand-in. Dead match, height and coloring. And she's like Radar O'Reilly, right behind you when you turn around. I don't have time for this shit, but the conversation does have its complications.

Jimmy creams every time he sees Lena. They're both hard bodies, both young, handsome, full of themselves. Perfect for a connection. Except for me. Do I want Jimmy to continue to come to the Sunday parties? Hell no. Can I say this? Fuck no.

"I'll talk to Alison. How're we doing with the young girl fighters?" I ask. We need a rotating group of young girls, between fifteen and twenty years old, to play the Women in White warriors. Most of the action stuff will be shot before school goes back, so the under-eighteen can work an eight-hour day. But our goal is to get as many athletic young women over the age of eighteen who look much younger. The younger the better. Katie gives Lucille a quick, troubled look.

"What?" I ask.

"Well," Lucille rolls into it. "That Rooster is a curious sort, isn't he?"

"What do you mean?"

"He's asked me to dinner twice now!" Katie blurts out. "If my dad ever found out, it'd be like a nuclear bomb went off."

Rooster. I've been avoiding him since he got here. The Glove trusts him. Just give him his space, he councils. We'll see soon what he's thinking, if he's the right guy. We all think he's got something going on with Luanne's grandmother, which is impossible to imagine.

220

"So, do you have any picks yet? Anybody in training?"

Lucille speaks up. "He likes four or five of the girls, all over eighteen and looking fourteen to sixteen. But."

"He won't commit until he goes out with each of them!" Katie again jumps in. "He's sick. This isn't Hollywood. It's Bishop! Sixty-year-old coots don't take eighteen-year-old girls to dinner."

Lucille turns, quiets her down. "It's just a strange process." She turns back to me. "We need another voice, from the producer-side of things," she says.

"Yeah, like someone who understands NO doesn't just mean no, it means, go fuck yourself!" Katie says this loudly. As she does, Etta, our young PA, steps through the front door. She hears Katie's explosion, stops dead in her tracks. She looks at me, then at Lucille and Katie. Her face blushes bright red. She hurries into the production office.

I tell them, "I'll get Rooster straightened out."

Inside, I meet Fiona, tell her I'll be with Alison for about fifteen minutes, then I'd like to sit with her and Liz and go over some things for the next week and a half. I ask her to call Rooster, have him in my office today at five o'clock.

Fi jots this down on her notepad. "Nina told me he wants to move the rehearsal to Saturday morning, so everybody gets a clean Saturday night."

"Remind me when we get together."

Alison matches invoices and purchase orders on her desk. She's smiling. Lena stands by the window looking toward the White Mountains, cell phone to her ear.

"I don't give a fuck what she says! I never said that! I never would! If I wanted to curse her out, I would have done it right to her fat old face!" Alison smiles.

"The stand-ins can come to the Sunday party," I tell her.

Her smile gets smaller. "Just trying to protect you," she whispers. We both look at Lena.

"I might need it," I joke. Alison's smile gets even smaller. "Want to look at the cost report? First pass, at least?"

A movie budget has something like two hundred categories. Each with a number attached, based on the conception of how the shoot and post-production will go. Days budgeted; days made. Hours budgeted; hours worked. A blueprint, in other words.

The inherent farce of making a movie on location is you take the budget out into the reality of humanity, sudden sickness, friendly towns that turn picky with idiot politics, high winds, rain, and it always turns into a hot tub party with crazy people. Things change, weaknesses reveal themselves, car accidents, tornados, the whole ball of wax called Life. And the only thing that doesn't change is the bottom-line of the budget.

That first number is always the number.

I meet Rooster in my office at five-fifteen. He apologizes for being late. Who knew there was afternoon traffic on the far side of town? "Probably some cow in the middle of the road," I joke.

"More like a Mexican with a six pack in his gut," Rooster jokes back.

"I hear you want to run the rehearsal on Saturday morning now?" I ask.

"Yeah. Don't you think? Then all the work is done, and everybody gets a Saturday night." I agree with him, but I hedge my bet and tell him I have to check with the Glove.

"Tell you the truth, between you and me?" I nod. "Janie, the woman who owns the place, said there's no way any work is going on at her place on the Lord's Day. Said she'd pull out of the deal. I guess you know she's a woman of her word."

This pisses me off. Never wanted to agree to this location from the start. But I got overruled. I swallow my anger. "So, I see you're bringing in three stunt guys tomorrow. Why's that?"

"Give 'em a day and a half to see what I'm thinking. We want this sneak attack to be exciting. And complicated. These three are my best boys. Truth is, we're lucky to get 'em. They all should be coordinating themselves."

"I just signed a check for twelve hundred dollars for a used Ford sedan, and then one for seven hundred to put a roll cage into it. What's that about?"

His eyes narrow. "For the rehearsal," Rooster replies. "If what I'm thinking works, it's money well spent. Is there a decent picture-car budget on this?"

"Should be enough."

"That's why we got to have this rehearsal! Once we know exactly what we're doing, then me and my team can work on a number. Look..."and he fumbles for my name.

"Larry."

"Look Larry, I'm sixty-three and believe me, I don't need to do this shit anymore. I got a ten-thousand-acre ranch outside Boulder, Colorado, paid for and all the grazing leased out for ten years. "

I stare at him. I don't like him. He's one of those old-timers who played for the team and realized the team didn't give a shit about him. Now it's just about money. His money.

"I do this because it's still fun. It's a movie, for god's sake. Not a script or a book. It's what your eyes see. Exciting. Scary. At least when it's good. When it's great, it's all that with some close-your-eyes stunts that make your asshole freeze up like bad catering food."

"I still don't see why you won't tell anybody what you got in mind. You're not the director, remember."

"But that's just the point! If I tell you, it's a conversation, not a reaction. A reaction tells everybody the truth. It works, it doesn't. It works but it needs to be extended, toned down, what-the-fuck ever. I told the Glove this is what I wanted, how I work these days, and he agreed. Did he tell you that?"

"He did."

"Then let's set it, you and me, for Saturday at nine o'clock at the location. Director, the Glove, cameraman, AD, you, transpo, stunts and effects, PAs with charged walkies. Definitely a view finder, or maybe a camera body with some long lenses. Sound right?"

"We'll make the call sheet," I agree.

He stands, turns to leave. "Thanks, Larry. See! I remembered it this time." He smiles, his old eyes boring into me to make sure I agree and won't go back on anything. I forget to ask him about date nights with the eighteen-year-olds.

He's a powerful presence. Most big shots in the industry are. They dazzle you with their confidence. I sit back, chuckle. My phone buzzes. It's Liz, telling me Craig the prop master is on line five. "Lar, it's Craig. It's going around there's a stunt rehearsal on Saturday. Any truth to it?"

"Yeah. Rooster just left my office. It's to work out the attack on the compound."

"I'm assuming you want me there."

"Not really necessary. It's for the director, cameraman, the AD, Effects. This is supposedly about the broad strokes. Once we get a plan, there'll be a more specific meeting."

"Look, we've been friends a long time. I love you like a brother, but I've worked with Rooster a couple of times. 'Oh right, I forgot about that' is on the first page of his vocabulary. I don't care if you pay me or not, I want to be there just to ask the questions the team might not. And the first aid guy wants to come too."

I love Craig. When we were young there was no one wilder after wrap. A flare gun battle in D Block on Alcatraz pretty much says it all. When it's about business, I listen. He was trained by one of the all-time best, and he's right up there in that category. I agree to have him with us on Saturday, on payroll. And the first aid guy. Nobody works for free on my crew.

THE GLOVE – LINE PRODUCER

Last night Clemencia and I just got tired of each other. We were at KC's dancing to jukebox music, laughing and kissing, and suddenly she stopped and looked me in the eye. Hard look, sincere look. Need-an-answer look. Wanted me to take her and the kids to the stunt rehearsal tomorrow. Her boys would love it.

I felt like I was caught in a spider's web. All my choices wrapped up in some sticky mess. A wonderful location fling turned into an ultimatum about commitment. I realize she has no idea about the rules. When the show is over, the circus moves on. The tears of the clown. Harsh, agreed. But the way it is.

We sat in the corner and had it out. She said all I wanted was sex, and I said all she wanted was a rich man to take care of her and the mess she made with her family. She stood up to leave several times, and each time I reached out for her, pulled her back to our table.

I don't want to hurt her. But I'm not going to commit to anything. I don't know how. Never learned. Certainly not to a woman with two little boys living in Lone Pine, California. I'm fifty years old. I've made it this far without any worry about a family. Plenty of women are the same. We have sex; we have fun. We go our own way.

My family was a cold, heartless group of selfish people blinded by the bright lights of Chicago success. When my mother, and then my father, died, I felt very little. I was always on my own. At least that's how I feel. Some shrink would say I'm still in adolescent-hurt mode but fuck that. Every bridge I burned, I burned with complete understanding I was burning it. Clemencia reminds me of my feelings of being heartless. Not good memories, but honest ones.

She cried all the way back to her house. She begged me to come inside, stay the night. I wouldn't. We kissed. She reached deep into my mouth, but I didn't reach back. She pulled away, started crying again. I turned and left.

Back in the hotel, I try to sleep but finally give up. Go on the internet around two o'clock. Never go back to bed. Around four I start to cry. Lost. Then Matthew texts me. He is back in LA with his Russian partner and they are getting in a car and racing to our set to see the rehearsal. Thought he'd make it by ten o'clock. Could we wait?

I'm so confused, I can't respond. Finally, I say of course, come ahead. I don't have a clue this is one of those moments in life where it all turns. Finally, I fall asleep on the couch for two hours. Alarm wakes me. Don't know where I am, who I am.

I feel deep sorrow about Clemencia. Angry about this Saturday morning rehearsal. Fucking Rooster. When I called him and he said he was available, I thought it was my lucky day. He's a tough old bird, finicky and stubborn as a dog with a bone. But he does a great job. His second units always cut perfectly with the first unit. And they always surprise you. This rattles around in my brain. Surprise is the enemy of production, after all.

ARLO – KEY PRODUCTION ASSISTANT

I did have a golf game booked this morning with Bishop's mayor and some LA guy who wants to buy land for a sports complex out by the course. The mayor, a friend of my dad, thinks I can get in on the ground floor with this guy and start a career. Dad always said it's better to be a good golfer than a good student.

I went to Luanne's last night. She was panicked about the stunt rehearsal this morning. Panicked, I think, about what's happened to her grandma. She asked Gus for advice, but his jaw is so wired we couldn't understand anything he said. He was on the sofa in the front room, slurping soup from La Fiesta and glowing like an evil space rock about to blow up the world.

His stare, his fire, is why I'm on Grandma's porch at seven o'clock. The morning is cold, but it's supposed to warm up later. No one is around; the house is quiet. A red-tail hawk circles the area. I wonder about the crew I saw working on the cell tower outside Benton. Reception out here has always been sketchy. My phone is dead.

Tim arrives in his van with three stunt guys and some blond in cutoff jeans and a jacket. She clings to one of them. They pile out and cluster in the driveway, warming their hands on the styro coffee cups they hold. Checking their phones. No reception.

Rooster arrives in his black Range Rover. Larry in his Subaru with Rainman. Xavier and his first assistant in a van driven by Junior, who's back with us. They unload the cases that contain camera body, tripod, lens cases. Rooster tells them to set up on the porch, looking out toward the driveway, straight down the barrel. Luanne arrives in her Camry, followed closely by the Glove in his Suburban with the director.

Kenny, the Effects boss, pulls up in his truck with two of his guys. One of them has a young dog on a leash. Nina is right behind, with her guy Cody. Craig comes blasting in with The Clash, 'I'm Lost in the Supermarket' on the stereo. The set medic rides shotgun staring out the window likes he's trapped with a crazy man.

It's barely eight o'clock and over fifteen people are here, wondering what's going to happen. Louie, the craft service guy, pulls his truck around the back of the house and sets up a table with donuts, bagels, hot coffee, juice, and an ice chest of bottled water.

The Glove is trying to make a call on his cell phone. With no luck. He asks me if my phone works. I tell him I saw a crew working on the cell tower out on Hwy 6 when I came in this morning. No one's phone seems to be working.

"Is there a land line here?" he asks.

Luanne walks up. "Grandma pulled it out when she got her cell. Said she didn't know why she had to pay two bills when one phone was enough."

"Is there better reception out by the highway?"

"Not really," I say. "Least, I don't think so." He looks at his watch, wondering if he can get to the highway and back before all this begins. Rooster walks up.

"You want my cell phone?" he asks the Glove.

"Does it work?"

"Nothing works out here. They can tell you when an astronaut farts on the Moon, but as far as making a phone call out here, good fucking luck."

"The head of the company is on his way from LA with his Russian money guy. He had to change a lot of plans because you moved this to Saturday."

Rooster looks at him without a care in the world.

"They got stopped in Ridgecrest this morning doing a hundred and ten miles an hour. He's not in a great mood."

"Yeah, but Sunday was gonna be a bummer for the crew. Early call Sunday, no Saturday night."

"This guy pays your salary. All our salaries! Without him, none of this happens. Fuck the crew's Saturday night." Never seen the Glove this hot. He's the big boss, never seems ruffled. But he's got a look on his face like a cornered animal.

Rooster steps back, lets the storm blow past. "You want to hear what I'm planning?"

"I want to hear where my boss is. He said if he couldn't get here on time to just go ahead. But he'd love to see it, see how his team prepares for the big stuff."

"That's what I want to see, too! I've worked with Effects before, and you, of course, and my guys. And Tim, the transpo guy. All top notch. Don't know this Mexican AD, but

I can break him in, and if he ain't up to it, we'll bring my guy from LA."

"Can we go at ten, instead of nine?"

"Rather not, got a lot to get through. But for you, absolutely."

Larry wanders over and the Glove jumps in his face. "There's no cell service here! How did this happen?"

Larry checks his phone. No service. He looks at the Glove, busted. "I don't know. Let me ask Rich, Luanne." Rich steps up.

"I just got back from the crew working on the cell tower down the highway. They said everyone was notified with a flyer that came out four days ago. They thought they'd be done by ten, ten-thirty. Sorry. Nobody told me."

Rodrigo walks up, a donut in one hand, coffee in the other. Nina and her shadow Cody are behind him. "So, what's the plan?" the director asks. Rooster looks around. He crows to the crew gathering at the front of the house.

"Hey everybody! Let's get together over here, make a plan." The herd slowly starts rolling toward Rooster. He steps up on the porch so everyone can see and hear him. The Glove pulls Larry off to the side. He's furious.

"What the fuck? We're doing stunts and we have no communication with the outside world! Are you the Production Manager or some pimp fucking the accountant?"

I hear this and see Larry turn away, trying to swallow his own rage. He turns back. "You're the one who said let him have his way! Not me! Yeah, I walked away from this. He's a dirtbag blowhard. Your choice! Let me see what I can do about the phones. At least we've got walkie talkies."

Larry storms off.

"Morning everybody!" Rooster says. "I know you all are wondering what I'm thinking. This is the end of the movie. What the ride's been building toward. The women here know the big bad is coming, but they don't know when or how. The law knows exactly where the target is, but they got a choice to make. Surprise attack, probably at night –" I catch Xavier give the Glove a stern look. "—or just a clear-cut power move, show of force. Quien es mas macho. Which is what they decide. Balls to the walls."

Rooster pauses to let this sink in. He looks to Rodrigo, who nods to continue. I hear something above and look to the balcony. Grandma has stepped out from the house, in a bright white blouse, and stands tight against the railing, her face stern. I look at Luanne, who stares at her in total bewilderment. I catch a glimpse of Rodrigo, who smiles, shakes his head. Rooster continues.

"The leader of the Women in White is watching from the upstairs balcony—" everyone looks up, sees Grandma in character – "as she sees this dust storm of cop cars coming down the driveway. There's a ridge about halfway from the highway to where we are right now, so all we can see is the dust cloud created by the squad cars. What happens next is what we're gonna show you this morning."

Everyone seems to be looking between Grandma and the driveway. Then back to the director. Rodrigo stands, thinking through the plan, going back and forth between the balcony and the road from the highway. He nods, indicating Rooster should continue.

"This has been worked out with effects and my stunt guys, so you'll only see one car come over the ridge. Xavier, my guess is you'll want to be on the balcony with the camera. I looked, but I couldn't be sure whether the ridge was high enough to hide the oncoming cars. If not, maybe we can build it up.

"We just want to see dust. Create the fear of something's coming. After this, we'll get into the hand-to-hand stuff around the house, the young girls running and shooting, all the other surprises Mama White has in store."

I look at Luanne, who is still staring up at her grandma. Rooster turns to Rodrigo. The director seems excited. He nods yes.

"Okay!" Rooster calls out. "Let's pass out the walkies and get in position. It's eight-twenty-five, let's aim for lift-off at nine o'clock."

The Glove hears this. "I said let's go at ten." Rooster glares at him.

"Let's get in position, see where the boat leaks, and maybe you'll have an idea where your man is. Okay?"

The Glove, still trying his phone, nods yes.

Jump, the young stunt guy, shouts out, "Tim, is the car here?"

Tim shakes his head. "On its way. Be at the top of the driveway in twenty minutes."

Rainman opens the back of Larry's Subaru. The two cases of walkie talkies are side by side. He opens them, starts passing out the walkies. He tries to keep a record of who gets one, but it all happens so fast he's lost.

There's only nine, per Rooster's request. One goes to Rooster, one to Tommy, one to Jump, one to Rickie, the third stunt guy just brought in. One goes to Kenny, and one to Ellis, Kenny's man at the ridge, the one with a young dog on a leash. Tim takes his. Renan grabs his. The last one is up for grabs. The Glove looks at Larry. Larry turns away. The Glove takes it. This is starting to feel personal. And not in a good way.

Ellis and his dog jump in the driver's seat of Kenny's truck. Rickie, the stunt guy who's going to the ridge, gets in the shotgun seat. Tim loads up his white van with Tommy and Jump and the blonde groupie, on their way to the head of the driveway where the action starts. Arlo motions for me to go with them and I climb inside.

Xavier and his assistant organize equipment to move to the second story, and Rooster, Rodrigo, and the Glove huddle on the front porch, going over the timing of all this. Nina slides into the group, and I notice Cody walking over to the tall pepper tree to the side of the house. He looks up, then out the driveway to the ridge, measuring the view from higher up. He quickly jumps, grabbing the lowest limb. Before Tim can get the van turned around Cody's fifteen feet off the ground in the leaves and branches of the tree.

We follow Kenny in his truck down the driveway toward the main road. At the ridge off the drive, there are four traffic cones. The cones are red. I drove around them this morning, not knowing what they were. As we go past the cones, watching Ellis toss them aside, he exposes an explosive.

Tim stops the van and Jump hops out. I hear him and Ellis talking about how big the bomb is. Jump is smiling, shaking his head in agreement. He gets back in the van. Tommy and

Jump share a look. They smile. "No guts, no glory," Tommy says. I catch Tim's eyes in the rearview mirror.

"Is something gonna blow up here?" he growls.

"That's why we put the roll cage in," Jump laughs. "Don't want to mess this pretty face up, you think." He winks at the blonde and she scrunches her shoulders and giggles. I think I recognize her from high school.

We park at the top of the driveway. Tim and Tommy test the walkie talkies. They call the house, asking for the Glove and Rooster. Nothing but static. Tommy tries Rickie, halfway down the drive, and gets some scrambled words back that he can't understand. He stomps over to the other side of road, calling Rooster on his cell phone. That doesn't work either. I start smelling panic.

The communications are turning into a nightmare. Tommy and Tim are stomping around the dirt like two cocks ready to fight. There's a muddled transmission from Rickie, saying (we think) that the explosive has been armed. Then Tim's phone pings. It's a text from JB, saying a black Escalade just went past him at eighty miles an hour.

As Tim tells Tommy, the Escalade screeches off the highway onto the dirt drive. Tommy leaps out, stops it. The driver's side window comes down. "Get out of the way!" a voice from inside screams. It's foreign to me, like maybe Russian. Tommy tries to explain what's going on here, but the driver is furious and yells back.

"The big bosses are inside! Get out of my way or I'll run you over!"

A small man, maybe five-foot-six, jumps out of the back. "I'm Matthew Kaufman! I'm the producer of this! Call the Glove! We're going through!" Tommy looks at the walkie. Drops it in the dirt. He sees the stunt car flying down the highway toward them.

"I don't care if you're the fuckin' queen of Sheba, you're not going anywhere!" he screams.

The man called Matthew leaps back into the Escalade and the driver hits the gas. Tommy leaps out of the way. He, Tim, and I all look at each other. We reach for our phones, knowing it's a futile effort. We're straight up terrified now. Tommy's walkie squawks from the dirt. It's Rickie. Tommy lunges for it.

"We've got a bogie coming down the driveway!" Tommy screams. "Says he's the producer! Doesn't know about the IED!" All transmissions go quiet. "Do you read me! The big shots are racing down toward you and they don't know about the bomb!"

The four of us jump in Tim's van and give chase. JB blasts in off the highway in the picture car and follows fast on our heels.

The Glove gets a voice mail, garbled. The system must be coming back on-line. "That's Matthew in the Escalade!" he screams at Rooster. "Don't roll until he gets here! Don't roll!" He throws Larry a furious look.

"There's a bomb buried in that driveway," Rooster says to the group.

"What?"

"That's my surprise. First car over the rise hits the IED and goes BOOM! into the air."

The Glove freezes. Then his face turns bright red with hot anger. "Jesus fucking Christ! Why'd you keep this secret!"

Suddenly Junior, Captain Eddie's kid, fires up his van and roars out of the driveway a hundred miles an hour. Everybody looks at Rooster. He leans into his walkie. "Anybody know what the fuck is going on here?!!"

I catch Rodrigo motion to Xavier to start rolling the camera. Grandma comes back on the porch, alarmed by the commotion. She leans over the balcony, straining to see what's happening.

Kenny is trying to get a hold of Ellis; he gets nothing but static. He and the Glove sprint for the suburban. They jump in, fire the engine. Blast out of the driveway kicking dust and pebbles everywhere. This is war. Bad shit is happening.

I race up the stairs to the balcony. Xavier is rolling the camera. I can see the dust trails speeding toward the house and away from it. The meeting in the middle will not be nice.

Suddenly, the white van comes into the picture, aimed right at the ridge with the IED. Junior's on the left side of the drive, the same as the Escalade coming toward him. I flash he's trying to get to the explosive before the big shots do.

As they both fly toward the ridge, Rickie jumps up from his hiding place, back to the house, waving for the Escalade to stop. The van doesn't slow down. It's like a shark going for the kill.

The van reaches the ridge fifty yards ahead of the Escalade. It hits the bomb. BOOM!!! Junior and his van go flying in the air. They hang there for one, two, three seconds, then crash down onto the front of the skidding black Escalade. Xavier keeps his eye to the camera. I notice Cody, high in the tree. He's dropped his head to his chest.

THE GLOVE – LINE PRODUCER

I don't even know if I put my car in park, I'm out the door sprinting for the Escalade. Dust is everywhere. The smell of explosives chokes my throat. The van rests on the front of the SUV. It heaves and rolls over on the dirt. This is Rooster's fault and I'm going to kill him for this. Him and Larry. Junior is pinned in the driver's seat. He's trying to release the seat belt, but it's wedged between twisted metal. His head is cut and his shoulder is bent in a grotesque way.

The driver of the Escalade isn't moving. Probably dead. In the backseat, Matthew and another guy are starting to come around. I reach for their door, but the metal is jammed tight. I yell, "Hang on, we'll get you out!" Then I wonder if anyone called 911, or if anyone fucking can.

Tim rolls up with Tommy, Jump, and Luanne at the same time Rooster arrives. Kenny sprints to the back of his truck where his metal toolbox is, rips it open and grabs bolt cutters. Tommy and Jump run to Rickie. He's okay. The blast knocked him sideways into the ditch. The back of his shirt is scorched, his flesh tore up pretty good from the explosion, but he's standing.

"Tim!" I yell. "Anyone call 911?"

Rooster charges Tommy, his son. "You had one job! Nobody gets through when the bomb is hot!"

Tim yells, "We need the jaws of life! Junior's fighting to breathe!"

Kenny squeezes, pulls, tugs at the Escalade door trying to pry it open. Finally, the metal gives, and together We pull Matthew out. Kenny and I go back inside and gently grab the other man. His head is ripped up and bleeding badly and it looks like his ankle is broken. We lay him on the dirt beside Matthew.

Matthew groans, leans over him. "Vlad, are you okay?"

Vlad smiles. "Is like Russian bachelor party... my driver, he's dead, right?" Matthew looks toward the front seat. "Yes. At least it looks like it."

"Glove," Matthew asks, shock now turning to anger, "how did this happen?" He asks again, anger building, "How did this happen?"

Kenny is now with Tim, trying to get Junior out of the van. It doesn't look good. Craig and the medic are tugging on the metal door. Crows circle in the sky. From far off, we hear the faint sound of a siren. Maybe two. Hopefully two.

Larry shouts: "The cell tower is back up! I called medivac!"

PART SIX – LOOKING FOR THE HEART OF SATURDAY NIGHT

RICH – LOCATION MANAGER

I'm desperate to do laundry. Wearing dirty clothes is not in my program. What I hoped would be a four-hour day just ended after ten hours. The Russian driver is in the morgue. Which, one cop laughed, in Bishop might be the freezer at the Chinese restaurant by the airport.

Junior is in the ICU by medivac to Northern Nevada Medical Center in Sparks, outside Reno. The paramedics stopped the bleeding and the jaws of life cut him out of the van. He lay stable in the ambulance for nearly an hour until the helicopter arrived.

I just talked to Tim, who is at the hospital. Junior's vitals are strong, might be a broken pelvis or back or just a bunch of cracked ribs. They're waiting on x-ray results now. He had a sudden impulse to reach the IED before the bigshots did.

In other words, he took one for the team.

Matthew and his Russian partner choose to go back to LA by ambulance to Cedars Sinai Hospital. The Glove, Larry, and I followed Sheriff Conrad to the sheriff's station in Bishop. Since the location is technically in Mono County, the sheriff there asked Conrad in Inyo County to run the investigation. Because our business is based in Bishop, in Inyo County, I guess.

Four hours later, questioned together and individually, we're released. The sheriff doesn't think it looks like homicide, but criminal negligence is obvious. The blood in each of our bodies turns ice cold. We huddle together in a strong wind in the parking lot. Fear, blame, mistrust, all the macho spices in a bloody war, surround us.

The Glove is the least involved in the planning. He was always busy bird-dogging the director to make his day. He rarely had any detailed involvement in future plans, especially once the schedule was solid. Besides, he trusted Larry completely. Larry should have stopped it all when things turned to shit this morning. But he stayed quiet.

And I, in charge of the location, should have realized how important radio communication was. At this ranch, its vastness is the heart of its magnificence. But when Gus went to the hospital, I was left with Arlo and Luanne. Zero experience. I had to cover the first unit. I wasn't allowed my LA assistant, who would have screamed bloody hell about the crap cell service at Grandma's. And who would have told me to forget about walkie talkies unless we put up a relay station. When will the bean-counters ever learn? Never, I know. The finger of blame is still just the finger.

It's decided. The three of us will meet in the office tomorrow morning. Larry will call off the Sunday BBQ. The Glove already told Rooster and his team to pack up and go home. We'll sleep on what to tell Grandma about the location.

Larry is adamant we must find another one; the Glove wants to talk with the director first. Larry doesn't give a flying fuck what the director thinks, we have to get as far away from that evil woman and that evil place as possible. It's been a curse since day one.

I mention we have a contract with Grandma, and she has one with us too. We bail, we eat the money promised. No question about that. A rabid dog never lets go. Larry doesn't care. One man is dead, three others are in the hospital, and we haven't started shooting there yet. He has a point.

The Glove is silent. Finally, he says: "It's the director's call. That's final." Less than 24 hours ago we were the Three Musketeers. Now we're the last rats on a cursed ship, fighting to see who gets off first. Or last.

I start toward the hotel. On my way I see Craig's two prop assistants ducking into Rusty's. All this happened because Rooster wanted the crew to have a free Saturday night. Do it on Sunday morning as originally planned, the money guys are already here, I've been out to the location on Saturday, probably the communication problems are exposed and dealt with. All goes smoothly.

Before I turn into the hotel, I change my mind, decide to go to the office. It's still daylight, and the wind has picked up and it's cold. Not the kind of night to sit in your room and wonder what the hell just happened. The devil's already between my ears.

The office is ablaze with light. I step inside the main door and hear David Bowie singing from inside the production office. I cross the corridor and peek in the glass insert in the school door.

Liz, Etta, Lena, Jimmy the stand-in, and Boyzie have pushed two desks to the side and cleared them. They're all dancing their buns off. Etta is bright red. Boyzie climbs up on one of the desks, motions for Etta to join him. Etta struggles up, and Boysie lifts her up on his shoulders. She's laughing hysterically. First time with alcohol, I'm guessing. As I step closer, the music pounding:

'Misses a step and cuts his hand, but
Showing nothing, he swoops like a song
She cries Where have all Papa's heroes gone
All...'

Boyzie leaps with Etta on his shoulders, in perfect rhythm to the music, to the other desk. Sticks the landing. '...Night! She wants the young American...'

Boyzie holds his arms out like an Olympic athlete who just set a world record. He's looking for props, looking away from the door toward Liz and Lena and Jimmy as I step inside. They freeze. He says, "What?" and turns. Our eyes lock.

First, I smile; then he does. Etta scurries down and hustles to her desk. Liz and Lena burst out laughing. Etta pretends to sort papers. Jimmy stares at me. Boyzie just stands on the desk.

"We needed to do something to get the bummer out of the air," Boyzie says.

"We heard what happened," Lena says. "I sent Boyzie to Von's for some tequila once Rooster left. He and I had a ten-minute toe-to-toe. He wanted to get paid for tomorrow. Double time. And keep his hotel room tonight."

"That's when I thought we needed some music, some dancing music." Boyzie says.

It's so funny, the young ones thinking you're the authority, you're older, the serious one. The parent. You stay in the film business so you never become the parent.

"Any tequila left?" I ask. Boyzie looks at Lena. I guess he bought her a bottle for later. Lena nods, and Boyzie gets an unopened bottle from his backpack. Liz pours me a double. I sit down, take a big sip, and tell them what happened.

Later, in my office, I go over the schedule for the next couple of weeks. We're solid if we make our days. We have a small window of opportunity to look for another location. But we must start right away. And I need Gus.

I wonder what Rose would say if we came back to her. Nina will freak out if suddenly she must create the nerve center for the Women in White both on location and on stage. The art department always gets the shaft when big changes come down during shooting. Grandma's place is perfect. Except for Grandma...and Rooster.

Liz knocks on my door. "You okay?" she asks.

"Just trying to sort out...man, what a fuckin' day."

"So, what do you think is going to happen? Are we shutting down?"

"The Glove is talking to Matthew about that. But it really makes no sense. Everything in front of the camera is intact. We just have to figure out what to do with that location."

"We can't go back to that crazy woman."

"Believe me, I know. She held a shotgun on me, swore she'd blow my nuts off if I didn't agree to her demands. But there's one thing..."

"And that is?"

"It's a great location and the director loves it."

"Oh fuck," Liz groans. "We're toast."

"Hope not. We both know production is all about eating crow, but this – this is like eating a whole flock of crows."

"They call that a murder of crows."

She smiles. Murder? No shit. How are beautiful women always so smart?

THE GLOVE – LINE PRODUCER

I feel paralyzed. Murderous. I want to start throwing furniture out the window, set fires, get in my car, drive into the mountains and fly off a cliff. Shoot Rooster point blank in the hotel lobby. Shoot cops, shoot some fat couple from Escondido here for the birdwatching, shoot myself. I don't know what to do.

My phone rings. It's either Matthew, Rodrigo, Larry, the Sheriff, or Clemencia. I'll talk to all of them except her. It's Matthew. I answer. Crisp and cold. He's at Cedars now, in a private room. After the niceties, I ask, "So what do you want to do?" The twenty-million-dollar question.

"What are the police saying?"

"No murder charges. But criminal negligence probably."

"Only if someone presses charges," he says. His voice gets quiet. "Listen, this has opened up a hornet's nest you know nothing about. The driver was in the country illegally. Arrested for murder in St. Petersburg, fled the country. My partner is about to go on Interpol's wanted list. The money he's bringing here is all dirty. A spotlight is the last thing he wants. He's pulling all his strings to wipe out the driver's death."

I try to understand what he's saying. "We need to make this seem like an accident. Which begs the question: was it?"

Yeah. It was an accident. We tried to communicate with Matthew's car, tried to stop it from coming down the driveway, tried to stop it from hitting the explosive. But in my heart of hearts, it doesn't feel like an accident. Forget the law, the technicality of whether it was an accident or not, it comes down to who fucked up on the team?

Matthew erupts in a coughing fit, and a nurse takes the phone, informs me the call is over. Click. Feels like a lot more than the call is over. I'm in jail now, a prisoner in my own head. I'm a white male who grew up in the sixties and seventies, where lonely heroes were on posters in our bedrooms. Easy Rider, Cool Hand Luke.

I know I have to face up to Larry. I am the captain. I should go down with the ship. But Larry...? This morning was the definition of a cluster fuck. Nobody knew what was going on. Nobody was prepared. He'll say it was because I had total faith in Rooster. He was told to stay hands off. I say he didn't press the issue enough.

When Rooster asked for nine walkies, did Larry question what they were for? A junker with a roll-cage? I was a production manager for years. You're supposed to be like a pit bull with a stick in your mouth. Don't give up until you get all the answers. That's the fucking job!

The phone rings again. This time it's Clemencia. The older you get, the harder it is to say, 'I can't talk right now.' You're an adult. You deal with life; there's no avoiding it, no 'I'll call you back when I'm in a better mood.' There is no better mood than the one you're in now. But right now, I'm poisonous. I don't want to break her heart, yet I don't know how not to. I answer the call.

"Are you okay?" she whispers.

"Not really."

"Where are you?"

"The hotel."

"Will you come here?"

To be honest, I don't trust my anger. My blood is boiling, my teeth are grinding. I'm ready for war. She'll want to take the pain and confusion away, but I need them to stay. I want to hit myself so hard that the tears and fear come bursting out of my skin like sweat from malarial fever.

"When I was little, in Mexico, the bad stuff would happen and the villagers would say, *somebody switched the tracks.* That happened to you today." I smile. Somebody switched the tracks. No shit.

"I love you," she says. "Get through this, and I will still be here."

Before I can respond, she hangs up. Angry? Disgusted? Or wise? I'm grateful she hung up. For a moment I want to call her back, say I'm coming. I can't stay in this room.

It was all going so smoothly; now it's like the aftermath of a mob hit. I can go across the street to the gas station and buy a bottle. That doesn't seem like a smart way to plow through the rest of the night. Eating alone in a restaurant would be the equivalent of going shopping at an after-hours gun shop.

I look out my window. I see the top of the bowling alley sign, COCKTAILS. I can only see the top half of it, but all of America recognizes that sign.

I cut across a parking lot past a quiet, low-rent motel toward the bright, noisy bowling alley behind, all lit up. The wide three-lane parking lot is packed with pickups. Outside the front door, maybe eight people, mostly young, all white, are hanging out, laughing and drinking from tall red cups.

To me, it feels like a drug market, but maybe I'm just an old geezer suspicious of malingering youth. Their eyes bore into me like I'm a cute girl walking into a pick-up bar. Only it doesn't feel like it's about sex. It feels like drugs. Want something? Need something? I got it man. Do people really score this way? Danger seems close. I lose sight of what I've come to forget. This is another planet.

Inside, the first thing that hits you is the sound of bowling. Balls on pins. Strike. Cheers. More balls on pins. More cheering. I look around. The restaurant is to the left. Check-in station. Straight ahead is the large, enclosed space that is the bar. Packed. To the right are the lanes, ten of them, all busy with happy people chugging beers and gobbling burgers and chicken wings. I can't help but smile.

I spot Roger, the sound guy who DJs the Sunday BBQs. He always has a smile that both takes you seriously and knows you're full of shit. He sits in the bar area with a tall woman, pretty, blue-rimmed glasses fronting big brown eyes. My guess, late-thirties. I think I recognize her. A set teacher, maybe? The young actresses who are the trained killers with the Women in White arrive on Monday. School starts on Tuesday, as do rehearsals. I lost track of the fact the show keeps going on.

Roger sees me. "Glove!" he screams across the noise of the bowling alley. I slide my way toward him. "Mind if I join you?" I ask. I cram in next to them, get introduced to Cathy, who is indeed the newly arrived teacher. I flag down a waitress.

"Double whiskey, Jameson's. Neat. With a water back," I order. "We've worked together, haven't we?" I ask her.

She looks me dead in the eye. "On a horrible TV movie years ago called SCANDAL SHEET. You were the UPM. I only remember because that was my first job in the business."

I try not to flinch. "I've gotten better since then. Ask Rog. At least until today." She leans over, puts her hand on my arm. "I didn't mean you were horrible, it was just the schedule, the hours, the little brat I was supposedly teaching...it made me wonder what kind of masochistic jerk off would want to be in this business."

"Did you ever find the answer to that?" I ask, laughing.

"Yeah," she says slowly. "The two worst kinds. Ones who want dreams to come true, and ones who want to make a lot of money."

"Like Roger, right?"

"Hey, wait a minute," Roger says. "I'm in this business because I like strange people and living on the road. There is nothing masochistic about that!" My drink arrives.

"I gotta ask," Roger shouts over the din, "what happened today? I heard it was a first-class goat rope."

"It was," I say. "Let me sip this and I'll tell you all about it."

At that moment, time slows. I lift my glass and as I bring it to my lips the sound of a gunshot explodes in the room. What was a cacophony of bowling alley noise suddenly turns deadly silent.

Then the next two gunshots erupt, and like a movie, time suddenly gets real, and everyone is screaming and scrambling for the door or the floor. The three of us dive beneath our table. Cathy presses up against me. To my credit, I don't spill a drop. I notice she doesn't either.

The shooting is outside. Flashing red and blue lights from the police cruiser rip across the walls. The cops are screaming at someone by the front door, probably a drug bust but what the hell is with the gunfire?

Inside it's quiet. No bowling balls knocking down pins. The rock n roll on the PA is off. People start to look around, see if it's safe to get up off the floor. Roger wastes no time. He grabs me and Cathy and we hustle out of the bar toward the back, where the bathrooms are.

"I already checked this out!" he whispers. "There's an emergency door with a security alarm, and considering there's bullets and cops everywhere, I think we can call this an emergency." He bangs through the door, setting off the alarm. Out back he leads us to his van, parked on a side street.

"I was pissed there was no room in the front, but not anymore!"

We jump in the van. Cathy grins. "God works in mysterious ways!" The word God brings me back to the reality of today. One man dead, three in the hospital, criminal charges coming.

Okay, big Guy, let's see some mysterious ways. I've come here to escape some sort of life surrender; now I'm fleeing a gun fight in a bowling alley arm-in-arm with a pretty schoolteacher and a wicked stoner crew member.

It's then I realize I'm still holding my drink, no drops spilled. I look at Cathy. She's got hers too. Her smile brings mine alive. We clink glasses and she laughs. "Bottoms up!" I laugh. Roger starts his van.

"Up for a little adventure?" he asks. I look at Cathy.

"Sure!" she says.

"Then away we go!" Roger says.

And into the quiet darkness of Bishop on Saturday night we roll. As he tries to light a stubborn joint, he's explaining. "I talked with this Indian last Sunday, the one with the Designer. He's Paiute. Lives here on the reservation."

"Cody?"

"Yeah. Said he loved my DJ choices. Told me about this place we're going. Narrow canyon where the sound echoes forever. Was it Tuesday when we finished early? I came out here, played DARK SIDE OF THE MOON, ate tacos al pastor and drank cold beer. Just bitchin'."

He turns off the paved road on a gravel one, and we head into the White Mountains. We're on the rez now, no lights, no sound, no buildings, no nothing. Cathy turns back toward me from the shotgun seat, smiles like she's riding a rollercoaster for the first time. After twenty minutes of bumpy road, Rog pulls over to the side.

We're in a tight canyon. Cathy and I climb out of the van, stare up into the brilliant sky. Stars so close you think you can pick them like apples. Roger hops out of the van, speaker in hand, joint glowing red. He hands it to Cathy, puts the speaker on the ground.

I lean against the metal of the vehicle. Take a hit. First one in probably five years. And then I feel the way I felt sitting in the Salisbury Cathedral in England, listening to choir rehearsal for Sunday service. Like sneaking backstage into Heaven. Only this is The Doors.

Robbie Krieger's guitar sliding into my consciousness, then Manzarek's keyboard, John Densmore's percussion, the canyon, the night sky, the world peeling back to unveil something magical, vast, the crystal sound reverbing down the valley, and then the Lizard King himself:

This is the end, beautiful friend
The end...

I'm remembering the beginning of *Apocalypse Now*, stoned on mushrooms at the Cinerama Dome in the late seventies, with some office PA who couldn't keep her hands off me. Maybe this was the moment I fell in love with the movies, fell in love with wanting to be a part of something barbaric, something crazy and unforgettable, something that tears a deep scar across the culture.

The stars in the sky are brilliant. If I see one shooting, can I believe I actually saw it? This new pot is very strong. I had one hit. My life is careening toward a steep cliff, and I'm stoned listening to The Doors in a Paiute reservation canyon that echoes into eternity.

But Roger cuts the music off and quickly climbs up on the roof of his van. Cathy and I look at each other. "Cody told me this might happen," he whispers.

And we hear them. Owls. Hooting into the night sky, from all four directions, looking for connection, companionship. Echoing up and down the canyon. "It's summer," Roger says. "These are the young ones, exploring the world."

Roger cups his hands to his mouth, hears the rhythm of the last owl, and hoots "Hoo hoo, hoo-hoo-hoo". And in ten seconds, his call is answered. Hoo hoo, hoo-hoo-hoo. Cathy and I look at each other and start giggling.

Soon there is a symphony of owl calls, from east and west, north and south, crashing into each other. Roger is like a mad conductor, trying to answer each and every call. "Hoo-hoo-hoo hoo hoo!" The canyon is a concert hall. Above, the night sky glitters like diamonds on the dark bed of an Egyptian princess. The heart of Saturday Night has arrived.

LARRY – PRODUCTION MANAGER

When I'm frustrated and confused, which I am now, I like to walk. Power walk. Rage walk. Around the corner from Alison and Lena's house is a tributary of Bishop Creek. There's a dirt path along the water and, though it's dark, the moon reflects off the water so I can see where I'm going. To be honest, I'm not thinking about where I'm going.

The Glove and I have been through two projects together. WOMEN IN WHITE is the third. Alpha Males don't always get along. My older brother was a Marine; he also played college football, and he always told me never trust the ones who only praise you, all they want is for you to make them look good.

Trust the ones who keep coming back, keep giving you opportunities. They're the ones who see your strength. You may not like them, and they may not like you, but when it's game time, they're the ones you want by your side.

Okay, that might be a little exaggerated. But teams win in life. And the Glove and I are a good team. Or were we? This was a huge fuck up. A man died. Three others, including rich and powerful men, are in the hospital right now. A malignant boil that infected our team burst, and now several major things need to change, and change in a hurry.

We have eight young girls cast as the killers arriving from LA on Monday, ready for rehearsals that will mold them into believable fighters. They range from ten years to thirteen years old. Their world of unicorns and Taylor Swift is about to flip to knife-throwing and automatic weapons.

And the man we thought would teach them, a man who calls himself Rooster, just got fired and there is no immediate backup. In a way it's a blessing. He's a dirtbag who can't stop chasing skirt. We're a month away from shooting the final battle. Actors and stunt players all must be ready. Rehearsed. Focused. The time left is nothing.

I realize I could chew on this for hours, and probably will, so I turn back and head for the house. Tomorrow we meet at the office in the morning. Hopefully, Glove has talked with the director. We need to find out what's important to him.

As I turn on the street where the house is, I check my phone. There are eleven messages. The first voicemail is from Aida, the costume designer. She's pretty upset. She texted me and the Glove multiple times and no one is getting back to her. She heard there was an accident at the rehearsal this morning and Rooster got fired. She's got eight girls coming from LA on Monday, and no one has told her what to dress them in for rehearsals. Brian Dennehy is already in Bishop, came on his own to sit with the director over the weekend, and is ready for fittings Monday before he starts working on Tuesday.

Then her voice gets soft, hesitant. "I heard the Glove might be leaving the project," she says. "Before we commit to any final choices, is there a producer I need to include? Lar, we need some guidance here. All of us. We're ready for anything. We just need decisions." She hangs up.

The other texts and voicemails are similar. Rumors are flying. The easy part of the schedule is over. Actors are arriving. Stunt logistics need to be worked out and finalized. How many costume doubles for the actors? How many for the stunt performers? Aida heard from Rooster there might be some characters on fire when the final assault happens? Is this true? Does she need to build fire retardant costumes?

If this is her list of panic questions, I can't wait to hear how props and special effects and extra casting are freaking out.

I enter the house and it's dark, just a few lights on in the kitchen. I go through the living room to the patio. Alison sits at the table, computer open in front of her. "Hey," she says, distance in her voice. She smokes a cigarette.

"Is everything okay?"

"What do you think?"

I go back into the kitchen, pour myself some wine. As I come back and join her, she closes her laptop. We look at each other like we've just met at a funeral. "What's going on?" I ask. She smiles, lights another cigarette.

"Where's Lena?"

"Out."

"Out? Where?"

"Rusty's. She was at the office, then she came back here and the prop puppies came and dragged her out. Guess she and Rooster had a knock down drag out."

Just this morning, still dark outside, I woke to her moaning, lost in a nightmare she couldn't shake. I nudged her but she kept clinging to whatever was scaring her. Finally, I rolled her over into my arms and hugged her. Her eyes opened slowly. I never saw such a lost little girl. "Thank you," she says. "I was in a rowboat going over a waterfall a thousand miles deep."

Alison says, "The Glove called. Wants me at the meeting tomorrow. Got a bad feeling about this."

"Join the club."

"Are they going to shut us down?"

"I figure they're in way too deep now. We're still walking and talking; we'll get to the finish line. How is the Glove?"

"In crash mode," she says. "The way I see it, it's been that way for a while."

I look at her. Big dark eyes boring into me, a sly smile sneaking across her mouth. She's been a rock of stability many times for me. Does not suffer fools, or bullshitters, well. Always outspoken about what she thinks.

"I feel like I fell down a well" I say. "Everything I trusted just went to hell."

She sips her drink. "We used to say, 'better to be lucky than good!' Remember? I guess we just learned there's good luck and bad luck."

I drain my wine and turn to leave.

"Was Jimmy in the group Lena left with?" I ask. Alison smiles. Cheshire cat.

"I warned you. She had a day, too. Don't be angry."

The street is quiet. No lights in any of the surrounding houses. I decide going back to the hotel is a bad idea. Stay moving. I head south on 395 and before I know it, I'm at Rusty's.

I pull into the parking lot behind the building. Thinking about Lena. And Jimmy. Maybe this is the kind of night to get into one of those fights. Saturday in Bishop. Gus told me that's when the knives come out.

I lock my car and head inside. It's the back entrance, so I go down a dark corridor until I hear country rock n roll. Hank Jr. crying about some wrecked car and a dead girl. I stop as I get to the dance floor. The bar is on the other side.

I see Lena and Jimmy and the two young prop guys at a table, laughing and drinking. My head feels like it's exploding. I head for them when suddenly I'm grabbed from the side and whirled on the dance floor. Carrie is smiling at me, clear-eyed and saying, "Don't you dare!"

To my surprise, the music is great. The shit-kicker bar band is rocking some hard ass music. It steadily turns this feeling of murderous revenge I have into a laughing, 'what the fuck was I thinking?' reprieve. Lena can do whatever the fuck she wants. I got no claim on her. Carrie and I cut it up for a while and, when we're both out of breath, I look over to where Lena and Jimmy were. They're gone.

Carrie leads me to a table, and as I sit Craig slides into the chair opposite me. He's carrying two beers. She turns to the bar with a sly grin on her pretty face.

"You know, Lar," Craig says, "I've been around a long time, but today...man, that was like no other day I've ever seen."

"No shit."

"I know I don't have to tell you, but there's a lot of balls in the air right now that were supposed to land today. ADs, extras, poor Aida...nobody's talking to them. So they end up calling me. That's probably the strangest part of the day, that anybody thinks I've got answers!"

We share a laugh as Carrie joins us at the table, a bottle of Kentucky brown and three shot glasses in hand. "Figure we need to let confusion be done with," she says, pouring. Then toasting: "To next week, and the one after that, and the one after that, and so on and so on."

We clink our shot glasses, down the fiery liquid, and slap our glasses back on the table. She pours again. I have the feeling everyone assumes this is my last night on the show. But I'm not walking, and I don't think there's anyone with the balls to fire me. I am Spartacus.

ARLO – KEY PRODUCTION ASSISTANT

I'm sound asleep on the couch in Gus's living room. Last night, I tried to get some advice from him about what happened at Grandma's, but Luanne beat me to the punch with a bottle of whiskey. With his mouth wired and grunts coming from every part of his body, it was a waste of time. I pulled the blanket up from the floor and stretched out on the sofa.

It's barely light outside, the windows leaking a creamy white glow behind the curtains, but everything else is pitch black. I smell him before I feel him. Gus shakes me. He's still in the jaw rig and I can't understand what he's saying.

"Rizz just call, wants you at sum meetn' today of the office. U go in me place. Ten swmorning."

I look at my watch. It's five-forty. A shit storm is brewing, and I wish I was going fishing or golfing today. But I'm learning there are no days off in production. As tight as everything gets planned, it all seems to change like the breeze in the morning. Working on Sunday, I think, must be worth a couple of hundred. This keeps up and I will buy that new car.

I'm making coffee when Luanne comes into the kitchen, drowsy and frumpy. Her hair sticks up like some old-time comedy star. Gus has been in her room too. Rich wants us both at the meeting.

"Did he say what this was about?" I ask.

She looks at me like I'm some idiot with his pants on backward. "It's about Grandma's place."

I hate when I feel stupid. "Rich, Larry, and the Glove hate it."

"They hate Grandma and Rooster, not the place," she says. "The stunt doubles playing those girls with machine guns are coming to town tomorrow. Rehearsals supposed to start Tuesday. Changing the location messes everything up."

"What do you think your grandma's gonna say?" I look at her. We both smile.

"Double the money and Rooster keeps his job. Otherwise go screw yourselves."

She pours a cup of coffee with milk and sugar. "I've got a couple of petty cash envelopes to turn in, and I think Alison is coming too. I'm tapped, you?"

I thought she wanted to be a screenwriter, but now I see her as a producer. She's understanding everything and everyone. A couple of years older than me, but for the first time I notice how blue her eyes are, how beautiful they are. I'm gonna make her breakfast.

Gus wanders in smelling the bacon, eggs, and toast. Figured he would, so I laid on some for him too. He's taken off the plastic rig that holds his jaw in place. I know he wants to talk to us, which on the best of days is an adventure.

"She kill the whiskey last night?" he asks me.

"Yes!" Luanne shouts from her bedroom. Gus tries his best for a sheepish grin; it looks like Robocop trying to show he has feelings.

The two of us drive over to the production office. Fiona's car is there, and Lena's rental, and Etta's yellow smart car her Daddy gave her for graduation. Luanne smiles. Much easier to deal with Lena than Alison. I park and we enter the building.

Luanne immediately goes to accounting, where she walks in on a room of waiting department heads, each of them with petty cash envelopes and purchase orders in hand. Luanne thought she was early. These people are pros. Even Sunday starts early. Lena is at her desk with Aida, the costume designer, punching numbers into her computer. There's a cash box open on the desk beside her.

I wander over to the office bullpen where the coffee is. Fiona pours water into the machine. Her hair hangs long on her shoulders, her white shorts tight against tanned legs. She looks up, smiles. She's like the head nurse at a trauma center. Show no fear, no weariness. I realize this is what I admire most about our crew: they never seem tired.

"Were you there yesterday?" she asks.

"Yes."

She turns, looks. "So, what happened?"

"Still trying to figure that out," I say. "Seems like the planning got done on a wet paper napkin. Didn't hold up in the wind."

Craig wanders in, petty cash envelopes in hand. "Umm, coffee smells good. Hey Fi!"

Fiona looks at him, then back at me. "Go on," she says.

"It was all so spread out, and nobody could talk to each other. Then shit just started happening and nobody could stop it."

"Until the bomb went off!" Craig laughs. We all get quiet. This is no joke.

"I talked with Tim and Captain Eddie this morning," Fiona says. "Junior's in ICU with a severe head wound and three cracked ribs." She pours herself a cup of coffee, slides into the nerve center of the production office to her desk. She's real pretty in a business-like way.

I look at Craig. He winks at me. "Gimme the beat boy and free my soul/I wanna get lost in your rock n roll/And slip away…" he sings as he pours a cup.

LUANNE – LOCATION SCOUT

I'm still steamed at how Lena kicked out my receipt for donuts I bought at Isla's Donut Shoppe for the construction crew. I could have gone to Schat's and spent twice the money, but Isla is a friend of mine, and her parents struggle slinging donuts to big rig truckers while competing with Bishop's hottie tourist place. The receipt didn't look real to Lena. That's $23.79 she wants me to eat. No way.

Rich arrives and calms both of us down. Lena gives me the cash. Alison comes in, dark glasses hiding her feelings toward this meeting. She's got a Schat's to-go coffee in her hand. Larry and the Glove enter promptly at ten. Neither look at each other. Both pour a large coffee and head for the conference room. Rich, Arlo, Fiona, and Alison follow. Me too.

The Glove speaks first. "Thank you everyone for coming this morning. Just so you know, only accounting gets paid for today." Everyone laughs. "As you know, there was a catastrophe yesterday. I don't believe in blame, certainly not on the team. We cover for each other, end of story. But let's face it – it was a total fuckup.

"The man who is bank-rolling this project is in the hospital. He comes from production. He demands to know what the hell went wrong. But he wants to keep going forward. That's why we're all here."

"Is Rooster coming back?" Rich asks.

"I spoke with Rodrigo this morning, and then I spoke to Rooster. Rodrigo is upset, of course, but he likes Rooster's ideas, thinks he has a feeling for the Western in the story."

We all grimace. The answer to Rich's question is yes. He's coming back. Not good news, but it makes sense.

"Rooster wants production to step up, do their job and protect him," the Glove says. "It's all turned nasty, granted, but there's no choice here. We have to make it work."

He looks at all of us. No one wants to step into the void. I clear my throat, raise my hand. "Are we looking for a new location?"

He smiles. "Good question."

"If not, I know what my grandma will say."

"And that is...?"

"Twice the money and Rooster comes back."

There's a long pause. "Have you talked with her?" Larry seethes.

"Figured you have to tell me to do that. But I know her."

Larry looks to Rich. "We still have a contract with her, right? She agreed to the money."

Rich nods, but there's nothing positive in his body language. "Signed, sealed, delivered."

"I know my grandmother," I say. "She gets something in her head, it ain't going away less she thinks she's won."

"But she can't just change the rules out of nowhere!" Larry explodes. He immediately calms himself down. "This is why we need to find another location."

At this point, the door opens and Nina slips in.

"Sorry I'm late," she apologizes. Sits. "If we're talking about finding another location, can I just say something?" she asks.

Everyone nods yes. "It's the people-situation that's wrong here, not the place itself. It's the perfect location. Rodrigo and I agree we don't want to lose it. I think Xavier would agree too."

Larry explodes again. "Yeah, but there's bad juju everywhere around that place! Ask Rich, she pointed a shotgun at his balls and said pay up or talk like a girl for the rest of your life!"

"But until yesterday, it was all under control," Nina argues. "Admit it, if yesterday had gone smoothly, this meeting would not be happening. Rooster is a problem because he can hurt people, but he's a human being. He can be controlled. Lots of people on this crew have worked with him before."

Everyone looks at the Glove. This is his call. He sips his coffee.

"What Nina said is true. Rodrigo asked for us all to worry about the movie, not our egos."

Larry rolls his eyes. "You say Rooster can be controlled. Who's gonna do that?"

Silence around the table. Long silence. Endless. Finally, I can't stand it anymore.

"I will," I say. "I'm from this family, I'll take care of my grandma and her boyfriend. Trust me, you don't want to come at her with lawyers. Her brother in Sacramento was known as the Cocksucker of the Owens Valley when he practiced here. You get to that stage, figure to come back in five years."

Holy shit, I can't believe I just said that.

Arlo gives me a look, but I feel power. I stepped into the void and there was no resistance. The Glove looks to Larry, who's staring down at the tabletop, furious.

Alison clears her throat, speaks up. "Do we need to push?" Everyone looks at the Glove. I look at Arlo. 'Push?' I ask with my eyes.

The Glove thinks, speaks: "We're in good shape, the schedule is holding, the actors are coming in. The stunt situation is messed up, but that's going to get fixed. We keep going forward. No push."

"And how are we going to pay for all this? If we end up back at that crazy place at double the price?" Larry asks.

"Starting over will cost a lot more," Nina says.

"I'll show you after this meeting," the Glove says to Larry. It's clear these two don't trust each other anymore.

"Okay," Rich speaks up, trying to sum up the decision. "We're gonna try and make it work with Grandma, let Luanne be the point on this, and everything stays the same. We're still light on one location. Where Toni is run off the highway by the right-wing deputy. But that's it for locations. If Grandma's stays the same."

"Has anyone contacted the other place? With the pond?" Larry asks.

Arlo speaks up. "I called her this morning, but no answer."

"Call her back. Get an answer. We need all options on the table."

Fiona speaks up. "I've got eight actresses, four of them minors, travelling from LA and four local stunt girls starting tomorrow. What should I tell them?"

Larry scowls, looks angrily at the Glove.

"Tell them, welcome to Bishop," the Glove says. "Sit tight. It'll all come together."

And with that, the meeting is over. As we shuffle out of the conference room, Rich and Arlo surround me, wanting to know why I took on the responsibility of containing my grandma. So do I. It just felt like the whole parade came to a halt. I know my grandma. I know the backbone that has twisted our family's relationship with our neighbors in the Valley for years. I think I have a chance at this.

I know I need help. And I can't see anyone right now who doesn't have a crooked connection to the problem. The front door opens. I hear the wind pushing leaves into the corridor. In an instant, Frankie steps in, grinning like he's just come back from Club Med with a suntan and a hangover, all smiles and carrying a bushel of cut flowers. Perfect. Craig and Aida are there, smiling. "I wondered where everybody was! Working on a Sunday? Cha-ching!"

Fiona closes the conference room door and rejoins the Glove and Larry. There are no windows, but we all hear the voices inside start to rise. Then it gets quiet for a brief time, and suddenly Larry storms out. He sees Frankie, stops. He smiles and goes to him.

"Did it all get worked out?" Larry asks.

"I lost a wife, and two days later I lost a dad. If I stayed another week, I'd only have one leg and be thirty pounds lighter," he jokes.

I step up to Larry. "Can I talk to you for a second?"

"Wait for me in my office. Frankie, you too. I'll be right back." He goes toward accounting.

Fiona and the Glove step out of the conference room. The Glove goes straight to his office, not looking at anybody. We surround Fiona.

"Well," she sighs, turning to face us all. "Two big changes. First, the Glove is stepping down. Taking the fall for what happened yesterday." There's an audible gasp. "If there are criminal charges, lawsuits, whatever, he'll be the one standing up for the company, saying it was his responsibility, his fault."

Nina balks. "But that's not right. We were all there!"

"It's old, and sounds trite, but he said first in command falls on the grenade. The important thing is that production doesn't miss a beat. We keep shooting. With Glove leaving, Larry becomes the line producer. It's his job to make it work. That's what production does. Make it work. And Frankie, welcome back." She smiles.

"There's talk of you and Luanne taking over the second unit. Renan is doing a great job with the first unit. Second unit is where we need the help."

Wow. Silence. I look from Fiona to where the Glove just exited the room. Shit changes around here faster than musical chairs at a junior high dance. The door from accounting opens and Larry and Alison join us. Both are serious, grim.

"I guess Fi told you," he says. "This is fucked up, no question about it. But it's our job to never let what happened yesterday go down again. Never. Ever. Ever."

Frankie tries to lighten the tension. "Wow, I'm gone for three weeks, I come back to the Manson family!"

Larry ignores this. "Rodrigo asked to have a small crew party at Alison and Lena's backyard this afternoon, to introduce you to Brian Dennehy. He's skeet shooting with Toni this morning, but this afternoon, around three, just drinks and some nibbles. If you can pass the word to your crew, whoever you run into, it's appreciated."

The room is silent. Fiona says, "Just so you know, I just got a text from Rooster. He's on his way back from LA. The Glove told him about the get-together this afternoon, and he's going to be there with...Grandma. So forewarned."

Larry tears up, says, "I need you to know one thing about my friend. My friend of many years. In this fucking business he is the straightest shooter I have ever known. Always fights like hell for his team. And to make a great movie." Larry breaks down, tears streaming from his eyes.

Fiona grabs him by the arm and she and Alison lead him to his office. I glance at Frankie. I guess the gods have decided we're partners now. I know trust is earned, and we don't really know each other, but right now I'm going with the flow. What else can I do?

I think about going back to Gus's and telling him what went down, but instead I phone Rose Silvera again and get her answering machine. So, I drive over there. I know she won't talk to me. I know she'll never understand the cold-hearted business decisions that come after the wine-and-roses part. I'm just starting to figure it out myself.

Ranchers aren't like that. They deal with blizzards and plagues that take down herds in two days. The front gate is locked. I could climb over the fence, but that still leaves a mile hike down to the house, and one back out.

I turn around and find the back entrance to the ponds and the cabins. There is no gate here. I drive down the dirt road into the cabin area. Dogs come running out. Two women see me from the porch. There is nothing that feels like welcome. Two Mexican workers on horseback ride toward me. I park, get out, raise my hands and smile. "Hola!" I say, loudly.

"We speak English."

"I'm trying to find Senora Silvera. I'm an old friend."

"She's gone to her sister's. In Canada. Told us not to talk to anyone."

"For how long?"

"Not to talk to anyone."

I'm young but I know what 'fuck you' sounds like. I nod, turn, get back in my car. Rose's place is clearly not an option. I drive back off the property, worried about the movie, worried about how much like a spider's web in the wind it all feels right now.

I've worked so many hours for so many days, I'm tired. Exhausted. Watching an old movie on Sunday afternoon sounds perfect. But in my head, I'm spinning. What if Grandma goes ballistic? I come up on the 395 at Westgard, and before I turn right, back to Bishop, the Glove turns left in front of me. He doesn't notice, but I do.

The lonely feel of this Sunday is like a day where you can't catch a fish or make a putt. I turn around, head back into the White Mountains following the Glove. In a couple of miles, he turns right on Death Valley Road.

He's probably thirty years older than me. Maybe more. My Dad's probably younger. He's a leader. Been all over the world, persuading people he just met to work hard and make something that might last forever. My Dad always said the luckiest man in the world was the guy who invented the toothpick. But if your name's on movies, or for me on golf trophies, that's something, isn't it? The legends in the movie business, as Luanne explained to me, are legends because they did things. They delivered.

The Glove ranks up there. Check his resume. The greats should never falter. The greats should never trip and fall. They should never reveal they're just ordinary human beings. Luckier. Smarter. But still just human. They wear down. They burn out. They grow weak. Seems true of everyone.

The Glove just quit. He said he'd take the fall for all the crap. He's heading now for Death Valley. This does not fit my brain. I have to make sure nothing bad is going to happen. He's driving 45 MPH. I increase to 55 MPH. I'm about a quarter mile behind him when I see him pull over on a Caltrans turnout. There's a big pile of gravel stored for the winter snows, so the plows and can spread it over the icy road.

Now it's early afternoon in late summer, hot, clear, and there's nobody on the road ahead of us. Either direction. I slow down, pull over. He gets out of his car, a small case in his hand. Doesn't look back, doesn't see me on the backside of the road. Goes to the front of his vehicle and climbs up on the hood. Opens the case and takes something out. It could be a handgun.

I punch the accelerator (Toyota beater to the rescue!) and slide into the turnout. The Glove turns, confused. He's got a pair of binoculars in his hand. When he realizes who I am, he smiles. Waves me over. "What are you doing out here?" he asks.

"I went to Rose Silvera's to see if she's around. See if she's still a choice."

"Good luck with that," he laughs. Turns with the binoculars and stares east back down Death Valley Road. "When I first came up here there was a sign that said, 'Best BBQ north of LA', with an arrow down this road. Being the sucker I am, I drove here. I guess the sign was old, or a joke, but this is as far as I got."

We're sitting in foothills at the top of a gentle downward slope that eventually gets to Death Valley, the lowest point in the U.S. There's nothing ahead but scrub desert, faraway mountains, empty road. I give him a clueless look, and he grins to himself.

"You have your camera?" he asks.

"In the trunk," I answer.

"Go get it. This'll make you a star."

It's a Canon Sure Shot and the longest lens on the zoom is a hundred. Looking through the camera, it does feel like an old cowboy movie. Nothing moving. Nothing of interest but space. Just the sloping highway rolling out to forever.

"Imagine our good sheriff's car coming toward us, through binoculars, someone's watching her, getting closer and closer, and then the binoculars drop, and the camera pulls out on the road, siren rips through the sound, we hear a shotgun pumped, and there's no one to witness, no one to see what whoever has been watching is planning to do. It's as lonely a highway as there is."

He turns to me. "The last location. All yours."

"What do you mean?"

"Show Nina the pictures. Show Rich. Bring them out here tomorrow. They've been looking in the Sierras, at roads that twist and turn and around any corner there could be civilization, eyewitnesses, a fucking motorhome. Not an ambush spot. Then after wrap, bring Rodrigo and Xavier here. Close the deal."

He looks straight at me, challenging. "I have a feeling about you," he says. "You're naïve, granted. And young. But you see through the bullshit," he says. "You don't learn that. You can't teach it either. You need somebody who tells you, 'Go figure it out'."

He nods at me. "Go figure it out."

When someone like the Glove tells you that because he believes you've got potential, all of a sudden you imagine yourself in a limo with Brad Pitt smoking ganja and sipping whiskey on the way to some crazy party.

I ask him, "You a golfer?"

"I'm a lifelong hacker, if that's what you mean."

"You want to go hit balls at the club?" I don't know why I said this, but it's all I can offer in return for his compliment. It seems like he's thinking about it.

"Nah., I have to figure out what my next move is. I'm just a fifth wheel now. You, on the other hand, should go make your pictures look stunning."

Off my puzzled look, he explains, "Get it on your computer and push in, make the foreground go away like the road's farther off and more mysterious than it is to the eye. Then take it to the party, show Rich and Nina, and if they like it, make her show it to Rodrigo."

He puts his binoculars back in the case. Climbs down off the hood.

"Are you furious at all this?" I ask. He smiles to himself, kicks the dirt. Somehow, I feel he's almost relieved.

"Of course, I am," he says. "Mainly furious at myself. You plan...it's like an army travelling on a river. Logistics. Equipment. Crew. You set off from base camp, you better have everything. You know you can't control the weather. You know the artists will have their moments. You know humans will make mistakes. You build that into the planning. But the real leaders, the ones that last...that win no matter what, always trust themselves. Always trust their instincts."

He turns and looks at me as he climbs into his car. "I don't trust myself anymore, and that's what I'm fucking furious about."

He slams the door and sprays gravel as he pulls out.

NINA – PRODUCTION DESIGNER

I'm in the Chinese restaurant by the airport with Bryce, my Set Decorator. He's bringing beers to the table. Lovely man, calm and quiet. He knows I'm confused, that the people-bullshit has overwhelmed me. It feels like I've lost the spark.

The Glove is gone. Larry is in power now. The UPM. What's the phrase I've heard so much, 'the moral center of the universe'? Yeah, well where the fuck is it when the truly good guy, the one who tucks everyone into bed at night and promises there's no bogeymen in the closet, just gives up, folds his cards, and leaves on a midnight train to nowhere?

By standing up for Grandma's location, did I seal the Glove's fate? Do you fight for art even if it murders your friends? Last night I went to sleep in Cody's arms, him telling me about the great migration from north Africa to the middle east, north to China and the real east, then over the Bering Strait to the new continent. Our continent. And some of the natives went east, to the Plains and the eastern coast, and some went south, along the Pacific coast.

But the thing was, Cody explained, it was all about wandering. All about roaming. All about the restless spirit. Gypsies. Somehow it made me feel calm enough to fall asleep.

Sizzling rice soup arrives. Delicious. I ask Bryce what happens if we lose Grandma's location. He turns gray. The large living room we've designed to be quickly turned into a command center? When the cops first come, they'll see Grandma's sitting room, pastel fabrics of faded roses and crocheted armrests on old hardwood furniture.

When they leave, the room quickly turns into a command center, computers, maps, people at desks, extras crossing with papers in hand, army drills outside the windows. No set, no build. Just a fast redress.

Rodrigo loves the plan. Staying in a real location, even though it brings large lighting problems—start a scene with the sun in the east window, end it with overcast in the west window—always allows you to see outside. No backdrops, no closed shades all the time.

You're in a real place. A Designer's dream. But you roll the dice on weather. An afternoon rain and it all goes to shit. And, of course, say goodbye to any high over-head shots.

We're not ready to change locations. Not remotely ready to build a control-center set on stage. Bryce and I look at each other and know this could happen. Bryce ordered fried shrimp, and he dips one in the hot mustard. I watch him go quiet; then his eyes explode, his nose erupts with snot, and he wretches into his napkin.

"That good?" I ask, laughing.

"Amazing," he chokes out. He dips another into the mustard. The waitress brings water.

I know every department is thrilled to be working on a project that actually feels important. They've bought into the party line that because it's special, it has limited money. We've all been racking our brains to save money, cut corners on the little things, save our budget for the big-ticket items in front of the camera.

I once dressed a high school locker room for a TV movie set in 1985. I spent $1,100 on period gym shoes, in lockers and on benches, because they were friggin' important back then. Kids got shot over what they were wearing on their feet.

I got fired and the Designer won an Emmy. That's the thin ice we skate on with WOMEN IN WHITE, because the Glove kept saying skate on. Trust him. And we did. Now there's no Glove.

We get to the party, and it feels like a wake. One of the caterers is grilling finger food, sausages, onions, tomatoes, and bread on a kettle BBQ. The two local wardrobe girls are serving guacamole and chips from a side table. There's a large tub of iced beer and a modest bar set up next to the beer. No music.

It's hot, but there's a soft breeze that wipes the sweat from my brow. Catering tables are set up. Louis craft service has popped up four sun tents. Rodrigo is holding court under one with Toni, Brian Dennehy and Xavier. They're laughing while spearing sausages and dipping them in mustard and guacamole.

There aren't too many others here. Most of the tables are empty. Alison and Lena are on their patio, sipping wine and enjoying the sunshine. Larry, Frankie, Luanne, and Rich are under another tent, looking at something Arlo is showing them on his computer. Larry seems tired, angry.

Rodrigo looks up, sees us. "Nina!" he shouts. "Come. Join us!"

I smile, look at Bryce. He winks, shows me he's on my side, and together we're getting through this no matter what. We head for Rodrigo's table, but Xavier jumps up first.

He opens his arms like we haven't seen each other in years. He encloses me in his arms and whispers in my ear. "We heard what you did this morning. Fighting for the location. Rodrigo and I are in awe of your bravery."

I realize my thoughts are dark, and this is not what I feel about these people, or this project. Toni and Rodrigo are my friends, solid professionals, extremely nice people. The Glove worked with Brian when he was just starting out in Chicago. *PRESUMED INNOCENT*. Dennehy befriended him and gave him encouragement to plow on, believing in him. The Glove told me that.

Everyone at the table stands as we arrive, faces full of smiles and love. Brian is a seducer. Got that soft handshake and quiet smile. Rodrigo is glowing. I can't help myself.

"Is everyone so happy," I ask, "because the Glove is out, or Rooster is back?"

That pretty much stops the parade. The actors look at each other, then to Rodrigo. He knows why I said this. I don't. This is the world we artists run away from. The world of ego and betrayal. Back-stabbing for breakfast. No-phone-calls-returned for dinner. As adults, we learn this is the world that mostly exists. It's a hard lesson. My brain is at war with my heart.

"Listen," Rodrigo says, "it was a rehearsal that went bad. People got hurt. Terrible. But it showed us a real vision of how our movie ends. To honor those that got hurt, I think we must finish strong. I mean, what choice do we have?

Finish in a hurry? Give up on the quality? The Glove wouldn't want that."

"Besides," Dennehy chimes in, "my agent just told me his series in Wyoming got picked up. He's gonna be fine."

Fine? Fine? Life only matters if you get another gig?

Fortunately, Rich hurries up to us, wonders if Rodrigo and I have a second to look at Arlo's pictures of the last location to be selected. I look at Rodrigo. He nods yes, and we follow Rich to the table where Arlo has his computer. Luanne is there. Frankie is there. Larry stares off into space.

There are three pictures of Death Valley Road. Long, lonely, deserted. And straight. Forever. It feels like you could see into last year. Immediately, I know it's perfect. Rodrigo is smiling.

"We've been looking in the wrong place," he realizes. "Twisty mountain roads. The Sierra side of the valley. Not lonely. This is perfect. No one around for miles. Good job, Arlo."

I agree. It is Ambush Country. You could be all alone in the universe, or a hundred pairs of eyes could be watching you. You never know in places like this.

"Should we invite Xavier to see this?" I ask.

Rich jumps in. "Let's all go there at wrap tomorrow. Pictures are one thing, standing on the site is another."

There's a commotion at the gate and Rooster and Grandma, along with his three stunt guys, stroll in. Big smiles, big attitude. Dennehy sees Rooster, stands up with open arms. Frankie whispers to me that Rooster worked with him on *TOMMY BOY*.

Rooster and Grandma are swept under the tent with the talent. Welcomed like royalty. I sneak a look at Larry. Not pretty. The karma here needs a lot of help. The kind the Glove always brought.

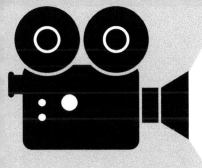

PART SEVEN – GUT-CHECK WEEKS

FRANKIE – SECOND UNIT PRODUCER

It was the summer between my freshman and sophomore years at college and my dad was producing a low-budget action movie shooting in the foothills outside Fresno, California. He gave me a job as key set PA. The picture was called *CASEY'S LAST SUMMER* and it's where I met Rooster.

One of the stunt men hired to do a big fall off a dam got hurt in rehearsal and Rooster was brought in last minute. He was mid-forties probably, but he didn't blink when he saw what the gig was. Horniest dude I ever met, including Billy Bob. The bar at the Fresno Holiday Inn made more money that summer than it did in the previous ten years.

His fall was stupendous. Tumbling... tumbling down into the water. Broke his shoulder. Should have broken a lot more than that from where I stood. That was a Thursday. He was back on horseback playing an Indian the next week on some other picture. I thought he was a god.

Now it's a little weird. Things went really bad yesterday, Rooster's day to shine. But I remember one thing Grandpa told me. The pros buck up. They get it done. No matter what it is, no matter how much it hurts the next day. The pros buck up.

I'm the new Glove (except of course for the salary and the title). I understand I need to be the healer, the one with soft hands on the reins. Line producers are rarely mentioned

291

when accolades for great film work are handed out. But we all know without great line producers, there are no accolades.

Rooster doesn't remember me. Which does not surprise me. Throughout a career you mainly remember the ones who continue to give you work, or the ones who never call you back. Like Mitchum's fingers. L-O-V-E/ H-A-T-E.

Toni is elated to see me again, thankful all the stuff in LA has been sorted. She jumps up and gives me a big hug. Rooster must accept me now. The Glove was his security blanket. Now it's a new ballgame. A life has been lost. A career is hemorrhaging scandal. I tell everyone about my experience on CASEY'S, how much I admire Rooster's bravery and commitment to getting a really exciting climax to the movie.

Rooster's son, Tommy, taps me on the shoulder. "Hey Frankie, the accounting chicks won't give us new start paperwork. We're on, right?"

"Absolutely," I answer. I looked at the budget once but don't remember it. They were on yesterday, why not now?

"Come on, let's all go over to this other table. Grab some beers! We've got a busy week to sort out." I motion for Luanne to join us.

We huddle in the sun. Rooster and Grandma come last. She pulls a chair from another table and sits away from us. There's Tommy and Rickie, who got hit with the blast and knocked into the ditch, and Jump, a young guy full of confidence who I've heard is a great driver. The cargo plane stunt in one of the FAST AND FURIOUS's? That was Jump.

"Okay," I say, "we've got three weeks before 2nd Unit starts shooting. A week after that, 1st Unit comes in with the actors. So, this is how I see it – tomorrow we go out to the location, work through what you've already planned, Rooster. Make as complete a shot list as possible."

Rooster looks at Grandma. He seems a little stunned. Probably started forgetting about this project yesterday, one minute after the Glove told him to pack his bags.

"Tomorrow the young fighter actresses travel, right? Tuesday their work starts." I continue, noticing Tommy lean forward, concentrating. "I think we take them out to location on Tuesday, walk them through the sequence, and make a list of workouts we need to get them started on." Tommy gets up and sits beside his dad. They whisper. Tommy nods his head.

"Any thought who's gonna run the workouts, get the girls ready for the camera?" I ask. Rooster nods to Tommy.

"Good," I agree. "I figure by Thursday or Friday we'll have our own rehearsal with the talent on location, and then—" I pause, make sure I've got everyone's attention—"next Saturday we'll run the whole sequence by the numbers for the director and cameraman."

"Who's doubling Sandra?" Rickie asks.

Good question. I look at Rooster.

"According to her assistant, she's got one from that TV series she likes, but this gal ain't answering my phone calls. I say we blow her off and get someone I know."

"Anyone in mind?" I ask.

"She can be here in three hours."

"Let me ask Larry," I say. "With the Glove gone, I'm not sure what the chain of command is. But I know one thing; we don't want to piss off the leading lady."

Grandma explodes from the last row. "She's not the leading lady! Toni is!"

I look from her to Rooster. "Well," I say, "let me get to the bottom of this. What's your choice's name?"

"Delilah Masters."

My balls drop to my thighs. She's a bull-legged Southern firecracker who couldn't look Asian even with a face transplant. I've worked with her many times. She can fall off buildings, run through fire, drive a Porsche or a horse-and-buggy off a ninety-foot cliff. Fearless. You can trust her with your baby going over a hundred-foot waterfall.

But full of herself. I think 'up yours' is her middle name. Old School. I want to see Craig's face when I mention her name. That's another story that should go in the Hall of Fame of Location Craziness.

Luanne listens intensely. She's realizing it all goes fast from this day forward. "We'll need toilets and crafty starting Tuesday," she says. "It's summer, we definitely need water." I like it, production instinct. Close your eyes and imagine the scene that will be on you like a hungry tiger in two days.

"Call Tim first thing tomorrow morning. Then call Louis. I'll sort the numbers out with Larry." Grandma scoffs at the mention of Larry. The stunt team seems embarrassed by her. This has to be resolved. Now.

"Look," I say, staring at her, "this is a team. We're the heart of it, but we're still part of a team. What's the old saying? Hang together or hang separately? We're missing at least a week of prep, I figure. But it's what we have. Everybody here's getting their rate, right? It's up to us to earn it."

Tommy looks up. "You're right, Frankie. We're with you. We'll get this done good as we can. But we don't just need toilets and crafty. We need communication. Walkies that work. Phones that reach outside. That's what fucked us up before."

Luanne nods yes.

I like Tommy. I get no feeling of judgment from him. I heard conflicting stories about how he froze when the money guys showed up at the head of the driveway. My instinct is he wants a career that stands beside his dad's, not because of it.

I look back to Luanne, who's making notes on her hand. She looks up, smiles. Runners to your marks. The race is about to go off.

ARLO – KEY PRODUCTION ASSISTANT

It's late Sunday and the final round of the US Open is on TV. Bubba Watson is carving shots no one has ever seen before around a tricky South Carolina course. I'm on my second beer when Gus enters. I'm still reliving my meeting with the Glove, and then the backyard picnic where I showed my pictures of Death Valley Road. I feel I belong.

Gus is free of his jaw rig. He's like he was before all the shit. Except he's pissed about everything. "Turn that TV off!" he shouts.

It's after four and he just woke up. Still on the pain pills, my guess. Full of the angry memories that hounded him out of Hollywood. I admit, this is confusing shit. I love the work, the driving around, sometimes in circles, to find the perfect place to film, where someday my family might say, "Arlo found that location!"

But turn on the TV. Hours and hours of perfect locations. The world is beautiful. Is this what I see for myself as I grow up? It's a way of life. Admittedly. I could build something, earn a living. Learn. Watch. I could become a manager or even a production manager. Maybe, if there's luck in the universe, a producer someday. I'm barely twenty and the road seems wide open.

When I got this job, I had $87 in my checking account. Rent was paid for the month. Now I've got $637, and the rent is paid for two months. No brainer, right? Eight more weeks of work, I'll have enough for the new car and a great set of clubs. If Luanne gets off her pedestal, I might even end up with a girlfriend.

Gus returns from the kitchen with two beers and a bag of Fritos. My stomach growls, but he doesn't seem interested in sharing. Finally, he hands me a beer.

"They'll be here soon, circling the wagons. They'll have a plan for success. They'll spit it out, wait for you to nod, say 'let's get this done!' But nothing's changed. We hit the reef once, let's keep charging toward it and maybe it'll all work out this time. Some plan."

"Should we blow off Grandma's location?"

He shakes his head in defeat. "No. It's what the director wants." Gus takes a long pull on his beer. "I ever tell you about this TV movie I did with Burt Lancaster."

"Who?"

"He was Elmer Gantry. Birdman of Alcatraz. He was Cochise. Jesus, you kids are so ignorant. We were shooting out in Acton, way the fuck out of LA but there was a ranch the director loved, so we rolled everything out there. And we ended up on a Friday night with a couple of hours to burn, the shooting going good. The AD said to set up the phone booth somewhere in Acton and we'll do the other side of a phone call with an actor named...Peter, I think, who's talking to Burt Lancaster on the other side, which we've already shot.

"I get a beep from the office. Call Burt ASAP. Me? Why not the producer? The UPM? The location manager? None of them are around, so I get to a phone booth -no cells in those days- and call Burt. That voice answers. Asks if we're shooting the other side of his phone conversation. I say yes, we are. Tonight. He wants the address of the location. And the time of the move. I say, but it's just Peter's side of the call. He says, 'Listen young man, making movies is a complicated puzzle, but none of it matters if the performances aren't solid. As an actor, I want to be there for Peter. Off-camera, of course, but there.'

"I say, 'But it's Friday night and Acton is a long way from Century City.'

I feel him smile. That Burt Lancaster smile. "Doesn't matter."

"So, what happened?" I ask. Gus rips the Fritos bag open, grabs a handful of chips.

"Burt and his assistant drive out on a stupid-busy Friday night to bum-fuck Acton, probably took him an hour and a half. I meet him at the location. The phone booth is set up, an electrician is lighting it, but I've heard from the set that the move might not happen.

"And here's Burt, to me one of the god-damn great movie stars ever, asking me what's going on? I mumble I don't know; things are getting weird at the ranch; it might not happen. He looks at his assistant/driver and gives him that smile. Looks off and sees a McDonald's. Says let's all go over there and get some coffee."

"Why the fuck did he come out there?" I ask.

"As we're sitting inside with coffees, he answers that question. Because he was a young actor once trying to make a space for himself, and some star he was working with told him to never care about anybody except yourself, because when your name opens a picture, that's the only thing that matters. Stars and the rest of you. End of story."

I look at Gus. Don't know if I understand his point.

"He said he'd played many generals, many war heroes, and all his research always said the same thing: it's a unit, a team, that wins wars. That's why he was out in Acton for a shoot that never happened."

"Wow," I say.

"Then some homeless old woman comes in, pushing a wire basket with all her earthly possessions. Stops when she sees him. She knows she's seen him before, but...and then the lightbulb goes off! She grins and heads for us. The assistant stands to head her off, but Burt stops him. 'Is it tonight you're gonna save me, Mr. Gantry?' she cackles.

"Burt gives her that smile, all white teeth and confidence. 'Probably.' he grins. It's good enough for her. She moves toward the bathroom. Burt says, 'let's get out of here,' and we leave."

At that point, Luanne and Rich barge into the house, big smiles and pizza boxes in hand, and then Larry comes in with a six-pack and a bottle of whiskey. They're all happy, ready to plan out the next four weeks until success is theirs.

The pizzas are spread out on the dining room table and the beers opened. Luanne goes into her bedroom and returns wearing a fresh blouse. She smiles at me like she's riding a massive high. I smile back. To be honest, nothing ever happened in my loins when I was around her before, but suddenly that's all changed. Her eyes are alive.

She takes the first slice of the veggie pizza, grabs a beer, and sits at the table. "So," she announces, "we just wanted to get together, the whole team, and pre-viz the rest of the shoot. The Glove always said if you can see it coming, you can deal with it. Sounds right to me."

I look at Gus. His jaw is open. I think he might even drop his beer. His little protégé has suddenly morphed into Michael Corleone. I never saw her do this before, but Larry offers her a cigarette and she lights up, takes a deep pull like a pro.

"Frankie and I are on the second unit, Rooster and Grandma patrol," she says, blowing out a steady stream of smoke. "That leaves Rich and Arlo, and hopefully Gus, with the first unit. The question is: is this enough team?"

I stare at Luanne. She's sipping beer and looking at each of us individually. I look at Gus. The jaw is open again. I can see the Fritos in his mouth, dry. His eyes are full of conflict. He doesn't know what to think. Neither do I.

It's Monday morning and Boyzie's waiting for me in front of Gus's house. We're going out to Grandma's to make a new deal with her. Boyzie is now working with the second unit as Frankie's assistant. Frankie is in the office with Rooster and Tommy making a schedule for the week.

My phone rings; it's Katie from extra casting. "I just heard you're wrangling the second unit! Man, things change fast around here!"

"Tell me" I say. "What's up?"

"Well, my phone won't stop ringing. Rumors are flying; Rooster's been fired; do I still have a job? The girls are silly-goose panicked. The summer jobs they gave up, the long apologies to their boyfriends, promises to their parents they weren't running away with the circus...blah blah blah. I'm like, grow up. Life is knocking on your door."

"Why are you calling, Katie? Tuesday is still on; Rooster and his team are back. The wardrobe people want to see your girls tomorrow at 9AM. Fittings for costumes and stunt workouts. The Glove quit. He fired Rooster and his team, but the Director persuaded Larry, who is now the line-producer, to bring them back."

"Wow," she says.

"Look, I gotta go. Have your girls here at nine for wardrobe. Tommy, Rooster's son, who seems like a pretty good guy, is running the workouts."

"I'm not sure how to say this, so I just will," Katie breaks in. "You need to know at least five fathers or boyfriends have told me if any of the stunt guys hustle their daughters or girlfriends, guns will come out."

This stops me. I laugh. Sort of. "Tell them if they think they're going to lose their women to a bunch of stunt roosters... they already did. Bye!"

So, this is how movie life works. You drop an atom bomb on Saturday, cart off the dead on Sunday, and back in the office on Monday morning. Somehow the fantasy of show biz and fun has become a thing of the past. This is just work.

I like Boyzie. He's boundless in his enthusiasm, supremely confident. Larry took him away from the Cielo Hotel in town to be the office runner. Guess he was an all-state athlete in Idaho, where he grew up. Dad was in the army or something. Gave himself the name Boyzie because he was the only Black man to escape the state without a football scholarship or inside a body bag.

As we drive out to Benton, he wants to know everything about my grandma. I don't know if he's laughing at my family or just curious. I choose to believe he's curious. We pull up to the house and she's waiting on the front porch. Glum look on her face, steel in her eyes.

"You wait here." I get out, smile. "Hi Grandma!"

"Come up here and speak your mind," she orders me. I climb the steps, our eyes locked on each other. I sit in the chair next to her.

"None of this would have happened if you hadn't listened to a Wilson. You know that, right?" she says.

"I guess you could say so," I say.

"So, what is it you want this time?"

"To talk to you about the extra money."

"I want double or nothing. No negotiation."

"But that's just wrong, Grandma. Something bad happened here on Saturday. People got hurt, one got killed. That's no reason to kick a dog when it's on the ground. You know that."

"That's not why I want more money."

"Then what is it?"

"They disrespected Rooster. Blamed him for the whole thing. He says it wasn't his fault, production fell on its face. And then blamed him. Fired him. In an hour the whole stunt world knew he got canned. That ain't right."

"But they realized their mistake. Rooster's in the office right now with Frankie and Tommy, getting ready to come back out here. It was a bump in the road. When it's all over, they've gone on to their next job, you'll have memories to chew on for the rest of your life."

She looks at me, a slight smile crosses her lips. "Who says you're so smart?"

"I'm not smart. But I am a Dieter. I see clearly."

"And what do you think is clear, here?"

"Seventy-five thousand. Clear. That's a jump of seventeen thousand dollars to you. And nothing has changed."

She looks out over the valley, chewing on my offer. She's a complicated one, my grandma, and now that she's older people might dismiss her, laugh at her. That'd be their mistake. The gears in her brain are still grinding.

"You know, I never really liked your mother. She was weak. Never stood up for herself. But you...you were a little firecracker from the start. Wouldn't go to sleep, wouldn't eat what you didn't like, just wanted to read books and play with your dolls."

She smiles, remembering. "Until you went to school. And then it was all laughing and fighting and running around like wild Indians. You brought energy to our family." She looks over to me. "And what'd we give back in return?"

She lets that little smile out again. "Tried to teach you to behave, be cautious. Polite. Christian." She laughs out loud. "Families can be so stupid sometimes."

She stands up. Looks me straight in the eye. "Okay, granddaughter, go back and tell them you got the deal. Tell 'em it was a cat fight. You want, I'll even scratch your cheek."

I stand up, hug her. "Thank you, Grandma."

FIONA – PRODUCTION OFFICE COORDINATOR

I like the Glove. I respect him. But I came in the door with Larry. It's a precision business to him. And I love the challenge of keeping all the daily changes together in perfect sync, all the new information made quickly available to everyone, creating the perfect 'effortless effort'. Prep doesn't stop when the shoot starts. The ones who don't make it in the 'biz never understand this.

So far, the split teams of Frankie, Luanne and Boyzie, and Rich, Arlo and Gus have worked out. We continue to stay on schedule. The actors are coming in from LA left and right. Finishing and going back home. The hotel situation is testy. The Fall Colors bullshit has taken over LA magazine coverage, and pushy people who want to see the colorful forest from their SUVs are starting to get political about a movie taking over the town's resources.

Larry's in the office. It's Thursday and Alison's got questions before the payroll goes out. Last weekend was a five-alarm shit fire, and she's unclear who, if any, should get paid for Sunday. Many of us were here in the office for at least half the day, some even longer. Alison and Lena are putting in for it, but the location team? Me?

He comes into my office and plops down in the soft chair, all smiles. The week has gone smoothly. No backfire over the Glove's leaving. Rainman has found his calling. The cast loves him, the crew likes him enough to help him learn the Hollywood way of working. Brian Dennehy really likes Rodrigo and Xavier. And Toni is solid with a great assistant who is clear about any problem and uncannily helpful with a solution. Even Victor is starting to seem relaxed and normal. My Irish eyes are smiling.

"I have a problem I can't fix," Larry says.

"Lena?"

He's fallen in love with her, and he's afraid. She's adorable. She's confident to the point of being scary. But I know one thing he doesn't. She's done with Jimmy.

She told me he asked her if he could get a month's advance on his salary. She asked him how he could be so sure he'd have a job for a month. She watched the idea roll through his brain. He got angry, grabbed her. She had a nail file by the bedside, took it and stabbed him. He squealed like a baby—her words – and grabbed his clothes and ran from the room. But he made the call on Monday, bright and cheery. Go figure.

"Whatever you do, don't show weakness to her. Something happened when she was a kid, who knows, but she's a fighter who only respects fighters."

He thinks about this. "So how do I say I'm sorry? I mean, I don't know what I'm sorry for, but whatever it is...."

I smile at him. Many miles together for us. He's a good man but choosing a career of being in the hot seat with all the money-and-people blarney that comes flying at you as the production manager, the hysteria and insecurity that gets injected into your blood, it's easy to see how you end up a beautiful, battered pound-dog that doesn't trust love or kindness anymore.

"A touchstone for me is the Otis Redding song 'Try a Little Tenderness'. She told me Jimmy's young. A prospect. She doesn't need a prospect, she needs someone who laughs at life, has been places, who isn't afraid of her. Will buy her a new dress."

At that moment Alison barges into my office. "I heard you were here! The paychecks are going out today, I need to know what to say to those who question Sunday."

I look at Larry. He's lost in thought.

"What?" Alison wants to know. "Is this about Lena?"

I nod.

"Well, forget it. She's done with Jimmy; claims she's done with boys in general. Wants to talk to you." She looks directly at Larry.

"Really?" he says.

"Yeah, really. Do you still understand English?"

I say, "Do you understand hurt, girl?"

"Hurt?" Alison responds. "Please. She's a big girl, not her first time on the playground. She jumped the fence, snagged her knickers. Who hasn't?"

"I'm talking about his hurt."

We both look at Larry. Alison says, "Look, you just met her and hit it off, we're here on this gig, she's young, beautiful, you're her boss, powerful and older, you two hook up. What's the flaw in this picture?"

"Temptation," I answer. They both look at me. Smile.

"Exactly," Alison says. "But you're still tempting, you're still the boss, and Jimmy is just a big kid with a hard body."

Lena enters the office. She's got a pile of bills in her hand that need approval. She looks at me, then Alison. I see anger all over her face. Anger that really is embarrassment. Finally, she looks at Larry, who hasn't looked anywhere except her since she entered. She says, baby-doll style, "Do you have time to look at these?"

"Of course," he says softly.

She gives him a smile that would make a cactus drop it spines. She flips the pile of papers into his lap, says, "I'm ready for my closeup, Mr. DeMille." Then jumps on his lap. On top of the bills. We all laugh.

Until Etta knocks on the door, opens it.

"Sorry, but there's this man..." and suddenly the door crashes open and Etta is knocked into the wall to the side of me. Like a snorting bull, some burly fifty-year-old man wearing jeans and a Pendleton long-sleeve barges in. Larry seems to recognize him.

Larry jumps up. "What the fuck?" Lena hits the floor, papers flying like a flock of pigeons spooked from the roost.

"I want to know where Mike the propman is! Right now!"

Mike the propman? Alison and Larry look at each other. We all think Craig. He's famous for that name in bars on location. Larry says, "There's no propman named Mike."

"You!" I scream. "Get out of here right now!" Larry gives me a look – calm down, this could get serious. It's America. Angry people fire guns in workplaces.

The crazy man ignores me, focuses on Larry. "I remember you."

"And I remember you," Larry seethes. "Officer Cummings."

He doesn't like being recognized. He goes cold, calculating for a moment. But then the rage comes back. "My daughter's been out with this dirtbag two nights in a row. Didn't come back last night."

"How do you know he's with us?" Larry asks.

"This," Cummings answers. He pulls a long sheet of paper from his shirt pocket. A 2nd unit call sheet. "He wrote his number on the back. Right there – Mike Props. I called it a dozen times. It's bullshit. There ain't no number like this."

Larry reaches for the paper. On the top of the front side is the word "Jump". Rooster's stunt driver. He hands it to Alison, who hands it to me.

The two men face off. "Let me make this perfectly clear, you bullshit slingers," Cummings says. "If my daughter don't come home tonight, there will be blood." He pulls a pistol from behind his back. Pumps a round into the chamber. "You can't just come in here and steal everything. We fight for what's ours."

Larry turns to me, says, "Call 911".

The man smiles. "Please do. As the chief here knows, I'm a sheriff's deputy. My daughter is missing. Your company is harboring a criminal."

And with that, he turns and storms out.

"Fuckin' Rooster," Larry groans.

Etta speaks up. "I think one of the stunt girls is named Candy Cummings. Probably that guy is her dad."

"Candy Cummings?" Alison remarks. "Sounds like a stripper name."

"Should I call Craig and make sure?" I ask.

Alison jumps in. "We need to take this seriously. A sheriff's deputy just pulled a gun on us. One of our crew is banging his daughter. Daddy don't seem to like that."

Larry is frozen. Thinking. "You're producing now, Larry. This is a big one," Alison says.

We all look at each other. Even Lena has no opinion.

LARRY – NOW LINE-PRODUCER

When you're young all your friends are solid. You drift down the same river together. Compete. Try to learn the same lessons. That's how I feel about the Glove. He was ahead of me, but he gave me a break and said, come on, let's figure this out. He taught me to be cautious in my words and decisions, then allowed me to voice them and make them. Learn to lead.

But he never taught me how to deal with an asshole like Rooster.

I get in my car. Call Rainman, tell him I'll be gone for a couple of hours. If there's a crisis, call me. I'll be back soon. Things are smooth on the set. Rodrigo has hit his stride.

I go to the sheriff's office. I'm thinking about what Alison said. 'You're producing now, Larry.' As the UPM, you deal with department heads about money. You push to make the schedule. When the road gets bumpy, you bust your ass to fix it. Now I understand as the line-producer, it's about making different decisions. If we hire a security detail to finish the movie, it probably adds $20,000 to the cost. But if someone gets shot?

I arrive at the station and park in the back. There are two other cars parked in the lot. One belongs to the Glove. I get out of my car as he exits the building. He sees me. Looks down at his feet and keeps heading to his vehicle. I don't feel right about this whole thing. I call out to him. He stops, looks up at me. Briefly smiles.

"What's going on?" he says, finally.

"Here to see the sheriff. Some deputy's daughter got hooked up with someone on our crew, and he barged into the office demanding to know where this guy was. Ended up pulling a gun."

"Who is it on our team?"

"She told him his name was Mike the propman."

We look at each other. Then slowly crack a smile. "Craig," the Glove guesses.

"Probably not," I say. "This asshole threw a call sheet at me with 'Jump' written on the top of the front side."

"Oh God," Glove says. He turns away. "I guess it's too late for sorry?"

"Sorry has nothing to do with this. I can't have crazy fathers with guns threatening our crew. As you know, we didn't think we needed security here. Nothing in the budget. Now we do."

The Glove looks away, smiles the smile of a veteran when they're remembering shit nobody will ever understand.

"So how do you read the sheriff?" I ask.

"He's out investigating a big rig accident north of Lone Pine. That's his day. Tell the deputy inside you need to talk to him right away, leave your number. Then go get rid of Jump."

He looks me straight in the eye. "Sorry. Do what you think is right. Not my call."

I get to Grandma's late morning. Frankie has his arm around Rooster, trying to focus him behind the house. Luanne is on the porch, sipping coffee with her grandma. I see Jump leaning against a pepper tree off to the side, texting on his phone. As I walk toward him, he looks up.

"Well, well," he says.

"You know Candy Cummings?"

"Might."

"Met her father this morning. Said his daughter didn't come home last night. Was out with someone named Mike the Propman."

"Sorry. I ain't no propman." Goes back to looking at his phone.

"Mike wrote his number on the back of a call sheet. That had your name on the front."

This gets his attention. Suddenly a tall teenage girl drops down out of the tree.

"I'm Candy Cummings. What'd my silly Daddy do now?"

"He came to the office and pulled a gun. Said if you didn't come home after work today it'd get messy."

Jump stands up. "How old are you, girl?"

"Eighteen."

"According to the law, she's a free woman. Ain't nothing her daddy can do."

I smile. Constantly amazed how stupid people can be.

"He's a deputy sheriff, you idiot."

Jump looks at Candy. She nods her head. Luanne, Grandma, Rooster, and Frankie wander over. "What's going on?" Rooster asks.

"One of your 'God's gift to women' has a deputy sheriff looking to shoot his ass off if he doesn't leave his daughter alone. That's what's going on," I answer.

Rooster stares at Jump, then turns to me, starting to get agitated. I know the feeling. "What you thinking we should do about this?" he asks me.

"Send him home right now. And that's not a 'should do'."

"No fuckin' way!" Jump yells.

Frankie steps into the middle of this. "Guys, guys. No need to panic right now, but we do have to deal with this. Obviously, Candy's Dad is pissed. And armed."

"He ain't the only one with a gun," Jump says.

"Jump," Rooster says, "shut up and listen to Frankie."

"Maybe you ought to go back to the hotel, lay low. See if this blows over," Frankie says.

"You're Candy Cummings, right?" Grandma interrupts. The girl nods her head.

"I've known your dad a long time. Used to shoot together at the range. He's not full of shit. If he's looking for you..." She turns to Jump, "he's on his way."

Boyzie clears his throat, and we all look his way. He motions toward the driveway, where a plume of dust is heading toward us. Jump picks up his backpack and starts toward the white 2nd unit van. The car that approaches goes over the ridge and it's a sheriff's car. Jump runs to the van, hops in and slams the door.

Thankfully, it's not Cummings. It's the sheriff himself, Conrad, and he wants to know what's going on. As I explain, the white van drives past us, heading back to town. Jump rolls down the blackened window. I look at Luanne, who smirks and smiles.

The sheriff says he'll talk to Cummings. But when his men are off duty, he has no control over them, which I realize is the big fuck you. Cops. You want them to be kind and caring, but you're never surprised when they're sullen and cold.

"What kind of guy is this deputy, Cummings?" I ask him.

"I guess I'm like most sheriffs these days," he says. "My team is solid. Officers who actually care about safety and protection. But there's always those who think their badge means, I don't know, they're the cop, judge, and executioner. The rest of us tolerate them. Don't like them. Don't trust them."

"Is that who Cummings is?" I ask.

"Afraid so."

"So, what if he shows up on my set pulling a gun?"

He gives me a weary smile. "I'd call the cops. But first I'd try not to make him angry."

It's the big day, take two of the assault-on-the-compound rehearsal. An hour before the vans start arriving, I'm at my grandma's watching crafty set up a big spread. It feels much more organized than before. Like an army is about to come through.

This will be much more expensive. Everyone is getting paid. And from the call sheet, there are probably twice as many people as the first time, including an ambulance standing-by at $95 an hour. Larry knows this, agrees to this, and moans loudly about this.

We put in a cell-phone relay station that also boosts walkie-talkies. Ready for any and all bullshit. Rooster and his team arrive first. Frankie is with them. Jump is not. Candy is not. There's a new stunt woman, older, robust and smiling. Her name is Delilah Masters.

Frankie pulls the case with the stunt walkies from the back of the van, clips one to his belt, gives the rest to Boyzie to pass out. He's got a clipboard and a smile that would light up Vegas. Rooster makes a beeline for the food tables where Grandma has his coffee waiting. With honey and a little Kentucky B.

Told me he learned to love that brew on a film in the eighties outside Louisville. Burt Reynolds picture. Thirty straight nights, middle of winter, freezing cold, gunfights on a river. Frankie comes up to him. I'm right behind. Gus told me to try and know what's happening before it happens.

"So, when everybody gets here, let's gather them in front of the house. Explain there's no need to start at the beginning, this is what happens after the lead sheriff's car is blown up. Cool?" Frankie asks.

Rooster nods yes. "Then we'll go to the side of the house, start going through our shots one by one. First slow, by the numbers, then at speed with the doubles. No costumes today, so the sheriff doubles are in dark clothes, the girl fighters in their workout grays. I think Xavier is bringing two video cameras, so there might be some time between the walk-through and real time."

"Fuck him," Rooster says, sipping his coffee. "I'll go along with it, but on the day... it's gonna be my way."

"Of course," Frankie says.

I realize I'm learning something important. If you want chaos and excitement on screen, you must be pedantic when you film it. Shot by shot. Inch by inch. Go slow, plan tight, squeeze all the air out of the bubble. No stone left unturned. Did I hit all the clichés?

Once everyone's had their coffee and bagels, we congregate in front of the house. Frankie explains what's planned for today. A rehearsal that starts with the attack on the compound after the car blows up.

Tommy and Rickie will double all the police in each shot, and the group of women playing girls in white is large, eight from LA and five from around here. Craig and one of his guys are handing out toy rifles; effects have small dirt bombs ready where the real explosions will take place on the day.

The talent seems well-rehearsed, and Frankie runs a tight ship. Gus told me stunt directors always like to go fast, get more shots, and Frankie is up to it. Boyzie is by his side with the shot list, and Renan is beside Rodrigo making a first unit shot list.

Before you know it, three hours go by. We've established how the police attack the compound, where the booby traps are, how the young women use their training to fight back, how they get outmaneuvered in the end, how the house catches on fire. We take a break for a snacky lunch and catch our collective breath.

Boyzie asks Nina to get her crew to set up a tall ladder that reaches to the top of the roof. Frankie is with Rodrigo, who squints as he listens to Rooster. Arlo sees the ladder going up. "Gus said there'd be a surprise."

"Wouldn't be a day in show biz without one," Rich chimes in. "I heard it's about the last scene. Rooster wants the house on fire, Sandra Oh tries to escape through a window to the roof, and she and Toni face off on the roof of a burning building."

"They're gonna burn my grandma's house?"

"Movie tricks."

I see Rodrigo turn away, quiet, thinking.

"Come on." Arlo taps my shoulder. The three of us step off the porch and walk toward the group. Rodrigo turns back to Frankie and Rooster.

"Look," Rodrigo says, "I appreciate all this work you've done, Rooster. I really do. I just think if we have the final showdown between good and evil on the roof of a burning building, it turns the ending into..." He pauses a moment, struggling to say this diplomatically, "...an action sequence that overpowers the meaning of the story. It feels like Hitchcock, that scene on Mt. Rushmore."

"You don't mind being compared to Hitchcock, do you?"

"What was the movie called?" Rodrigo asks Frankie.

"*NORTH BY NORTHWEST.*"

"Exactly. What was that movie about, Rooster?"

Probably only Frankie, Xavier, and Victor have a chance at answering that. I don't. Arlo doesn't. Maybe Rich. Rooster is caught. Not a clue. Good guys running from bad guys? Rodrigo is strong. He clearly doesn't want to create a split in his team.

"It just becomes another good guy/bad guy story, nothing more than that. Bruce Willis world. This is trickier. It's issues, not who's the baddest one of all."

There's a long pause. No one looks at each other.

"So, what do you suggest?" Rooster asks.

"The writer called me this morning. She had a dream about a horse, a white horse she said." Rooster looks at Grandma. She gives him a tiny smirk. He turns back to Rodrigo.

"She got me thinking about a barn, maybe on fire like you suggest. Sandra trying to get on this horse that's freaked out by the fire. As she tries to get on the horse, Toni stops her. A war of words, a war of beliefs, not one of muscle and courage."

"If that's what you want, that's what we'll give you," Rooster says, not looking at Rodrigo.

"I want you to agree with me," Rodrigo replies. "See what I'm going for."

Rooster takes a pause, clearly not used to being second-guessed in front of a crowd.

"You got it, bossman," he says. He and Grandma turn, walk away from the group. Rodrigo turns, fury slowly consuming his normally smiling face. Frankie looks at everyone else.

"Well, I guess that does it for today. Nina, we'll need a fully enclosed barn with a hayloft and... let's say six stalls in three weeks when we start shooting. And a white horse that's movie savvy. Effects? I'll let you know about any fire as soon as it gets decided."

LARRY – NOW LINE-PRODUCER

I'm praying the Glove answers his phone. Rooster just called and said he's got an offer for a big movie in Japan and he's leaving. He wants his son Tommy to take over. Rooster is one of the biggest assholes I've met in this business, and I only know him because of the Glove. But the Glove quit. Said it's all my decision now. Yet the last piece of his dirty underwear remains. Which puts me, and the production, in a fucking hole.

Never in a million years would I have dreamed I'd be fighting to keep Rooster on the show. But if he leaves, what happens with Grandma? Who runs the second unit? I must talk him out of it, get him to stay for another month. This thought shoots bitter bile into my stomach.

The Glove finally answers. I tell him what's happening. Tell him he needs to come to our meeting in an hour, persuade his guy to stay the course. Finish the movie. He's reluctant. "This is how you learn." I tell him to fuck off.

There's a long pause on the line. I don't know if he's in Lone Pine or Bishop. Getting his dick sucked or thinking about jumping off a cliff. Finally, he says, "Okay. Where and when?" I tell him the conference room at Cielo. Ten o'clock.

Rooster arrives with his team like Ike Clanton at the OK Corral. Narrow-eyed and angry. They grab most of the Danish and some coffee. Rooster is like a rattlesnake pulled out of his winter hole. Frankie is in the corner of the room, texting. The Glove arrives. Weak smile and straight to the coffee. Nobody says anything. Finally, I speak up.

"Rooster says he's got another movie and wants to leave. Says Tommy can replace him." I look to the Glove for a reaction. There is none.

"We're a little more than two weeks from second unit at the compound. I say, much against my will, that you" -and I look right at Rooster- "must stay. Finish what you started."

Rooster looks at the Glove. "This cocksucker hates me and he's trying to screw this whole thing up. I'm leaving, no matter what anybody says."

The Glove looks at Rooster. Looks the way an old lover remembers the good old days.

"But I'm willing to leave my whole team," Rooster says, "with Tommy running the job, making sure it all goes down right. I don't see how it gets any fairer than that."

All eyes return to The Glove. He sips his coffee, thinks. "Tommy," he says, "what do you think about this?"

"Dad and I talked it over. I can do this. I know what he wants, what you want as producers. We'll give an exciting end to the film, make the director happy, stay on the budget, walk away heroes."

The Glove and I stare at each other. Frankie looks up from his phone. No one wants to make this decision. "If you leave," Frankie asks, "will there be any problem with the location?"

"Problem?" Rooster asks too innocently.

"You know what he means," the Glove says. "Guarantee that, go ahead and leave. If you can't, stay here and finish the job. Or we'll see you in court."

Rooster stands up. "You motherfucker. I ain't working with some Mexican director who wants talk over action. That's the final line."

"Answer Frankie's question," the Glove persists.

"Will Janie agree to let it go forward? Only if you agree to what I want!"

The Glove looks at me. Reluctantly, I nod my head yes.

"Tommy, sure you're ready for this? Directing second unit is not like crashing a car. It's telling a story."

He looks at Frankie, the Glove and me. Serious. "I can do this," he says. "I was born to do this."

Rooster turns to leave.

"Hey Rooster!" I ask. "There isn't any Japanese movie, is there?"

"Be in the theaters before this piece of shit." He looks at the Glove. "Thanks for nothing," he growls.

LENA – ASSISTANT PRODUCTION ACCOUNTANT

The party is in full swing. The smoker is back, sending mouth-watering aroma of roast lamb and skirt steak over the neighborhood. The sound system rocks with Roger spinning tunes, a mix of dance and folk today. The wardrobe girls sling their guacamole and chips. Carrie and her daughter serve their delicious chili. The ice chests are full, the liquor table well-stocked, and the prop boys again brought a plate of pot brownies. This time I had a little piece. Don't tell!

There's probably seventy people here, including three neighbors who have returned from Hawaii all tan and ready to party. Tables and chairs are set up; two popup tents cover an area reserved for the bigshots, actors, director, husbands, wives, and girlfriends. I notice Aida, the costume designer, is sitting next to Rodrigo. Hmm.

The other tent is taken over by the DP and his team – camera, electric, and a couple of grips. I see Craig and the new stunt woman, Delilah, at a table with tall glasses of beer, laughing their asses off.

I'm upstairs looking out my bedroom window at all this, on my cell to the office, where Etta, the young rock star of the production office, has become my new payroll clerk. Half the crew worked yesterday so we're getting the timecards in dribs and drabs, and I taught her to break down each card into straight time, time and one-half, and if there is any, double time. The hours on this show have been light so far.

Fiona is at a table with her husband, SkyDiveMan, who is in town for the weekend. He's gorgeous-she scored. They seem to be having a good time. Larry and I are back together, and I see him huddling with Tommy, Frankie, and Luanne. I know Rooster quit this morning, supposedly got some big movie shooting in Japan. Godzilla vs Roosterman, or King Dong Rooster. Who knows? Who cares? All the hens in the coop are safe now.

After the fuck-off meeting, Larry went into production manager mode, thousand-yard stare in his eyes, wheels turning in his head. He can deal with the logistics of the change; that's what production managers do. But now he's the line producer, and he's thinking about how to tell the director and the actors; how to avoid a creative panic because one of the key players just quit.

Etta jumps back on the line. "The grip cards are all the same with one exception. The Key Grip, Galen Howser, is putting in for Saturday. He wasn't on the call sheet."

"Okay," I say, looking down at the crowd. Don't see him at the DP's table." I make a mental note. "What else?"

"The drivers' hours are long, but I guess that's normal. That's what Alison told me. Otherwise, to my eye at least, it seems pretty clean."

"Thank you so much, Etta. You're a godsend. Get cleaned up and get over here. You earned some fun."

"I'd love to, but actually, it's Sunday and I have to go home and help Momma with Sunday dinner. That'd be a heartbreaker if I didn't do that."

I have a flash that not all America is like L.A. Sunday means something. "Yeah, well, that's too bad. I so appreciate what you did. Saved my ever-expanding butt."

"Oh my God! You're beautiful. You don't need any saving."

"Well, have a great rest of your Sunday. See you tomorrow bright and early!"

I step outside. Alison waves me to where she's sitting on our patio. She's got a plate of lamb and chili and guacamole in front of her. "You have to try this lamb. It's from some local ranch, Basque people, been here for a hundred years."

But I'm watching Larry. He sends Frankie over to Rodrigo, who asks if he'll join the group at the stunt table. Rodrigo gets up, follows him. I head for the table, curious. But I'm cut off by Arlo, who says, "It's not really open to the public. I know you know what's going down. Give them some space."

I look at him, and then I look at Luanne. Three months ago both of them were cruising 395 looking for a way out of town. Both so young. Both suckered into thinking they're now on the inside. They don't understand.

I smell the BBQ, head over for some eats. I pass Goldie, the video assist guy, who's laughing with one of the actresses who just came in.

"...when they're that young you just crack 'em open like crab's legs..."

Waldo, the caterer, is carving up meat from the grill. He lights up when he sees me. Of course, I pay his bill every week. He's tall, his smile big and toothy. I guess in the eighties he was known as Frosty the Snowman because he always had cocaine, at least what was left after the night before. I missed those days. Heard it was a drug that ruined sex. Definitely not for me.

I take my taco and get some guacamole to add to it. Then a stop at the liquor table, a glass of tequila on ice, and I look for a table. Craig is alone, abandoned by Delilah.

"Can I join you?" I ask.

"Please. The brownie is kicking in. My tongue is loose. I need an anchor."

I ask how he knows Delilah. He chuckles. "Does anyone really know Delilah?"

He smiles, thinks. "We were shooting in downtown LA. Skid Row. She'd been hired to fall two flights of stairs after she gets shot. It took forever to light. God bless and good riddance to film. My boss, the prop master who couldn't stand stunt people, told me to go make sure her pads and harness were on correctly. I knocked on the stunt trailer door and she answered.

"She grabbed me by the shirt, pulled me in. Said she couldn't get ready because she had all this sexual energy. I was newly married at the time. I thought forever. Before we left the trailer, my pants had been around my ankles for twenty minutes and I was sharing her coke and whiskey.

"The AD called a lunch break because it took so long to light the set, and Delilah and I decided to go up on the roof, look out over downtown LA. We had another couple of toots and another hit on the whiskey bottle. Suddenly she was on my pants again, unbuckling, yanking. I couldn't stop laughing.

"At the end, when the ADs finally found us, we were thirty feet in the air on the neon sign for the hotel. Thank God there weren't iPhones then."

Wow is what I say. Sounds kinda fun.

"Still could be," he says with a wicked smile. "If you can sneak away for a little while."

While I'm thinking about that last comment (did he just flirt with me?) I notice everyone stops talking and in unison turns toward the gate. Even the music stops. Candy Cummings and her dad walk into the backyard.

ARLO – KEY PRODUCTION ASSISTANT

Everybody on the crew knows who they are. Everybody has heard the stories. Jump and her. The cop in the office with the gun. It's America in the 21st century. Mass murder isn't just a TV news event. It's on everybody's mind. They should replace E Pluribus Unum with Lawless, Loaded, and Looking.

I look at Rich, wondering if he's thinking the same thing I am. Does the killing start now? But Candy seems embarrassed, and her dad is shy and nervous. Frankie, Larry, and Tommy are in heavy discussion with Rodrigo. Rich and I go over, greet them. Explain there's food and drink, and they're welcome to join in.

Cummings coughs, starts to explain he's grateful that guy Jump left and he's sorry for his behavior the other day. Rich stops him. "Let's wait until Larry and Frankie can come over."

I lead him to the BBQ table. He moves slow, eyes searching the crowd like he's Hannibal Lechter at a garden party being brought to the stage in chains. But he gets yapping with Waldo, who goes on and on about this local lamb he's carving up.

Cummings laughs, says he once raided a Basque camp in the mountains where this shepherd, some crazy Spanish guy, was shacked up with a twenty-year-old tweeker who was so loud during sex that the other shepherds in the camp called the cops. They were keeping the sheep awake and all the dogs.

He seems to relax. As does everyone else. Laughter seems to do that. A man laughing is not a man who will kill you. Or so you'd think. Out of the corner of my eye I see Larry leave the table where Frankie and Rodrigo carry on. Rich gets his attention, motions him over to our table.

I get Waldo to serve up two lamb tacos and direct Cummings to the guacamole, then back to our table. I ask him what he wants to drink. He says, "vodka rocks, deep."

"So," Larry says, "to what do we owe this visit?"

Cummings looks to his daughter. Smiles. She is clearly the apple of his eye. High school cheerleader, gymnastic competitor at the state finals, Homecoming Queen. With that blonde hair and big smile, she could be on TV. She smiles back, then looks at Larry.

"I guess we want to see if there's a chance I can come back to the team," she says.

"Now that Jump is gone," Cummings adds emphatically. "Look, I know I overreacted. I'm really sorry about that."

I set his drink down in front of him. He takes it in his hand, swallows.

"Pulling a gun on people when you're pissed off? What do you mean?" Larry asks.

"Do you have kids?" Cummings asks.

"I don't. But I have about a hundred people on my crew."

Cummings stares at him with razorblades in his eyes. Then he grins like a good ol' country boy and says, "I guess I just went crazy in this tired old head of mine, you know? Talked myself into believing I was about to lose my little girl to some Hollywood freak. Might turn her into a sex doll or something..."

His calculating eyes go around the table to see if anyone is buying this. I don't think so. Frankie joins us at this moment. He laughs. "Did I hear somebody say sex doll?" Larry and Bryson both look at him with darkness. Frankie gets it instantly.

Rich speaks up. "I think she wants to come back to the team."

"And...." Bryson whispers, "maybe I can bring some of my fellow deputies, have them play cops in the film. I got a cousin in LA works the movies, so I got a fair idea of how it works."

Larry is cold. Pull a loaded gun on somebody, that's not an easy thing to forget. But Frankie is deep in thought. This could be a godsend. Extras who actually know how police behave, body-language, holding and firing weapons. Save bringing stuntmen from LA.

"Things change in production," Frankie says. "Schedules are a concept. Somebody twists an ankle, somebody gets the flu, their kid is in the hospital...we need flexibility. Can you guarantee that?"

"If I say it, you can bank it." I wonder what Gus would say if he was here. In the end we all agree to let bygones be bygones. Take two, like they say on set.

Candy has a smile as wide as her shoulders. She hurries over to Tommy and Rickie, giving each a big hug. Bryson

Cummings hands Frankie his business card with his cell number on the back.

"Call me with the details. Do we bring our own weapons? Uniforms? Vehicles?"

"We'll take tomorrow to get organized. Figure to show up for work Tuesday. How many men can you guarantee?"

"What do you want?"

"Want? Fifteen. Need? Seven."

"Same ones every day?"

"Everybody's in uniform. It can all rotate. Actually, that might be better."

"We all look alike, right?" Cummings laughs, but nobody laughs with him.

PART EIGHT – FINISH STRONG

LARRY – NOW LINE–PRODUCER

Craig finds me on set Monday morning. Pulls me aside. I've got a major problem I'm frantic about, but we've been friends for a longtime.

"Carrie called me last night. I guess she works at some bar in Lone Pine when she's not with us. That stunt girl, Candy, well her dad came in last night. Gus was there, nasty as ever, and there was a confrontation about redneck cops hating the Hollywood crew that... let's see, what'd she say, 'come like rustlers riding out of the mountains.' Love that image."

I barely listen to him, but then I go back, hear it again.

"Second unit shoots in two weeks," I say. "But they start rehearsing tomorrow. Who you got going with them?"

"Probably Bruce. He's my best gun man."

"Let him know there might be a problem. Keep his eye on Cummings. If this is an ambush, I can't see it happening in rehearsals. I'll tell Frankie and Tommy."

"Maybe we should just say no thanks to his help?"

I look at him. He's sincere. I am too. "You mean whack the hornet's nest with a shovel?"

"Okay, I see your point. Keep the bad guys where you can see them."

Like I told Craig, right now I have an even bigger problem. After the BBQ yesterday, Toni went back to her condo. Her assistant, who was baby-sitting Toni's little dog, said something weird happened, like the dog got bit in the park and seems lethargic, confused. Toni comforted little Squeezy, went to bed early with her, and the dog died in the middle of the night.

She was supposed to work today, but she called Rodrigo at four a.m. in tears, saying she really needed a day to get over this. The dog was with her for fourteen years.

Rainman called me at four-thirty. Rodrigo wants to give her the day off. Without her we can fill up half a day's work. Rodrigo and I had breakfast an hour ago. Brian Dennehy talked with Toni, completely understanding. With a broken heart you can practically do any job, even direct a movie, but you can't do it if you're acting. He had a suggestion.

"The county sheriff is going to die in the first wave of the charge," Rodrigo explains. "They have two powerful scenes, one before the charge, the other after the explosion. He suggested we find a house that is his character's, and we shoot half a day of him getting ready for the big day, leaving his house before dawn with a feeling that maybe he isn't coming back."

Actors. Their solution to everything is more scenes with them. This is major. We make a creative decision without a "creative" producer, and we add a day to the schedule, and thus to the budget. As a Production Manager, this would really piss me off. But as a producer, and a human being, I listen respectfully.

I call Rich. He brings Arlo and Gus into the conversation. They both get in their cars and head out on the hunt. I forget to tell Nina, who confronts me on set. I apologize. We're in panic mode now. She's already talked with both Gus and Arlo. They know what she would like. She wants to see everything before the director.

"Hopefully before lunch," I say. "Then we'll take the director and cameraman at wrap." Bryson Cummings stops being my focus. The snake slithers away.

Somehow it all works. The scouts come back with two strong choices that Nina likes. She asks if we can show the director and the cameraman at lunch, so the decorator has a chance to make something happen in the afternoon. With any luck we start tomorrow back here and finish what we didn't get today with Toni, and then move to the new location and finish in a day. I get a call from Alison. She's ready with the cost-to-date through last Friday. She needs to send it to LA by the end of the day; says it looks like we're under about $200K, mostly because the hours have been light, and the grip and electric rentals and purchases are way low. That will pay for the extra day.

I tell her to add another day of shooting to the budget and take a $100K savings. In the end we'll take it out of the music budget and wait for the money people to fall in love with the project, put the money back. Oldest game in town, I know. But not if you're sitting at the table with rookies.

The angry cop comes back into my mind. I've known a few men who carry a grudge until it consumes them. My Dad being one. They don't think straight. They get lost in crazy. I live in LA; like most people, I don't own guns or rely on them to sort out my problems. I know I'm naïve. America lives on top of a powder keg. One pissed off guy with a badge and an arsenal is not who you want on your payroll. Yet, how do I prove it? Should I call Matthew? Just cold turkey him there's another catastrophe building on his shoot. Create another shit storm of hysteria?

We've basically finished our work for the day as we break for lunch. It's Monday, so it's rib eyes on the grill and a great salad bar and some sautéed broccolini. Rodrigo, Nina, Bryce, and Rich get in a Suburban with Tim and head for the location choices. I follow in my car with Rainman and Xavier.

Everyone loves the first house. An old, weathered, two-story home at the end of a cul-de-sac in Bishop that looks out toward the Sierras. There's a perfect den, a small patio, a large master bedroom. Three shots and we're out. Nina wants us to at least see the other choice, so we caravan north to Mammoth.

The house belongs to Marat Pilonski, who made a gazillion dollars selling Halloween face masks of Britney Spears and Ryan Gosling when they were in the Mickey Mouse Club. The house, which Gus found - of course - is multi-level and virtually all glass. You don't feel walls. The outside is inside. Or should I say, the lake outside and the trees surrounding seem to be next to where you're standing. It's chrome, masculine, simple and austere.

Nina is smiling, wickedly I might say. Rodrigo, who loved the first place, is gob-smacked. At first, we all thought why are we even coming here? But standing in the space, slowly being overwhelmed by the balls to build something like this, it starts to get silly. The director and cameraman walk around, whispering about the windows and the three levels.

Xavier is the first to come to his senses. He asks Rodrigo if this is where he thinks Brian Dennehy lives. The bubble pops! Rodrigo smiles, says, "Of course not," and before you know it, we're back in our cars heading to set and lunch.

At the base camp, I sit next to Frankie, Tommy, Luanne, and Delilah. They're finishing as I sit down with my food. "We need to talk," I say to Frankie.

He smiles. "Privately?"

"No," I say. "This involves all of us."

Tommy sits back down. All eyes are on me. Delilah laughs. "Candy Cummings?" she guesses. I look at her for the first time. We only met briefly on Sunday. My guess is she's fifty, with short auburn hair, broad forehead, a little wrinkled and deeply tanned. Strong and sexy. Must have been a stone-cold fox back in her day. She looks at me with a friendly challenge in her eyes. I like her immediately.

"More like her dad," I say. "You know he pulled a gun on me in the production office. Yesterday he apologized for that, asked to join the team, and bring some off-duty sheriffs with him to be in the movie. We went for it. Saves a chunk of money."

"But?" Tommy says.

"Well, last night he went into a bar in Lone Pine where Carrie works, and he and Gus our location scout got into it.

Carrie called Craig, said she got a scary vibe from him, like he was thinking about something... Pay us back for whatever."

Tommy stands up, turns away. "Fucking Jump."

Frankie says, "Let's just get rid of them. Both."

Tommy agrees. "Really. This is a no-brainer."

Delilah clears her throat. "What's that phrase? Keep your friends close and your enemies closer? We're in a small town, guys. You embarrass some hothead with a badge, there's gonna be a response. Guaranteed."

"We made this decision already," I say. "We keep 'em, watch 'em closely, cut 'em no slack. I mean NO SLACK. Anything more seems weird, dangerous, I want to know about it. Agreed? Settled?"

The group collectively nods their heads. Tommy laughs. "Jump always brags about never wearing a condom." He shakes his head. "Let's hope he was shooting blanks when he was peeling her clothes off and telling her about travelling the world with the best stunt driver in history. Fucking Jump."

LUANNE – PRODUCTION ASSISTANT

On Monday I leave the location and go to the office, $1,347.89 in petty cash receipts in hand. The coolers are near empty. I glance at the upstairs balcony where my grandma has taken roost. Since her cocky boyfriend left, she's been in her rocking chair overseeing what the effects and stunt guys are doing.

She never cared much about people, as my mother always said, but I can see something different. She's heart-broke and there's an anger building in her that maybe Rooster isn't coming back. A lonely woman watching the ocean for her lover to return from the sea.

Frankie asked me, when I get to the office, to check in the gym where Delilah and a couple of effects guys are working Bryson Cummings on a wire. She tricked him to be the sheriff who runs, hits the ground, rolls over firing his pistol at the deadly Women in White. Movie history shot, she told him. He'll learn to roll and fire, suspended on wires. I like her. When someone says we got to get this done, she's the kind who's already on their feet and figuring out the solution. Delilah has decided Bryson is her project. That's her solution to this threat.

Lena's in her usual mood: fire-spouting dragon somebody woke up too early. I try to be nice, understanding, explain there's no drinking water at the location, no food, I'm here early and I can get to the market if she can help me with some cash.

"Go get water from crafty. They're shooting close by. Come back, I'll have your money. Don't skate so close to thin ice next time!" I look over, see Etta at her desk in the corner. Matching POs and invoices. She smiles at me. I roll my eyes.

"I forgot! Got to deliver something to set. I'll be back in twenty minutes!" And off she goes, before Lena can rage-stop her. I know she's going for the cases of water for me. I go to the gym. I've never seen a cable-rig, as I learn it's called. Simple. It's rehearsal, after all. Bare bones.

Delilah is with Bryson, holding him as he floats on the wires. She's rolling him back and forth, getting him comfortable in the air. She motions for Rob the effects guy to gently roll him over. She grabs his gun, raises it, and aims.

"Pay attention!" she demands. "You're trying to kill before they kill you! Keep your eyes on me, the gun pointed at my forehead the whole time. I'm the camera."

I see him laugh. He's a very uptight man, but even he seems to appreciate the comedy in all this. He wiggles and twists and the rig stops. Delilah steps back. "Too much for you?"

"Do I look like an action figure?"

"Actually...no," she answers.

"How does this work on location?"

"It won't be on location. It'll be against greenscreen here. But first, you have to get much better. Or they'll just dump the shot. That's all you are, a shot. But it's a shot that could be in the movie, the trailer certainly, maybe in movie history."

She sways the rig like he's a little boy on a playground swing. "You're a cop," she says, grabbing his gun. "This is a weapon put on earth to end life. You don't take it in your hand like some popsicle. You take it to kill something. Fuck this up and you're dead. Understand?"

"It's a stupid movie." he says.

"What's stupid about it?" she asks. He's four feet above ground, cabled to wires holding him up. With Vicious Dolly in his face.

"Come on, tell me what's stupid about this story? That some jerk-off with a leaky dick can knock up a young girl, ruin her life, twist her mind about who men really are? That's better than learning to fight back?"

The cop tenses, stares her down. "Let me down," he growls. "This is fucking hell."

"Oh, we haven't even started with the hell part," she says.

Bryson tries to twist and turn, eyes wide, panicked, doing his best to get out of the rig. But it's not happening. Delilah is in his face, holding the wires that control him.

"Back in the day I ran with a motorcycle gang. Knives and guns. No bras, no rules, just drugs and weapons. Man, that was fun shit. Wish I could remember some of it."

"I quit. Get me off this thing."

"Not that easy, Bryson my boy. I'm determined to make you a cinematic legend."

"Fuck you."

"There's no chance of that happening. But I could tell you stories about famous people who tried. Some even got there. And some are still my friends.

"This is kidnapping. I'm a sheriff!"

"My," she says, gently pushing him on the rig, trying to calm a four-year-old screaming for his mommy, "such a temper from a man with a badge."

She turns to Rob. "Time for a break." She leans down into Cumming's face. "We'll be back."

"Get me out of this, you bitch!" he screams.

They leave him suspended in the gym and head for the coffee room. Only two local Mexican seamstresses are in the room, sewing badges on ND sheriff's uniform jackets. He calls out to them. "Hello! Can you get somebody in here?" The seamstress's look at him. They know he's not their friend.

"No hablamos Ingles," they say.

I can't help but ask Delilah how she got him on the rig.

"Simple," she says. "I told him he could be a star. Men are not that complicated."

FRANKIE – SECOND UNIT PRODUCER

We are moving fast. Like worker-bees going from sucked-out flower to full-load flower. No hesitation. A wild dance with a skipping record. It always has a back beat about how things fit into the movie. Big picture, small details. And, not to blow my own horn, I'm rocking this gig. My jaw hurts at the end of the day from smiling so much.

Tommy seems happy with the energy of our team. Nobody is surprised about what's up next. We're going through the shots with the 2nd Unit DP, here from LA. The three of us set up the viewfinder for a shot, run the stunt puppies through it, once at half speed, then at full speed. If there are no adjustments, we move to the next shot and repeat the process again. Boyzie has a detailed shot list from when Rooster was around. Tommy agrees with it, but part of this rehearsal is to make sure the son likes what the father set up.

All the girls playing the fighters have taken their workouts seriously. They are strong, prepared. They know the cues, the actions, the attitude. Everyone's hungry to impress. They hang on every word. They watch Tommy like groupies watching the lead singer, hoping to be asked to the after-show party.

Luanne pulls up with water and food. It's a little after eleven. We decide to take a break. She lays the spread out over the crafty tables and makes a plate for her grandma. I ask if she needs help. She hands me the plate and wonders if I can take it to her. "She's on the..."

"We know where she is," I answer, cutting her off.

I make Boyzie come with me. He needs to meet Grandma. After all, she's the owner of the property and a powder keg looking for a reason to go boom! It's a beautiful mountain day, cold this morning, turning warm as the sun rises. Summer is starting to pass the baton to fall. Yellow sneaking into the trees. We step out on the balcony and Grandma jumps, turns and stares.

"Luanne asked us to bring you some food and water."

Grandma relaxes. "Thank you," she says. She looks at Boyzie. "What's your name?"

He tells her. When this confuses her, I continue: "It's where he's from. In Idaho."

A dreamy smile spreads over her face. "We used to have a family of sheep herders from Idaho. Basques. Hard-working men. Short, but rugged. Loved to laugh," she remembers. "The government came through in the eighties and arrested them, sent 'em back to wherever Basque is."

"Yeah, governments do that."

"Does your cell phone work out here?"

"Absolutely. They put in a transmitter system, and we can call anywhere we want. Do you need my phone?"

"No. I'm waiting for a call, just wanted to see if calls are coming through." She turns, stares back out toward the driveway.

"Anything else I can get you?"

She sits up, raises the binoculars to her eyes as a plume of dust rises from the driveway. It's a stunt team SUV. A tiny grin creeps over her face. We watch it come closer and closer. It stops in the front yard and Delilah gets out. Grandma puts the binoculars down. We smile, each of us hope the rest of the day goes well, and Boyzie and I leave.

Luanne is laughing with Delilah by the back porch as Boysie and I join them. A teamster is moving a set wall with a tractor close-by so the four of us head to the craft service table.

"Where's Cummings?" I ask. She's supposed to be with him.

"Probably on some cow road jacking off to what I told him."

"What?"

At the crafty table Delilah grabs a banana and a water.

Luanne is persistent. "Where's Bryson?"

So she tells us about after the break at the gym, letting him down, helping him shake his spine back into a livable position, feel his legs again. Challenging him to stay with the team. The magic question arrives: what's in it for me? The spider smiles.

"I ask him when he was twenty years old, which actress did he jerk-off to? He blushed, got pissed off, turned away, then thought about it. I told him I'd put him back on the wires if he lied to me. Finally, he broke, said Farrah Fawcett."

I look at Luanne and Boyzie. "Do you know who this is?"

Luanne thinks, then smiles. "From Charlie's Angels?" she asks.

Delilah smiles. "Back in the day, the heartthrob of the world," she says. "Someone told me her poster is still the biggest selling one in history."

Luanne looks at Boyzie. "You know, the blond with the eighties haircut in the red bathing suit."

"If you say so."

"So I tell him a story," Delilah rolls on. "About Farrah. Sweet girl, doubled her twice. Never seemed like she got why the whole world was crazy for her. She had a big part in a TV movie. Had to die jumping off an ocean cliff. I think it was San Pedro, whatever those cliffs are called.

"I was a little larger than her, if you know what I mean, but in a quick cut it wouldn't matter. She had just given birth to her son, and her tits were filled with milk, so the difference between us was not that noticeable."

Luanne drops her eyes, kicks at the dirt. Women don't like to talk about this kind of stuff. But Delilah is surgical.

"This is where I got him. She was a new mother. Her tits were lactating. Every twenty minutes they had to change her top. Wardrobe was going crazy. Her nipples dripped all over the costume. She was huge. Maybe the greatest nipples I ever saw. Red and ripe."

"And then?" Luanne asks.

"I told him the wardrobe girls ended up calling her 'Pair of Faucets.' She couldn't stop leaking. Those nipples should have been painted by Van Gogh. Or Dali. Bryson was thrilled to the gills with this story."

"Is that true?" Luanne asks.

"Of course not. But if you're not in the game.... He creamed. Farrah Fawcett's nipples! If his knees buckled it wouldn't have surprised me. I honestly don't think he'll shoot anybody, but there's still a lot of time. And I still got a lot of stories."

She takes a bite of the banana. "Like Eddie Norton and Brad Pitt. Fight Club? He'll go crazy."

ARLO – KEY PRODUCTION ASSISTANT

My fifteen-year-old brother, Robbie, asked me if we could go to the driving range on Sunday and hit balls. He's on the high school golf team and a scout from Cal State Long Beach will be at his next match against Carson City on Thursday. He wants me to tune him up.

He's good. Strong and coordinated. Can outdrive me but he's wild off the tee. Not good for a competitive golfer. And he's full of himself. The leader of the school's jock-posse. Goes out with cheerleaders. Blinded by the light.

I get him to stay on his toes in the backswing, to pause a half beat at the top of his swing. The ball flies off the clubface like a rocket, straight and true. He grins at me. I'm still his older brother, still his idol.

We finish and I store the clubs in our locker. Robbie's in the bar getting cokes. In the bathroom I hear a familiar voice at the urinal. It's Bryson Cummings, the angry cop. He's with a friend, another cop I'm pretty sure.

"Well, at least it's not in that fucking warehouse with that batshit crazy woman," he says.

"I heard she's hot for her age, though," the other one laughs.

"Man, get between those legs, you come out charred and stuttering," Bryson laughs.

"Still..."

"Safer than sorry, my friend. Safer than sorry."

"What time's the call tomorrow?"

"Eight AM at the location."

I join Robbie in the bar and Bryson Cummings and his friend are right behind me. They climb back on their stools with another friend, grab their beers. They're watching a 49er's preseason game.

He sees me, tries to place me. "Hey, aren't you Colin's boy?" he asks, a little beer-drunk slur in his voice. "Didn't we meet at the BBQ last Sunday, for the movie?"

I smile, wave. "Hey!"

"Who's this?" Bryson motions to Robbie.

"My brother. He's got a tournament this week against Carson City, wanted to hit balls, get some pointers."

"Oh, that's right. You used to play, too. Right? Maybe even all-state?"

"My senior year, yeah."

"You want to be a golfer when you grow up, kid? Or some movie pimp like your brother?" One of the other cops touches his arm. Bryson continues to stare at us. Robbie don't take no shit.

"Hell no, I don't want to be a golfer," he says. "And my brother's not a pimp, mister."

I reach for Robbie's arm; try to avoid what I know is coming.

"What is it you want to be then, hotshot?"

"I want to be a cop," Robbie says loudly. That gets the attention of the other two.

"A cop? Why?" Bryson asks.

"So I can fuck with people. That's what cops like to do, right?"

Bryson grabs his beer, slowly takes a sip. He's got powerful arms, and right now they look like they're wanting to start crushing things.

"You got that right, little pissant."

We hurry out before we get tossed from the club. Once I drop him off at our house, I head straight to Gus and Luanne's. Nothing about this seems right to me.

Luanne, on the phone with Larry, ignores me. Gus is watching the same game Cummings was. He listens. Thinks. Shakes his head. Nothing about this feels right to him either.

I tell Larry. I tell Tommy. I tell Frankie. I even call the Glove. But all anybody can do, really, is wait and watch. Gus says nothing is going to happen until the last day of filming anyway.

THE GLOVE – LINE PRODUCER

It's the final day of the shoot. My bags are packed and I'm heading home before someone persuades me to go to the wrap party. I heard they're bringing in a band from Reno and catering it with some fancy L.A. team, dressing up the gym at the production office for dinner and dancing.

After the work is finished everybody packs up, cleans up, gets fucked up and parties. First one I ever went to I was the production manager and I got told off by three different department heads for being so cheap. Came in on budget and got hired back, though. Even hired back a couple of those same department heads who'd cussed me out. That's how it works sometimes.

Before I check out, there's one thing I need to take care of.

The call is eight o'clock on location. To be safe, from Bishop, you need to be on the road by seven. I leave my packed bags by the door, grab my phone, wallet and keys, and head out of the room. It's six-fifteen. Very little traffic, just a couple of big rigs going south. Before the golf course, I turn right into a small residential neighborhood.

I staked out the house yesterday. A light burns in the kitchen. Bryson Cummings' police cruiser is in the driveway. I park across the street. No coffee, no radio, just me and my thoughts. Six-forty AM.

I learned in grade school not to fear bullies. Usually, they go away bored or frustrated. If not, throw the first punch and aim for the nose. They're bullies because they're weak. They want to humiliate you and chase you away crying. Then they gloat over something they barely raised a finger to accomplish.

This guy pulled a loaded gun in the production office, classic bully. Flashed his badge. Again, classic bully. Fiona told me Delilah took him on as a project, convinced him he could be the star of an iconic movie shot, probably in the trailer, the cop rolling and firing his gun non-stop at the bad guys. Been done a hundred times, but he fell for it. Classic bully.

A week ago, Delilah had him on the rig in front of a camera for five hours. He had to sit for another hour before he had his balance back. Told Delilah he'd see her on set on the last day, and the way he said it made her nervous.

She called me. Before we hung up, I asked her if they really filmed him. She laughed. "Hell no! He's an uncoordinated lump of shit."

It's six-fifty and the front door opens. I start my car, and as Bryson Cummings strides out to his car I pull into the driveway and block him. He turns, glares at me. I get out, slowly walk toward him. I hear the front door open and glance over as his daughter Candy steps outside.

"I want to talk to you."

"I'm late for work," he growls. "Get the fuck out of my way."

"Not before I say what I came to say."

"Listen—" he says, but I interrupt.

I'm face to face with him now. "No, you listen."

"Who the fuck are you?"

"He's the producer who got fired, Daddy," Candy says from the doorway. My legacy now, like a big pile of dogshit on the bottom of my shoe.

"What do you want?" Cummings growls.

"I want you to forget whatever's brewing in your sick head."

He gives me a cold, steady stare. "Go fuck yourself. We're gonna be late for work."

"I'm asking you to forget work today."

"You got no say anymore. They dumped your ass."

"You won't get away with it. They're on to you."

A harder stare. Anger brewing. "Don't know what you're talking about."

He steps toward his cruiser. I block him.

"You certainly won't get past Delilah."

"That bitch," he grunts.

"She's had three different last names since I've known her. She can never go back to Mexico. Know why?"

He stares at me.

"Because one night on location a big-shot Mexican producer raped one of her Mexican stunt women. He was found dead in his room two days later with his dick in his mouth."

"Get the fuck out of my way."

"You might beat justice, but you'll never beat Delilah."

"My daughter got raped by that piece of shit stunt guy. Raped!"

"If that's true, call the cops. You know the number."

This is happening too fast for his brain.

"Have you asked her? Have you?" I demand. "You demand revenge, and you haven't even asked her if it's true?"

He looks at his daughter on the porch.

"He didn't rape me, Daddy," she says softly.

"No, he seduced you! An eighteen-year-old girl just out of high school? Same thing."

"Immoral, definitely," I say. "Illegal, doubtful."

"So, what should I do, Mister Big Shot?"

"Are you pregnant, Candy?" I ask her. She sucks in breath. She wants to go back inside but seems afraid to leave her father alone.

"Be a father and support her," I continue. "She's an adult. She was when it happened! Sometimes you grow up quick. In my experience, that usually produces the best people." Cummings looks toward the highway, probably at better days now long gone.

"Soon it'll be over," I say. "The circus leaves town. Then all that's left is good memories or nightmares. Your choice."

I turn and walk back to my car. He charges and hits me hard in the back of the neck. I stumble, hold on to the hood to break my fall. I turn, and he hits me again, this time in the jaw. I smile at him.

"Dick. In. His. Mouth." Blood streaming down my front.

He swings again and I roll left. He misses, fist glancing off the car hood. He loses his balance, lands on his knees on the driveway. He gets up with his gun in hand.

"Daddy!" Candy cries, racing toward him.

I smile. It's weird; somehow, I feel at peace. "Go ahead. Just be sure to say goodbye to your daughter, your grandkid, your career, your pension, the rest of your miserable life."

Candy gets to him, but not before he shoots me in the leg. She's screaming, he's struggling to stand up, I'm crawling away from him as fast as I can. He fires again. Misses. But I'm bleeding like fucking hell.

I hear Sandra Oh is freaking out about working around a horse. They rehearsed half-speed and the white horse, Snow, who has wide-nostrils and bug eyes, looked a little crazy. Freaked her out. She told Rainman she needed to go back to her trailer.

She has not come out since.

Rodrigo talked with her. He came away and asked Lex, Snow's owner and one of Hollywood's top horse wranglers, to try. She scooted him out immediately. Stalemate.

Rainman comes to me. "She's freaking out," he says. "Something happened with a horse when she was little."

"What's the plan now?" I ask.

He smiles at me. That smile always means, 'you're the producer, you're the only one who can fix this.'

I knock on the trailer door. Sandra's assistant opens it.

Sandra's on the couch. Glum. Like a tired, cornered animal. With still enough fear to be hostile. The trailer is like something from Las Vegas, mirrors with gold streaks and fake marble counter tops. The AC unit hums from the roof. The bedroom door at the back is closed. I smile at her. We know each other, like each other. Hopefully, we trust each other. "I hear you're freaked out about the horse."

She shakes her head. "I know it's crazy. I know it's on the page. I know I didn't say anything. But this morning, rehearsing, that horse going back and forth with that crazy look in his eyes... I know it's the last day. This is so fucked up."

Show biz. Sometimes it just doesn't make sense. You freeze. You're human. Everybody sees this. Everybody knows this feeling. But there's a lot of money on the line here.

"Hey look, you know who my grandpa was," I say. She nods. "He always told me the only thing that mattered was the comfort of the actors. A safe place to let it fly. So, tell me."

She stretches her legs, swings her right arm over her left shoulder, rolls her neck trying to relax. When she looks at me, her eyes are the color of beautiful river rocks. A tiny smile turns into a hesitant frown.

"It was when I saw this movie, BLACK BEAUTY, and my best friend and I wanted to be around horses. We were just little girls." She sips her tea, relaxes a bit.

"We got a job on Saturdays grooming horses at a riding school. My Mom drove us there, and we brushed and combed and sometimes washed horses for six hours. We each earned three dollars. The best Saturday ever."

"So, what happened?" I ask.

"Well, one day we were brushing this tall horse who was very restless. At the time I thought he was wild. And it stepped on my friend's foot and the two of us couldn't get him to move. I finally had to run for help, but by that time he was on her foot for around... fifteen minutes.

"When the trainer finally got him off her..." She looks away. "An ambulance came and took her to the hospital. My Mom came and we went there too. Her foot was broken. Shattered, actually. She was a great athlete. Could jump streams, climb trees, catch crazy chickens at my grandparents' farm, do anything.

"But after that, she could barely walk. She limps to this day."

We sit in silence for a moment. "My Grandpa loved to tell this story about the early days of movies." I look at her, she's listening.

"He was making a movie about Amelia Earhart. The actress was mortally afraid of flying, especially in one of those open-air biplanes from the twenties. Back in those days, who could blame her? Grandpa wanted a shot of Amelia flying in her first plane, a single engine wobbler, with her best friend, Lucy Baines.

"So, he convinced her to get in the plane. In the pilot's seat. But they'd rigged the flying controls into the back seat, where the stunt pilot would fly the ship. They mounted the camera on the dash, pointed toward the pilot but wide enough to include her passenger, and got both actors in their places. Then they taxied up and down the runway for an hour, until the women started to relax.

"On the last taxi, the pilot took off. The camera assistant, tucked under the floor on the passenger side, turned the camera on. The pilot was seated in the back, flying the plane. The camera saw him, but after a while he ducked down out of sight of the lens. They rigged a periscope from the back seat to the front of the plane, so he flew blind, but not really.

"There wasn't much air traffic in those days. And if anything came up, he could always pop up and fly. Grandpa gave the camera assistant a feather. Once the pilot was out of the frame, he started tickling both actors' ankles with the feather, and slowly the tension drained. They started giggling, then laughing. Perfect for the movie.

"The shot is in the Smithsonian today. In fact, it's what they showed when she was nominated for an Academy Award."

"So?" Sandra asks me.

"We've been making movies for a long time." I reach for her hand. "We know what we're doing."

As she stands, she laughs, "Did you bring your feather?"

"Never leave home without it!"

Last day of shooting. We're in the barn, flames surrounding the structure, Sandra Oh trying to escape on a white horse when Toni corners her. The white horse is freaked out, aggressively going back and forth between the two wranglers on either side of it, nostrils snorting fire, eyes wild with panic. This is the scene that lays it all out. The fight to the death over who has the right to decide the fate of an unwanted baby.

The actresses have already had a couple of scenes together. Blows my mind how nice each of them is. Then they go into this trance, and when Rainman says 'Action,' they become warriors. Frankie told me on *A FEW GOOD MEN* he got goosebumps watching Jack Nicholson go from happy joker on set to an evil, condescending brute on camera. He said no matter what we all did to get to 'action', it didn't matter if the actors didn't bring it. Sandra and Toni are bringing it. Katie, the extras coordinator, taps me on the shoulder. She's got a look on her face like she knows the world is going to blow up in minutes.

Rich has just given me a gift certificate for three days and nights at the Bellagio in Vegas, thanks for all the great work I've done. I'm in heaven.

"What?"

"The Cummings didn't show up today," she says. "No answer on their phones."

My heart freezes. It's like one of those movies where the birthday clown starts killing kids. I look for Rich, but he's on route from the office. I look for Tim Transpo, the one I can always rely on for sound advice. He's at catering, laughing with Delilah. I spot Nina.

She hears me, immediately turns and looks for Cody. He's by the corral with the other horses who might need to work in the shot. The wrangler on the show asked if he could provide background horses. Somebody waves money around in the Owens, there's a line.

Crazy men with guns are a real thing around here. I watch. Cody listens, turns to his helpers, tells them to stop working the horses and spread out. Find out if the asshole sheriff is anywhere near, hiding, getting ready for an ambush.

Larry stands by the camera, smiling, encouraging the team to get it done. Don't feel I can interrupt him. The filming goes on. Presents are coming out of the woodwork. Thank-you gifts from the leaders of departments to their crew, from the actors to everyone. The catering tables are overflowing. Steaks on the grill are taking over the smell of late summer hay in the valley. I know Sandra is flooded with fear, but she doesn't show it at all. She listens to the wrangler's instructions intently.

I look up at the balcony. Grandma is now standing, stoic. Like some scary character in a Stephen King story, about to release a firestorm. Suddenly Rainman is on the bullhorn.

"Everybody! We've come to the second to last shot! Please come and celebrate this incredible experience!"

Delilah, doubling Sandra Oh, will ride the underbelly of the white horse, burst out of the burning barn, and Toni will step up and put a bullet in her head. She'll drop to the ground. Story over.

It's a big deal to rig Delilah under the horse. Canvas straps the color of the horse's hide. She gets in the rig, squirms, adjusts, gets her gun and her balance, and finally she's ready. The wranglers work to steady the horse, calm him down. Focus marks are taken. Two boom mikes go up in the air. Tommy and Rickie are by camera, focused on Delilah strapped to the horse, ready to jump in if anything goes wrong.

The wranglers need a moment to settle the horse with Delilah rigged underneath him. I look up again at my grandmother. Her eyes are cold. In her head I know she's blowing things up, summoning all the bitterness that made every social occasion a powder-keg in our family. I grab Arlo and hurry upstairs.

The crew is ready for the big shot. Second camera will get a close-up of Toni firing the gun. All that will be left is a close-up of Sandra in the dirt, a bullet in her forehead. She's hustled into the makeup trailer to apply the head wound.

We get to Grandma on the balcony, and she whirls on us. "Rooster stole my heart," she says. I hear Rainman shout, "Places, everyone!"

"Grandma, listen to me," I say. My eyes bore into her and reluctantly she turns and meets my stare. "Rooster didn't steal your heart!" This freezes her. Years of being the hard ass betrayed woman washes over her face.

"He brought it back," I continue, "My whole life, we never had love coming from you. Us kids were terrified of you." Something melts in her. "But then I saw you on the roof, in blue jeans and boots and your name was Janie, and you were dreaming about making a TV series, and you were giggling and jumping off ladders.

"I didn't know this person. But I liked her. For the first time in my life, I liked my grandma."

Grandma looks away. Down the driveway one last time. Nobody's coming. "He said he'd come back. We'd ride off into the sunset together."

"It doesn't matter," I say. "It just doesn't matter whether he comes back or not, it proves... that life can be fun. You just got to find where that fun is. Go for it."

"Too late for this old gal."

Rainman calls 'Rolling!' on the last big shot of the movie. We get it in one take, which I hear is Delilah's pride and joy. Sandra comes out of the trailer with a fatal head wound on her forehead between her eyes. Looks very real to me. We punch in for a final close-up of her, dead in the dirt.

The end of WOMEN IN WHITE.

We're herded to the front porch for a crew picture. The office van arrived with ten minutes to spare. All the girls, dressed up and smiling. Rodrigo, Xavier, Toni, and Sandra are on the porch, along with Larry and Frankie. At the last minute a car pulls up and Brian hustles up on the porch with them.

The rest of the crew is gathered around the base of the porch. On the balcony above it are Grandma, Arlo, and me. Above us on the roof are the stunt players. I don't think I've ever been around a happier group of people in my life. No one seems to understand the dream is over. Including me.

Grandma spots something in the distance, a car coming toward the house on the driveway, kicking up a tornado of dust. She quietly slips back into the house as Arlo and I watch the approaching vehicle. It quickly becomes recognizable as a police cruiser.

And then the Cummings' squad car flies over the ridge heading for the house.

The stills cameraman is on the tall ladder, framing the crew shot, when Bryson Cummings screeches up to the house and almost knocks over the ladder. Cummings, large and sweaty, climbs out of his squad car, gun drawn. His daughter Candy exits from the back seat. She's scared to death. A body is slumped in the passenger seat.

I turn and look for Cody. He's nowhere to be seen. His men are spread out over the property looking for the man who now stands in front of us with a gun in his hand. Brian D. smiles, raises his hands to let Cummings know he's not a threat. Cummings raises his gun, points it straight at him.

"What's going on?" Brian asks.

"This," Cummings answers. He opens the passenger side door and pulls the slumping body out of the seat. It is the Glove. His leg is wrapped in a blood-soaked towel. He can barely lift his head.

"My daughter was raped by one of your dirt-bags!" he screams. "This is what you Hollywood fuckheads call payback!"

Larry, on the porch with the VIPs, speaks up. "Don't be stupid, Cummings. Don't go down in history as one of those guys. Whatever happened to Candy is wrong. What comes next doesn't have to be."

Cummings grins, evil taking over his eyes, his hands shaking. He raises the gun and fires a round into the porch past Larry's head. Nobody's breathing now.

"I'm fucking done being talked out of how I feel. That's what you perverts do. You come in here like a bunch of pirates looking for gold and pussy." He pauses, again with the self-satisfied grin. "But all you're leaving with this time is lead…"

The Glove raises his head. Says, "Dick. In. His. Mouth."

Cummings struggles to pull him up, put a bullet in his head. But something spooks him. He looks up to the roof. Delilah stands there, hands out as if to say, 'Shoot me, you coward'.

They stare each other down. She's still in his head.

We all hear a rifle cock. Cummings looks down to the balcony, where Grandma's rifle points at him. He turns white with fear, struggles to get the Glove in front of him. She fires. He fires back. The rifle bullet hits him square in the throat, exploding out the back of his neck all over the windshield of his cruiser.

Cummings' bullet grazes the Glove in the cheek and hits the Stills Cameraman on the left leg. He squeals, grabs the ladder, swings out off to the right. It teeters but he regains balance and the ladder settles back on four legs. Then he drops to the ground, unconscious.

Cummings lets go of the Glove, who spins toward the car, trying to stay upright, blood streaming down his cheek. Cummings' throat spouts blood like a fountain. For a moment he looks around, trying to figure out what just happened. The gun is still in his hand. He blinks rapidly, struggling to see. His legs collapse, he falls to the dirt gasping for air. Nobody moves.

Then his body shudders, and Bryson Cummings dies.

Candy erupts in tears. She stumbles to the ground, crawling to her Daddy, and covers him with her body. The Glove falls beside her. Their eyes lock on each other. She screams, tries to pry the gun from her father's hand and shoot the Glove, but the teamsters and Craig are on her quickly. They take the gun from Cummings' hand.

The medic on the show pulls the Glove off to the side, screaming for someone to call 911. I'm in shock. I don't even know how my feet are working, but I hurry to him. I need to know he's still breathing. I need to know this doesn't end with him dying. This is not a movie. This is my friend who better be fucking alive!

And that's how this show ends. As the stills guy regains consciousness he says, "I got the shot."

ARLO – KEY PRODUCTION ASSISTANT

The cops came in force and made us all stay on site for hours while they interrogated, measured, diagramed, and whatever else they had to do. They seemed to enjoy talking with Delilah the most, since almost all of them had their turn with her and she left them all laughing.

The grips, electrics and camera slowly packed their equipment into the trucks, as did the props guys and the armorer. The cops talked to the actors and the big shots first, so they left early. Grandma was the last to give a statement. Most everybody agreed she'd saved a bunch of lives by shooting first, and the sheriff agreed not to arrest her or take her into custody. But she had to stay on the property until the DA sorted it all out.

Luanne didn't like that and spoke up. Our Wrap Party was tonight, and if anyone deserved to come to a party where production said THANK YOU to all who helped make this project, it was her grandma. Even the sheriff couldn't say no to this. Luanne was starting to get that reputation. No one could say no to her.

And, it turned out, she couldn't say no to me. We hooked up for real at the party. Didn't know her Dad played on the golf team at UNLV. She's smart, funny, really, really pretty. Gets things handled. And she wants a future that challenges her. Maybe kids, but first up is a challenge.

We learned the long haul is the backbone of making a movie. Believe in the dream, trust in the scheme, savor the crème. The Dude's motto. Larry gave Luanne and me each a five-thousand-dollar bonus for all the help we brought to the effort. We were speechless.

When WOMEN IN WHITE finally left Bishop, Luanne and I left Gus's house and moved together to Eagle Rock, LA. The ten large made it all possible. Leaving Gus was hard. But we all knew it had to happen. Luanne started working in post-production on the show, and Larry let me watch as the second wave of storytelling took over.

We learned the old adage that the last rewrite takes place in the cutting room. Finishing a movie is like finishing a symphony. Gotta hear it to finish it. The Sound Design team was awesome. The desert winds, the rivers and gunshots and big trucks, the crying from confused, frightened girls, it's all a big stew of tastes and fears and joys that aren't there when the cameras are.

Then the composer walks in. And the experience becomes a hundred minutes of great confusing sex. Here on the ankle; here on the ear; just closing your eyes and forgetting what the brain is feeling and the body craves. For us, it was mind-blowing.

For dessert, opening day. See what real people think about it all.

WOMEN IN WHITE is in two theaters in Century City. It's a warm spring day, and there's a line at the box office. The film got reviewed yesterday. Rave reviews. As I pay for popcorn and cokes, I look toward the tunnel where our theater is.

The Glove sits on a bench, staring at his phone. Alone. His cane rests against his leg. The scar on his cheek is no longer prominent. This is not right. I feel really sad. All our blood is in this effort. Especially his.

We follow at a distance as he slowly puts his phone away, opens the door to the theater, steps inside. The door closes behind him. I look at Luanne. She touches her hand to her heart. This is the man who said you can do it, kid. Now just go out and do it. The most important person in my life. Struggling with a cane, a career in tatters, nothing but lonely road ahead. And nothing I can do.

He used to say, "if you're looking for justice, you're in the wrong business." Somebody probably said that to him, and he probably ignored it. Think I will too.

EPILOGUE

RICH – LOCATION MANAGER

It's really hot and I don't trust my AC so I'm driving down to Palm Springs with the front windows cracked. Heading to Joshua Tree on a project for some thirty-year-old producer who heard I was great. It's about Hunter S. Thompson's death dream, where snakes and Indians and storm clouds all talk to each other.

My car has nearly 70K miles on it. There's no petty cash advance so I'm paying for the gas and the hotel on my own, but let's face it – I'm laughing. Earning a good living wearing flip-flops and shorts, driving who-knows-where...chasing the dream. Again.

I see a Holiday Inn Express. I'm tired and hungry. I pull off the highway. I've heard the desert around here is weird; gun-crazy drunks who shoot at guys in Subarus. There's an Applebee's next door. A cold beer and a shrimp salad sounds perfect. Shrimp in the desert? Hmm. Maybe just a burger.

I enter the lobby, smile at the young girl at the counter. "I'm with a movie," I say. "Might be bringing a lot of money here."

She returns my smile. Rates are $135 a night, she says. I choke. Really? In the middle of the bumfuck desert?

"But HBO is free in your room!" she giggles.

Okay, I tell myself. I'm not handsome, I'm not brilliant. My car is dusty. I'm the first one on the job, responsible for everything...in charge of nothing. Same as it always was, I laugh.

I put down my plastic. Straighten my *FEAR AND LOATHING* hat. Smile. Game on.

THE END

BIO

STEVE NICOLAIDES was born in Los Angeles in 1948. His father worked in the emerging industry called TELEVISION, and from an early age he was smitten by stories told on screen. In fact, his first job in "the business" came at age eleven when he answered fan mail for Mister Ed. He nearly graduated from the University of California, but when he became a father in 1973 he threw his hat into the entertainment ring and has been there ever since.

In 1984 he met director Rob Reiner and began a working relationship that included the films "The Sure Thing", "Stand By Me", "The Princess Bride", "When Harry Met Sally", "Misery", and "A Few Good Men".

In 1991 he produced John Singleton's Academy Award-nominated "Boyz N The Hood" and went on to work with John on "Poetic Justice" and "Shaft".

Throughout the nineties and the 2000s he produced several box-office successes including "The Forgotten", "The School of Rock", "Nacho Libre", and "Beverly Hills Chihuahua." He is married to Caroline Thompson, the screenwriter of

"Edward Scissorhands", "Nightmare Before Christmas", and "The Addams Family".

This book is dedicated to all the crew members with whom Steve worked through the years, the struggles, the sweat, the laughs, the tears...all with the goal of excellence no matter the project. No regrets.

CPSIA information can be obtained
at www.ICGtesting.com
Printed in the USA
BVHW031014181022
649726BV00011B/42